MADWOMAN

MADWOMAN

LOUISA TREGER

BLOOMSBURY PUBLISHING
LONDON · OXFORD · NEW YORK · NEW DELHI · SYDNEY

BLOOMSBURY PUBLISHING
Bloomsbury Publishing Plc
50 Bedford Square, London, WC1B 3DP, UK
29 Earlsfort Terrace, Dublin 2, Ireland

BLOOMSBURY, BLOOMSBURY PUBLISHING and the Diana logo are
trademarks of Bloomsbury Publishing Plc

First published in Great Britain 2022

A catalogue record for this book is available from the British Library

Library of Congress Cataloguing-in-Publication data has been applied for

ISBN: HB: 978-1-4482-1801-1; TPB: 978-1-4482-1802-8;
eBOOK: 978-1-4482-1803-5; ePDF: 978-1-5266-3716-1

2 4 6 8 10 9 7 5 3 1

Typeset by Integra Software Services Pvt. Ltd.
Printed and bound in Great Britain by CPI Group (UK) Ltd, Croydon CR0 4YY

To find out more about our authors and books visit www.bloomsbury.com
and sign up for our newsletters

For Adam, Imogen and Alexandra, with all my love.

Much madness is divinest sense
To a discerning eye;
Much sense the starkest madness.
'T is the majority
In this, as all, prevails.
Assent, and you are sane;
Demur, — you're straightway dangerous,
And handled with a chain.

From Life by Emily Dickinson

'I always have a comfortable feeling that nothing
is impossible if one applies a certain amount of
energy in the right direction.'

Around the World in Seventy-Two Days
by Nellie Bly

Author's Note

Madwoman is based on the biographical facts of Nellie Bly's life but is a work of fiction. Liberties have been taken with facts, characterizations, and especially chronologies, and where gaps exist in the records, I have felt free to invent.

Some readers may be offended by the use of terms such as *lunatic*, *maniac* and *mad*. Although they have acquired an offensive connotation, my use of them and other similar language is historical and not intended to suggest any disrespectful or derogatory meaning.

Prologue

1887

THE BARGE PULLED AWAY from shore, pitching and rolling. Some of the patients were whimpering or crying out, but the guards barked at them to shut up. There was a girl strapped to the bunk, weeping and shaking, her face smeared with snot and tears. Through her short, fair hair, raw patches gleamed on her scalp. Nellie got up to comfort her, but a hard-faced guard shoved her back onto the bench. No one else tried to help. Eventually, the girl's sobs turned to sniffles and she fell silent, her eyes strained wide with fear. Nellie opened her mouth to speak to her, but caught the guard's eye and let the words fall silent. The air in the cabin filled with stale breath.

She glued herself to the grimy porthole and saw schooners on the waterfront, gulls swooping low over the dark brown river that billowed and seethed like tea coming to the boil. Soon a handful of large buildings appeared on the horizon, strung out in a line on a long, narrow strip of land. The boat headed toward them and docked, bumping and creaking against the tires that lined the wharf. The women were led up a plank to shore. They stood quietly now; they seemed cowed, stunned.

Nellie breathed air deep into her lungs, trying to get a hold of herself. It was cool and fresh, smelling of damp earth. She could hear the staccato call of a thrush and, in the distance, crows were cawing. Coming from Manhattan, it was a relief to hear birds, to see all the green space, but they weren't given long to enjoy it. New guards began herding them into an ambulance.

'Welcome to Blackwell's Island,' one of them said. He cleared his throat and spat. 'Once you get in here, you'll never get out.'

Panic exploded in Nellie, turning her vision gray. She clenched and unclenched her hands, and her heart dragged at her ribcage. *What on earth have I done?* The Island was where they shipped criminals, paupers, the sick and the insane; kept them out of the way, out of sight, so that sane, decent people didn't need to have them on their minds.

The ambulance set off along the river road that ran along the sea wall. Trees writhed in the wind; the low, metallic sky was a lid pressing down. They passed a ragged man with a high-stepping gait, harnessed to a crude wagon made from a packing case. He wore a battered hat pulled low over his head and there was a horsehair tail pinned to his coat. He halted to let them by, pawing at the ground like an animal. He must be one of the madmen, Nellie decided, though he looked harmless and not at all like the howling monsters she was expecting. No doubt the real freaks were locked up behind bolts and bars. She shuddered with adrenaline and fear.

They drew up outside a set of wrought-iron gates, fastened by a huge padlock. A guard unlocked it and hauled open the heavy gates, and then they were driving through beautiful gardens, with lawns and flower beds, shrubs and willow trees and a pond, coming to a stop outside a tall, octagonal building made of whitish stone, with two wings jutting out at right angles. A nurse ushered them out – 'Move, ladies. Let's go' – and Nellie's pulse started hammering in her throat. But she straightened her spine and reminded herself that she had already learned not to break down. She would deal with this in the same way she'd dealt with all the misfortunes in her life. She would save it up and write it down, along with everything else she experienced in this place.

A memory came, of nestling on her mother's lap as a child, inhaling her smell that was like laundry dried in fresh air, and listening to her weave story after story. She thought about learning to read at Poppa's knee and, much later, getting to know the books in his study: *Ivanhoe*, *A Key to Uncle Tom's Cabin*, *Leaves of Grass*; books that came to seem like friends, lined two-deep on his shelves. She felt a pang of longing, but comforted herself with the thought that storytelling would get her through this. So far she had gathered scores of stories – almost too many to remember. She had to keep on repeating them to herself, fostering them, holding them in her mind until she could safely commit them to paper.

They walked up a flight of stone steps into a cold, narrow vestibule and the nurse locked the doors behind them.

One

1870s

NELLIE STOOD AT THE door of the farmhouse, her head the same height as the handle. Fruit orchards and fields were spread out beneath her, grass rippling in the sunlight. In the distance, she could see her brothers, Albert and Charles, taking turns to ride standing up on their old horse, Homer. It made her heart hungry and angry – she longed to be included in their games. Balling up the lengths of her pink dress, she tore down the hill, breathless by the time she reached them.

Charles was dismounting. 'Hello, hello. Why the hurry?' he smiled, but Albert pursed his lips, and said, 'What now?'

'I want a turn,' she said. 'Please? It looks like fun.'

Albert crossed his arms. 'You're only six. You'll hurt yourself and Momma will kill us.'

She tossed her head and said, 'I'm nearly seven. Besides, I can do anything you can do – spear fish in the river, hunt for birds' nests. Why, I can even spit further than you.'

'She's right, you know,' said Charles, and Albert shrugged.

She sat on the ground and pulled off her shoes and stockings, noticing that they were already grimed with earth. She tucked her skirts into her drawers, knowing how horrified Momma would be if she could see her.

Why did Momma insist on dressing her in pink frocks and white stockings anyway? Amid the other girls in their grays and browns, she stood out like a sore thumb. But she guessed she would have stood out anyway, with her tomboy ways and her outspokenness. She had been christened Elizabeth Jane Cochran, but the name never stuck. Everyone called her Pink.

She patted Homer's neck, whispering, 'Come on, boy. Help me out,' and he made a snorting sound that seemed to mean 'yes'. Charles gave her a leg up and held her while she scrambled into a standing position on the horse's broad back. And then he let her go and Homer moved off.

At first, it was exhilarating being so high above the ground, the wind in her hair. She breathed in the horse's pungent smell, felt the heat of his body and his muscles moving under her feet. But he soon broke into a trot – a jiggling, jerking motion that made it hard to keep her balance. Her feet slipped and her stomach reeled, but she managed to stay upright, not knowing how to stop or get down. From the corner of her eye, she glimpsed her brothers' grinning faces. She would not let them see her fear, she simply would not – she'd never live down their teasing. She was halfway across the field and beginning to think she might make it to the end, when Homer stumbled on a mound of earth and threw her.

The next thing she knew, she was on her back on the ground, bruised all over, with a cramping pain in her chest. Her lungs pulled with all their might to draw in air, but there seemed to be a tight band around them, stopping her breath. Panic erupted – her heels drumming the grass, hands scrabbling at the empty air. She was aware of Albert bending over her, heard him say, 'We're really going to get it now.' She thought her chest would explode, but slowly it eased, and she gulped in air that smelled of sun-warmed grass. Homer was grazing nearby, unhurt. Finally she felt strong enough to stand. 'I'm fine now,' she announced, hating the tremor in her voice.

'You had us worried, Pink. We better get you home,' said Albert shortly, offering her his water bottle. She drank thirstily; then Albert grasped one of her arms and Charles took the other, and they made their way up the hill, half supporting, half dragging her. They reached the farmhouse at the same time their father arrived home from the courthouse. The boys greeted him and slipped off to their room.

Poppa seemed to tower above her, taking in her grubby, dishevelled appearance. He was a lean, erudite-looking, kindly man, who seldom got cross. There were ten grown-up siblings from his first marriage, and he sometimes told funny stories about the scrapes they had got into as children. Even so, Pink held her breath, fearing that this time she had overstepped the line. At last Poppa grinned and the tension melted away.

'I'd like to sit with you in your study,' she said. 'Can I? Please?'

'Yes, of course you can.'

'Let me wash her first. I mean, just look at her,' said her mother, who had just joined them on the porch. Sunlight glinted on Momma's auburn hair, but her mouth tightened as she turned to Pink. 'How did you get into such a state? No, on second thoughts don't tell me. I'd rather not know.'

'Go with Momma. I'll be in my study when you are done,' Poppa said and he smiled at Momma, the secret smile that was just for her. Poppa was a judge, and Pink knew that he was in charge of the courthouse, but their mother was boss at home.

Pink requested a cold bath, so as not to waste time heating water. Momma brought the tub into the kitchen and began filling it while Pink undressed. Momma drew in a sharp breath and asked, 'How did you get those marks on your back? You're going to have a fine set of bruises tomorrow.'

'I fell,' Pink mumbled, knowing that she would be in trouble with her mother if she revealed what had really happened. Her back was stiff and sore, and the water was so chilly it made her flinch, but at least it was over quickly. When she was dry and in clean clothes, she rushed to fetch Poppa's slippers. She guarded the task jealously, refusing to let anyone else touch them. The slippers were battered crimson leather and a faint whiff of animal hide clung to them, but she didn't mind.

Once the slippers were on, Poppa poured himself a glass of whiskey, put his arm around her and asked, 'What did you do today, Pinkey?'

His smell of soap, sweat, maleness enfolded her in safety. 'We rode Homer standing up,' she confessed, for she could tell him anything. 'I was pretty good at it, but then he stumbled and I fell off.'

The arm that was holding her tightened, so she quickly added, 'I'm fine, I didn't hurt myself.' She plucked at her hot, itchy dress. 'Why can't I wear trousers like the boys? It would make everything easier.'

He smiled, but she thought there was a trace of pity in it. 'It's just the way the world is, darling.'

'But why, Poppa?'

He shook his head. 'Look, we can only hope it changes eventually. But for now, I'm afraid you must accept your dresses.' A gleam appeared in his eye. 'Actually, there is a way to be as free as a boy.'

She sat up eagerly, which made her back twinge. 'Tell me?'

'Educate your mind. Learn everything you can through books and newspapers. Reading can take you anywhere in the world.'

Pink was confused – how could reading take her places? She had a vision of flying through the air perched on a book, but before she could ask what he meant, Poppa said, 'So, you must learn as soon as possible. It's time to look at your letters.'

She sighed. The alphabet was a bunch of lines and curls, as meaningless to her as chicken scratchings. But today she had a new sense of purpose and the lesson went better than usual. Poppa helped her sound out the letters C–A–T and an image of their cat, Daisy, flashed into her mind, like a match blazing in the dark. So this was reading – this delight in discovery, this sense of power. She began to grasp what Poppa had been telling her about books.

'I am thrilled with your progress,' he announced when the lesson was at an end. They packed up the cards and he said, 'It's time for me to do my own work now. Stay by all means, but we won't talk.'

'You won't even know I'm here,' she said, getting up to scan the bookshelves that lined every wall. She chose a book about horses and settled in the big leather armchair to look at the pictures, turning the pages very quietly so as not to disturb him. Quiet but perfectly contented as the deep, warm shadows lengthened in the early-evening sun and bees hummed in drowsy circles outside the open window, Poppa's pen scratching, scratching over paper.

The years flowed by peacefully. Around the time Pink turned nine, Momma began to tell her Native American legends about their area. These days, Pink's little sister,

Kate, sat on Momma's lap and there was another baby on the way. Pink missed being alone with Momma, but Kate was a sweet-natured child and Pink felt a fierce, protective love for her. The first legend Momma chose was about the covered wooden bridge that crossed the waterway, not far from their farmhouse.

'The story goes that a hair from a horse's tail dropped into the bridge's watering trough will turn into a snake,' she said.

'Really? Is that true?' Pink asked, believing and not believing it, both at the same time.

Momma gave a shrug. 'Well, that's what the legend says. Can't tell if it's true or not unless you try it.'

She hesitated. 'Did you know the bridge has another name?'

'No, what is it?'

'Amy's Bridge. See, when it was built, there was a girl called Amy. She fell in love with a man, but her family loathed him and forbade the relationship. They planned to meet at the bridge and run off together, but Amy waited for hours and he never showed up.' Momma made her eyes wide and lowered her voice. 'She was so devastated that she threw herself into the river and drowned. Now she haunts the bridge doing hideous things like shaking wagons, laying tree branches across the exits, and spooking the horses so they rear and buck.'

Pink's skin prickled and her palms went clammy. But the legend fascinated her, and so, the next day she persuaded Albert and Charles to test it out with a hair plucked from Homer's tail.

It was a cool day with low-hung banks of cloud gathering in the sky, swollen with unshed moisture. She told them Amy's story as they walked. Charles let out a breath.

'Better make sure it doesn't happen to you, Pink,' Albert teased. 'Pick a fella who treats you right.'

'You'll never catch me picking a fella. I'm going to do far more interesting things with my life,' she said loftily.

'Just wait and see,' said Albert. 'You'll have to get married because there's nothing else for a girl,' and both boys guffawed as if he had told a good joke.

Pink was still fuming when they arrived at the bridge. It was old and rickety, and bore the inscription: 'Pass Through At A Walk'. The interior was dank-smelling and crisscrossed with timber beams. Albert fished the horsehair out of his pocket and plunged it into the cloudy water of the drinking trough.

'May the Great Spirit of the River speak in the sky!' he chanted in a commanding voice, and the echoes came back to them. *Sky...y...y.*

'Breathe deep on this hair and change it into a serpent!' said Charles, sounding less sure of himself.

They waited for several minutes, but no magic happened. The horsehair remained a hair and Pink didn't know if she was disappointed or relieved. They heard hooves approaching at speed and there was only just time to press themselves against the railing before a horse and rider thundered through. Pink squinched her eyes shut and pressed her hands against her ears. The noise was deafening, and the planks shuddered and lurched so violently that she feared it was the ghost of Amy, trying to shake the bridge to pieces, wanting to catapult them into the fast-flowing river below. They returned home subdued, and Pink stayed close to her parents for the rest of the day, though she didn't tell them what had happened.

Supper that night was chicken pot pie, Pink's favorite. The pastry was cooked to perfection, cracking open of its own accord so that the creamy filling bubbled out, but the familiar, comforting ritual of Momma setting it on the table with a flourish only heightened the strangeness of what had happened at the bridge. At bedtime Pink lay awake for a long while, her mind filled with snakes, perfidious men and vengeful ghosts.

On Pink's eleventh birthday, Poppa gave her a blue leather notebook and a silver fountain pen engraved with her name. 'Now you can make up your own stories,' he said, and she was so overcome that she could hardly thank him.

'They're the most beautiful gifts I ever had,' she stammered, her mind alive with all the writing she would do.

Momma baked Pink's favorite plum cake and brought it to the supper table with slim pink candles burning on top. Pink blew them out and her family sang 'Happy Birthday'.

'I can't believe how big you're getting,' said Momma, and Albert added, 'Yes, you'll have suitors before you know it.'

Pink was angry, but she ignored him, concentrating on cutting the cake into thick wedges and passing them around.

When the meal was over and Pink had helped wash the dishes and Henry, the youngest, was settled with his milk, Momma said, 'Sit with me awhile. I'd like to tell you my own favorite story. In fact, I've been saving it for this day.'

Pink clapped her hands. 'Swell! What's it called?'

'"The War of the Ghosts",' said Momma, taking her place in the rocker, while Pink settled on a stool beside her. 'Are you ready?' Pink nodded. Momma took a breath and began to tell a terrifying story of a young man who was kidnapped by ghost warriors in canoes and forced to join them in battle.

'He was mortally afraid, but didn't resist, fearing for his life if he put up a struggle. The warriors continued up the river to a village on the far side. The people came down to the water and fierce fighting broke out. Men on both sides were killed. In the thick of it, one of the warriors warned the boy that he had been shot. Yet he felt no pain and, looking down, he couldn't see a wound.'

A log tumbled in the fireplace, making them both jump. 'Afterward, he returned home and told his people what had happened. As he finished, he fell into a deep silence and, by daybreak, he couldn't walk. His face contorted and black vapor came out of his mouth.' Momma glanced over her shoulder, her voice dropping to a thread. 'Then he died.'

Even though her words made Pink grip her hand tightly, there was such a thrill in knowing she was safe while terrified by the world Momma described. They sat quietly, letting the story settle, enjoying their closeness until tiredness took hold of her. Presently, Pink kissed Momma goodnight and went to visit Poppa in his study.

She peered around his door watching him work until he sensed her presence and glanced up. 'You look worried. What's wrong?' he asked, patting the couch for her to come and sit beside him. A coal fire cast a glow across the books and papers on his desk.

She shook her head and snuggled close to him, knowing that she stood secure in his rational, fact-filled world. But she also loved Momma's stories for their magic and mystery, and she could not give them up. Momma's stories stretched the boundaries of her world just as wide as Poppa's education did.

Pink watched Momma folding a huge pile of laundry, her calloused hands smoothing and stroking the linen as she worked. She sensed depths in Momma, weary and patient.

'Tell me a story,' she begged. 'Just one?'

Momma drew the back of her hand across her eyes. 'Sorry, darling, but I can't today. I've too much to do.' And Pink understood that she meant it and that there was no point in trying to persuade her, as she had so often done before.

Seeing her face fall, Momma added, 'Isn't it time you made up your own stories? You're twelve years old and have a wonderful imagination.'

Pink was already writing stories in the notebook Poppa had given her. But she kept it secret because her efforts were clumsy and laborious, and they lacked the magic of Momma's words and her knowledge of ancient myths. Why couldn't Momma see how badly she needed that magic? She ran out of the kitchen on the verge of tears.

That night, she lay awake, sad and unsettled. However often she changed position, she could not find a comfortable spot on the mattress. She could hear Daisy, now a full-grown cat, yowling outside. At last, she gave up chasing sleep. She got out of bed and opened the windows, watching the moon light up her room so that it seemed to glow gently. Cool air flowed in, stirring the curtains; tree branches made writhing shadows on the walls. The room seemed mysterious and alive, like something out of a ghost story.

She returned to bed dazed and fell into a waking dream in which strange visions entered her mind – a vengeful ghost, a haunted bridge and a handsome young man who crossed it every day. Slowly they shaped themselves into a story. The ghost was in love with the man, but however hard she tried to appear to him in human form, he could not see her. Eventually she realized it was hopeless and gave up, but she didn't want any flesh-and-blood girl to have him if she could not. So she stabbed him in the stomach with a hatpin – an invisible wound that was nonetheless lethal.

A pretty young girl, out on her morning walk, found him writhing in agony. She managed to heal his wound with magic herbs gathered from the forest, and he was so overcome with gratitude that he proposed to her on the spot. The ghost tore at her hair in fury, but was somewhat consoled when the girl said, 'Thank you for your kind offer, but I am going to see the world. I've no time for marriage.'

Momma, these days, was often tired and Pink's nocturnal storytelling hours became routine. She grew to treasure them, but her insomnia held a dark side too. So active was her brain and so strenuously did her faculties elude sleep that her condition became alarming. She grew pale and wan, was frightened of going to bed, and began to hallucinate in the daytime. She would be doing something perfectly ordinary like sweeping the kitchen, and strange shapes would come alive in the corners of the room – avenging ghosts, amputated stumps, children dying of invisible wounds.

Her father gentled her fears as best he could. 'Don't you worry, darling. None of it's real,' he said, putting his arms around her. 'Phantoms don't exist.' Then, frowning at Momma: 'I'm surprised you think it right to bother Pinkey's head with your fairy tales. That's what set her off in the first place.'

Momma flung up her hands and said, 'Actually, it's *you* who are the problem.'

Her parents seemed to have forgotten she was there.

'What do you mean?' asked Poppa.

'Stop teaching her about all the ugly things that are happening in the world. I hold you equally responsible.'

'There's a big difference,' Poppa said impatiently. 'You've filled her mind with fanciful nonsense, but *I* am giving her an education.'

'Oh, *Michael*,' she said, her voice softening. 'Listen to us – both so sure we're doing what's best for her.'

'It's what loving parents do,' he said, giving her that special smile.

She smiled back, but her anxious expression soon returned. 'All the same, she's exhausted. I'd feel better if Dr Smith came to look at her.'

Dr Smith arrived the following afternoon, a bald-headed man with a hollowed, angular face. He examined Pink, and asked about her dreams and daytime visions. At the end, he said, 'She has a mild case of hysteria.' Momma let out a breath. The doctor glanced at the pile of books beside Pink's bed, adding, 'Clearly, she's a keen reader. I expect she has an active imagination?'

Her mother nodded.

'I thought as much. Too much imagination can play havoc with a young girl's mind.'

Momma started to say something, but the doctor cut her off: 'It's a common enough problem, Mary Jane. No need to worry. In fact, I have just the thing for it.' He took a tinted glass bottle full of brownish liquid out of his bag and handed it to Momma. 'A spoonful every night should calm her down.'

The medicine had a bitter taste and Pink woke in the mornings groggy and dry-mouthed, but the daytime visions stopped. The fear of lying awake did not – she knew things shifted at night. In the moments before the drug took hold, she felt the air thicken, turn malign, and the horrors beneath the surface breaking free. Then wave after wave of drowsiness would wash over her, each one stronger than the last, taking the edge off terror and pulling her into dreamless slumber.

Pink stood in front of the looking glass in her bedroom while Momma brushed out her hair. Pigeons crooned throatily in the garden and the air flowing through the open windows smelled of freshly cut grass. *Swish swish swish* went the brush, her mother's lips pursed in concentration.

Pink was watching her own reflection in the mirror. She saw a face that was pert rather than pretty – reddish brown bangs curling over the forehead, hazel eyes framed by dark lashes, a tinge of stubbornness in the jaw, but the mouth wide and generous. Fuchsia ruffles at her throat.

'Momma, why can't I have a black dress like everyone else?' she enquired.

'Because, my special girl, you stand out in pink. Enjoy being different. Revel in it.' The hairbrush paused. 'And by the way, don't you think it's time to be more, well, lady-like? You're thirteen years old, not a child any more. When are you going to stop tearing around like your brothers?'

Pink pulled away from her. 'I don't want to be a lady. I want to be out in the world doing things. I want a job that makes a difference, like Poppa's.'

Momma looked at her pityingly. 'Darling, that's just not possible. Women don't do that kind of work.' To soften her words, she laid her hand on Pink's head and for hours afterward, Pink could still feel her mother's light touch. But she was in a flame of rage and frustration.

That was the summer her brothers went wild. Their bodies were changing, sprouting hair, growing hard and muscled; they were boy-men with more energy than they knew what to do with. Albert started to pomade his thick hair, which was the same color as Pink's, and he and Charles took to disappearing for hours without telling her where they were going. The pain of exclusion was sharp, and so when they invited her along to steal hoops from Samuel Jack's barrel factory in Apollo, she accepted at once.

They waited till nightfall, slipping quietly out of the house. They walked fast, without saying much. The misdeed they were about to commit – and the risk – weighed heavily on Pink. She couldn't stand to let her father down, and yet she was desperate to be included by Albert and Charles. The moon was nearly full, a transparent silver disc lighting their way. The town buildings loomed out at them, pale and black-shadowed, and the streets were deserted. Most people were at home, though they could see the huddled figures of men through the windows of Scott's Saloon – men who didn't want to be at home, or who had no homes to go to. As they made their way up the hill to the factory, the courthouse clock sounded its half-past chimes. Half-past ten.

The factory doors were padlocked, but Albert expertly took the boards off the window with a screwdriver. It was a side to him Pink hadn't seen before, lawless and uncaring, and she wasn't sure she liked it. Catching sight of her face, he said, 'Don't be a ninny, Pink. I knew we shouldn't have brought a girl along, but Charles wanted you to come.' He shot Charles a hard look, then said in a more conciliatory tone, 'Listen, we've done this lots of times before. It's fun, you'll see,' and he held out a hand to help her inside. After a short hesitation, she took it.

Moonlight poured through the window as Albert led them past the huge machines, made up of valves and belts and toothed wheels. The air was heavy with the acrid, oily smells of wood, tar and coal. A door slammed shut – they all gasped and froze – but when they crept over to check, there was no one there. The hoops lay stacked against the walls at the back, next to narrow strips of wood and piles of rivets. They gathered as many hoops as they could and left, Charles carefully replacing the boards on the window, while the bright moon carved his features into lines and shadows.

'This is the best bit,' Albert said gleefully, and he began to send the hoops rolling downhill to the canal. Chasing after them with her brothers, Pink thought the hoops looked like a herd of live creatures, scuttling and bouncing to freedom. The sky was seamed with stars and, once, a shooting star went streaking across it. She gave herself up to the long, luminous night, wishing she could be part of the boys' world for ever.

Two months later, Pink wandered down a quiet street in Apollo and was pleased to see Annie Gleason sitting on her narrow porch, which was just big enough for a couple of chairs. She was a bony, tired-looking woman with blonde hair pulled carelessly into a bun. One of her feet was scuffing the ground, back and forth, back and forth.

'Would you like company?' Pink called out.

'Yes, why not? Thank you, Pink.'

Pink took her place beside Annie, feeling adrenaline surge through her. She was gathering information for Poppa – it was the third time she had done this. He called her his researcher because she had a knack for asking the right questions, for prising pertinent bits of information out of families and neighbors; information that might not come out in a courthouse. Annie's husband, Joseph, a casual laborer, was the prime suspect in a series of livestock thefts, but he had not been convicted because Annie swore that he was always with her at night. The townsfolk were incensed and had ostracized them both. The thefts were continuing.

Annie asked after Pink's parents and her siblings. Pink told her that everyone was well, and that all the children were in school now, though her older brothers were impatient to leave and sometimes cut classes. That she loved English, reading and writing.

They fell silent, looking out at the front yard. It was that calm and tender hour when the birds were singing their

19

hearts out and the deepening of the light turned everything it touched to gold.

'And how are you doing, Mrs Gleason?' Pink asked, not looking at her so it didn't feel like an official enquiry.

'Well, things could be better,' Annie said, with a sigh.

'Do you want to talk about it?'

'Bless you, child. You're far too young to worry about my troubles.'

'But maybe I can help you? Or just be a listening ear.'

Annie's eyes met Pink's and the look in them was a blend of fear and resignation. Then her shoulders sagged and something inside of her seemed to crumble.

'All right, I'll tell you,' she said. 'I'm going half mad anyway, keeping it to myself. See, Joseph has been stealing animals.'

Pink's eyes widened as Annie told of the late nights, Joseph coming home scratched up and covered in muck. Annie nodded glumly and said, 'He swears he'll beat me if I tell the truth in court. Says I'll never survive if he goes to jail because I am ugly and useless. And you know what? He's right.'

She shook her head as if to clear it and tears started trickling down her cheeks. Pink comforted her as best she could, drying her eyes with her own handkerchief, promising to find a way to help. The lie hurt, but she knew what she had to do. Back at home, she carefully wrote up her report and presented it to Poppa, watching his expression change from surprise to satisfaction as he read it.

'This alters everything,' he said, looking up at her. 'You've brought valuable testimony and I am proud of you.'

She shifted her weight from one foot to the other. 'One thing, Poppa. I know I had to tell you about Annie's confession, but I'm worried. Will it go against her that she didn't tell the court the first time around? What will Joseph do to her when he finds out?'

He gave her a reassuring smile. 'Annie was threatened by Joseph, so she will be pardoned for withholding evidence. And he will go to prison, where he can't hurt her any more. But I like your grasp of the complexities.' He stopped speaking, his face entangled in invisible thoughts. Then he said, 'You know, you'd make a fine lawyer, if only people weren't so prejudiced against women lawyers.'

'Thank you,' she said, wondering if law could be the vocation she'd been searching for. She felt really seen by Poppa and a slow joy rose in her. But then she remembered Momma saying women don't do that kind of work, and she felt torn and confused.

Weeks later, after Joseph had been sent to the county jail and the parish had rallied round to support Annie, Pink sat with Poppa on the porch swing. The trees were turning and there was a scattering of leaves on the ground. The smell of smoke from a bonfire reached them. He said suddenly, 'It's good for a girl to have a career.'

'What makes you say that?'

'Well, for one thing, it will make her strong-minded and steady; stop her head getting turned by any romantic nonsense.' He paused, looking at the blazing colors of the trees. A group of young men was coming down the road, talking and laughing. 'If you want to study law, Pinkey, I'll do everything in my power to help you.'

She turned her eyes away from the youths to him. 'I've been thinking about it ever since you suggested it, and it's what I want above all else. I am not interested in romance.'

'It's settled, then. Good girl,' he said, and she was filled with the elation of finding her life's vocation. She vowed not to tell Momma. Not yet.

Two

O N A COLD, CRISP day, two weeks before her fourteenth Christmas, Pink and her younger siblings walked home from school, swinging their arms to keep warm, and looking forward to roasting chestnuts in front of the fire when they got there. The frosty ground crunched and crackled underfoot as they climbed the hill to the farmhouse. Homer was grazing near it with a red blanket over his back; he came trotting to greet them and Pink rubbed his silky muzzle, breathing in his warm smell. Then she climbed the steps to the porch and opened the front door. The instant she stepped through it, she knew something was wrong.

There was a funny odor in the air, sour and metallic. Momma appeared on the first-floor landing. Her face was white, her eyes were like dark holes. A chill ran through Pink, contracting her flesh. She sent Kate and Henry off to find the dogs and went upstairs. Without a word, Momma led her to the room she shared with Poppa. Pink halted at the threshold, shock slamming into her.

Her father lay inert on the big double bed. His eyes were half-open, glassy and unfocused; his mouth was agape. His features were like melting wax, collapsing in on themselves. Everything in Pink cried out, *No! This is not my Poppa.* Did she make a sound? She wasn't aware of it, but something made Momma look at her, tugged briefly out of her own desolation.

'What happened?' Pink asked in a low, appalled voice.

'He came home early complaining of a headache and nausea, but I thought nothing of it,' said Momma, wiping her eyes. 'I sent him upstairs to lie down, and when I checked on him half an hour later, he was like this.' She gave a shuddering sigh. 'I called Dr Smith. He should be here any minute.'

There was a peremptory knock at the front door. Momma was already on her way out of the room to answer it.

'I'm grateful to you for coming so quick, doctor,' Momma said, holding out her hands to him.

He took them in both of his, saying, 'I'll go to him right away, if you don't mind.' She nodded and he went upstairs, shutting the bedroom door behind him with a firm click.

The examination seemed to for last for an eternity, while they waited in fear and anguish. The older boys came home and Momma told them what had happened. They stared at her in disbelief. 'But he was perfectly well this morning. How could this have happened?' asked Albert.

Momma shrugged. 'I am sorry, boys. I'm as shattered and confused as you are. We must wait and see what the doctor says.'

They sat brooding on it. Charles was white-faced; a muscle twitched sharply in Albert's cheek. Kate and Henry were tearful, sensing something bad had happened but not understanding what. At last, Dr Smith came out and Momma hurried toward him with imploring eyes.

'What's wrong with him? Can you bring him around? Please say yes!'

He was looking at the floor. 'Michael has been struck by a kind of crippling, dumbing paralysis,' he said. 'I'll be honest with you – it's a condition doctors are still learning about.' He raised his eyes to meet hers. 'I've only seen it a few times before, but I do know this much – that there's not much I can do for him. I am so sorry to have to break it to you.'

A sound escaped Momma's lips, an animal expression of pain. Pink felt like she had been hit by a hammer in her gut. One minute Poppa was an upright, loving presence in their lives; the next he was a carcass. She heard the doctor say, 'The only thing to do is to keep him as comfortable as possible.' It was too much to take in.

In the days that followed, Pink refused to leave Poppa's bedside, though her siblings were too scared to cross the threshold. A change had come over their mother, too. She sat next to Pink, gazing helplessly at Poppa's motionless form, apparently incapable of doing anything to look after him. And so Pink took on these tasks herself: washing him, straightening the covers, moistening his cracked lips with a few drops of water. She felt compelled to do everything she could for him, and although he gave no sign of being aware of her ministrations, keeping busy distracted her from her own fear and grief. She talked to him and even read Walter Scott, his favorite author, trying to reach him, make him respond, return him to himself. But as the days wore on, she realized that it was futile. His chest rose quickly and fell slowly. She could hear the breath whistling in his lungs, but there was no other sign of life. Was he somewhere inside that rotting body, or had his spirit departed completely? Where had he gone?

Sitting at Poppa's bedside hour after hour, Pink couldn't stop thinking about how hard he had worked to allay her fear of the uncanny, ignited by Momma's stories.

But despite everything he had taught her, this calamity had fallen on them from nowhere, without any reason or solution. Poppa's world of rules and justice had come crashing down around their ears, plunging Pink into that other world, where ghosts sought vengeance and innocent people suffered invisible wounds. She felt all her fears come flooding back; she was lost and helpless. Poppa was like the boy in 'The War of the Ghosts' and she wondered what inner damage had been inflicted on him and why.

Two weeks after the paralysis came on, Pink woke to find that the whistling sound in Poppa's breath had turned into a horrifying rattle. Momma called Dr Smith, who came at once. He took one look at Poppa and said, 'I am so very sorry, but this is the end. It could take hours, or it could take a couple of days.' He gave Poppa a shot of morphine to keep him comfortable. As he packed up his equipment, he said, 'It's a terrible loss to bear. Michael was one of the finest men I have ever known.' He brushed a hand over his bald head. 'At the same time, I can't help thinking it's a merciful release.'

Pink resented and rejected his words, only wanting the old Poppa back. Weren't doctors supposed to cure people? But she said nothing because she knew he was trying to be kind. After he had gone, she and Momma sat in sombre, anxious moods, listening to Poppa's labored breathing. It went on and on, with no change.

Pink heard her siblings' footsteps on the stairs, a door banging shut. Somewhere Daisy was wailing – the others must have forgotten to feed her. Momma went downstairs to fill her bowl, moving slowly, as if it hurt. She came back with two hot, sweet cups of tea and handed one to Pink. Pink was grateful for the comforting liquid, but she knew that the taste of tea would always bring her back to this dreadful time.

Toward nightfall, Poppa's ghastly death-sound began to slow until, eventually, it stopped. Momma collapsed into sobs. Pink's eyes were dry, though she was full of a feeling that was like a wail, or a shriek. The unthinkable had happened. Poppa was gone, and although all fifteen children had come to sit at his bedside, there had been no chance to say goodbye.

Afterward, it was Pink who held the stunned family together. She made sure Kate and Henry got dressed in the mornings and went to school, cooked and washed for them all, because Momma stayed in her room and did not come out for many weeks.

And then one day in spring, needing a break from the endless round of chores, Pink went for a walk in the woods. The leaves were fresh, young, glossy, with sunlight splashing gold between them. Bright coltsfoot and violets stretched at her feet, thick as grass. Towhees warbled noisily and, high above, a buzzard drifted on enormous wings. Perhaps it was the smell of sap and warm, moist earth, or the mildness of the air on her skin, or perhaps it was simply having enough time to think, but a realization hit her that was surprising and devastating.

Her father was never coming back.

It was as if, all this time, she had believed him to be upstairs with Momma or away on a trip, and when he was ready, he would step back into family life. And now she saw that he was simply gone. Even her memories of him were fading with a speed that was frightening.

So this was what grief felt like. It was darkness rushing through her, cracking her apart. A cloud slid across the sun, casting a shadow on the land. The wind came up, making the tree branches twist and whisper. The woods seemed eerie and insubstantial, filled with the ghostly beings of her stories. She could sense them in the trees and undergrowth and walking silently behind her, sure she would glimpse them if she turned her head fast enough. The terror she had known as a sleepless child came rushing back and she hurried home, casting uneasy glances over her shoulder along the way.

The next day, Momma got out of bed. She took up her place again and did all the things she was supposed to, but was there was something vacant about her, as if she wasn't properly inside herself. It frightened Pink. Momma hardly spoke, except when they were washing up the lunch dishes together.

'That black dress doesn't suit you half as well as pink,' she said suddenly.

'Maybe that's true,' said Pink, elbow-deep in soapy water. 'But I can hardly wear pink for mourning.'

'No, of course not. It was just an observation. You'll go back to pink when the time is right.'

Pink dried her hands and turned to face Momma. 'I don't want to. I've given up pink for good. It's just not me.'

Something flickered behind Momma's eyes. 'But it *is* you,' she said plaintively. 'It flatters your complexion far better than dark colors.' She carried on in this vein, but Pink kept her face averted, pretending total absorption in her task. She felt guilty for ignoring her mother, but also as if she were fighting for her life. When Momma gave up, she felt a weight roll off her. They finished drying the dishes in near silence, and then Momma went to change into her good dress and hat because she had an appointment at the attorney's office.

She returned hours later, looking pale and sick. She sank into a chair and put her face in her hands, which were shaking.

'What's wrong, Momma? Are you ill?' the older children asked, gathering around her.

Momma lifted her face and said, 'No, I just had bad news. It might shock you, but you have to know how things are.' She took a breath. 'Your father died without making a will. I've been searching high and low for it, but it's time to accept that it does not exist.'

Dread settled into Pink's chest, like lead. 'What exactly does that mean?' she asked.

'He hasn't left us decently provided for.' Something like a sob ran through Momma. 'His estate will be divided up between you and your step-siblings. We'll get the furniture and other household possessions, one of the dogs, and an income of sixteen dollars a week. How am I going to manage on that?'

The ground was sliding from under Pink. She wanted to swallow, but her mouth was dry. This was more than a shock – it was betrayal.

'I – I don't understand,' Albert stammered. 'Poppa was the most rational and intelligent man I know. How could he have done such a thing?'

'Perhaps he didn't want fortune hunters coming for Momma?' Charles suggested.

'Perhaps,' said Momma. 'But more likely, he thought he was invincible.'

There were strands of gray in her auburn hair. Her face looked pinched and shrunken; tendons stood out in her neck. The unthinkable was happening – Momma was getting older.

'What if he didn't think at all? What if it was a lapse of thought so gigantic, it practically amounted to lunacy?' Pink brooded to the others.

This was the most disturbing possibility of all and they fell silent, considering it. The pendulum of the clock swung back and forth and a dog howled outside as Pink realized that her view of Poppa had changed for ever. He had always epitomized the principles of right, truth and justice, and yet he had turned out to follow none of these things. She felt dazed, as if something had been cut from her brain. The man who had never failed her did not exist, and there was nothing left to hold on to.

Up until this point, Pink had assumed that she would still become a lawyer, even though Momma disapproved. But now there was no money for Pink's studies and she was forced to give up her hopes of a career. Over the following months, she endured the painful inner adjustment of letting go of what she'd believed she must have in order to live. There was little comfort or support from her mother, who said, 'I am sorry for you, but I always thought law an unwise ambition for a girl.'

'But why?' asked Pink, putting down the knife she was using to peel carrots. 'I never understood what you have against it.'

Momma was making bread. 'We aren't suited to that kind of work,' she said, folding, turning, kneading the dough. 'It strains a woman's mind, makes her hard and dried up. Remember when the doctor had to come because you weren't sleeping? We just aren't built for mental stress. You'd do better to settle down with a husband, like I did.' Sighing, she molded the dough into a loaf shape and set it in a pan with a damp dishtowel over the top.

Pink felt hurt, angry and misunderstood. But she knew that Momma was struggling through her own process of grief and adjustment. They had to sell the family home and move into a two-story frame house in Apollo, on a street where the houses were cheek by jowl, with no driveways or yards, and scarcely enough room for five children and a lively collie.

Their loss of status was instant and painful. Was it possible that Mary Jane, the judge's wife, had put on airs and lorded it over the townsfolk a fraction too much for their liking? Certainly there were those who made sure that the Cochran family was acutely aware of its fall. There was no overt hostility, but people who had greeted them on the street now crossed to the other side to avoid them, or melted away into shops.

Whenever this happened, Momma would give a helpless sigh and a shrug, and say, 'People should be kinder, they really should.' And Pink understood that her mother was ashamed of their life, ashamed of what they had come to, and at these times, she couldn't help scorning her a little. There was no denying that there was a lack of backbone to Momma's view of life – that you were swept along a course which could not be altered, that fate was indifferent, tossing you here and there, mocking your fond plans and dreams. Pink rejected it utterly. She would never be so ready to surrender. Yet it also created a surge of protective feeling toward her mother.

Even with two older brothers, Pink felt increasingly called on to keep the family safe and cared for. Albert was showing a worrying fondness for alcohol and girls; Charles was steadfast, but he lacked enterprise. However, Pink clearly didn't do a good enough job of protecting her mother because, by the time summer came, Jack Ford was hanging round their house, with his doggy eyes and beery breath.

Three

J ACK HAD FRECKLED SKIN that was prone to burning, soft fair hair and soulful brown eyes. He was a Civil War veteran, a sometime cooper and sometime farm laborer who had tried his hand at gold panning out west in the fifties. He would ring their doorbell and Momma would take him to sit on the porch in the moonlight, unaware that Pink could hear everything through her open window. She soon realized that Jack was taking Momma into his confidence, telling her about his bad experiences with war.

'I stood up to my duties like a man,' he said one warm, fragrant night, 'but it was harrowing. I saw and did unspeakable things. They haunt my dreams – I'll never get over them.' Peering through the window, Pink saw him bury his head in his hands.

Momma rubbed his back gently. 'Oh, Jack,' she sighed, 'what a brave man you are. I am sorry for what you went through, but look how wonderfully you've come out of it!' And Pink understood that he had succeeded in making her heart ache for him.

Her own emotions about the romance were mixed. She knew how lost Momma felt without Poppa and was glad that she had a new man to lean on. She hoped that Jack would help Momma get back on her feet, so that

Pink's household responsibilities would ease, giving her time to concentrate on her studies and make something of her life.

Jack bought the children candy and chucked the younger ones under the chin, telling them how sweet they were. At these times, there was a mushy sentimentality to him that Pink distrusted, just as she distrusted his courtly manner toward her. 'How are you, young lady? I hope you're not studying too hard,' he would ask with a half-bow. She would smile and say, 'Great, thank you,' and 'No, not at all,' but she resented him for trying to take Poppa's place.

Momma and Jack began to plan a modest wedding, with only the children and Momma's friends, Millie and John King, present. The Kings were one of the few who had stuck by Momma despite her change in fortune. Millie was a large, calm, pretty woman, with soft tendrils of blonde hair escaping from her bun. Two weeks before the marriage, Pink came home early from school, and overheard her and Momma talking in the kitchen. Pink stopped in the hallway and Millie said, 'I am happy you're happy, truly I am. But what's the rush? Why not give yourself time to think it over?'

'What is there to think about?' Momma replied.

Millie cleared her throat. 'Well, Jack is a nice enough man, but he is hardly Michael's equal, socially or career-wise.'

This echoed Pink's view and she felt relief, but Momma said in a tight voice, 'He is a good man and he loves me. I know what I'm doing.'

Silence fell. Pink was scared that they might come out and find her, so she shut the front door loudly, making a show of being home.

On the day, Jack turned up in a tight, uncomfortable-looking blue suit, but Pink thought Momma had never looked so beautiful in her gray silk dress with flowers in her hair. Pink sat through the ceremony with her arms around Henry and Kate, and a fixed smile on her face that hid confusion and regret. Jack moved into their little house right afterward.

Things went on very well at first. Jack called their mother 'Beautiful', as though it were her baptismal name. 'How was your day, Beautiful?' he would say as he came through the door in the evening, laying his hand on the back of Momma's neck, beneath her hair, in a gesture so intimate and tender that Pink could hardly bear to watch. But she was relieved to see her mother happy once more, her face rapt and luminous. It seemed that Momma was made to be a wife. The house was spotless and there was supper on the table every night.

Jack was hired by farmers in the area to work on their land, and he would spend the periods between jobs at home. On his free days he often went to Scott's Saloon to get away from the children and their racket; he said a man deserved some peace on his hard-earned days off. As time passed, the visits to the saloon became more frequent, and he began to show up late, or not at all, for work.

Within six months, he had got a name for being un-dependable, and the jobs started to dry up. When he was home, he was consumed with irritation most of the time, and his mood billowed through the house.

'I can't *believe* I ended up with such a pack of brats to feed,' he said through gritted teeth, as the children helped Momma clear up after supper. 'Why do you eat so much? It makes me sick. Someone should have crushed your skulls at birth.' His voice rose and, without warning, he hurled his bottle of beer against the wall with a tremen-dous crash.

The terrified children watched the spilled liquid pour down the wall and gather into a puddle that spread over the floor, mixed with shards of glass. Next thing, their feet were wet and sticky, and Kate had cut her heel. Instead of comforting her, Momma sent them all upstairs. 'Why must you bother Jack?' she cried, her voice thick with reproach. 'Why can't you stay out of his way?'

Pink saw distress mixed with anger on Momma's face and it filled her with confusion. Why was Momma angry with them, but not with Jack? It was left to Pink to pluck shards of glass out of Kate's foot and bandage it, though she was shaking with fear and rage.

Before bed, Pink made up a story for the younger children about two baby robins whose Momma flew off to find food and didn't come back.

'They grew hungry and frightened,' she said in a hushed voice, conscious of Jack downstairs and not wanting to set him off again. 'Their Momma had to come back, she simply had to. Just as they gave up hope of ever seeing her again, they spied her flapping through the sky, with two juicy worms in her beak. After a joyous reunion and a good meal, she told them about the trials she had met on her journey home. A mean boy had wanted to put her in a cage, she had been hunted by a vicious raven, and a flock of pigeons had plucked out some of her breast feathers and chased her away. But she had overcome it all, determined to return to her children. And do you know why?'

'No. Tell us,' said Henry.

Pink put her arm around him. 'Because she loved them more than anything else in the world and it was her job to keep them safe,' she said, trying to set things back into their proper place. And it worked well enough that they were able to fall asleep, though later she heard them both whimpering in their dreams and, in the morning, there were urine stains on Henry's mattress.

Over breakfast, everything fell apart again. Jack made Momma hand the housekeeping money over to him and he accused her of lying when she said that that was all there was. Convinced she was hiding dollar bills on the sly, he went through her dresser drawers, flinging her underclothes all over the floor and getting even angrier when he didn't find any money.

For days afterward, Jack went around with a face like thunder, while Momma was cowed and tearful. Pink felt furious, afraid and wild with pity for her mother. How had she turned into this abject woman with pleading eyes? And what was Pink supposed to do about it? Kiss her, give her a hug? But there was something shut-off in Momma that made Pink hesitant to touch her.

Eventually Momma and Jack made up. But each time he wanted cash for beer, whenever she did the shopping or served a meal, the muttering about the hidden housekeeping money started up again. And even when he was cheerful, there was always the memory of the berserk times, and the fear of what he might say or do next.

Momma told the children to keep their voices down and stay out of Jack's way – particularly in the mornings, when he woke up with a sore head and a worse temper. They weren't to breathe a word to anyone about what went on. Their family, the complicated web of love and loyalties that bound them together, was not something that an outsider could understand and it was best kept private. If the children would hold their tongues, everything would come right in the end.

They held their tongues. They made themselves scarce, taking care not to pound up and down stairs, or slam doors, or play loudly in the yard. Kate began trailing round after Pink, a second shadow. Henry, a slender boy with the darting movements and alert brown eyes of a small bird, developed a stutter. No one watched out for them and told them to wash or put on clean clothes or do their schoolwork. It was a life of tenuous appearances and scraping by; their mother a different person, subdued and pale, as unavailable as a stranger.

Pink began to drift; she felt light-headed and strange and disconnected from herself, as though she were floating outside her life, observing but not part of it. She thought it must be how the boy in 'The War of the Ghosts' felt – mortally wounded, but numb. She was having trouble with the rules at school and she couldn't understand why everyone else accepted them. Why did they have to sit up straight and memorize facts they would never use and recite endless lines of poetry? She contemplated running away, but there was nowhere to run to and, besides, she could no sooner abandon her younger siblings than she could cut off her own arms. She started talking back to Mr Davis, her teacher, and skipping classes. Mr Davis would send her to Owens' Wood to crack willow rods off trees for her own punishment. But she didn't mind because the woods were her favorite place.

As soon as she got there she would run and run, until the world began to fall away and she stopped feeling like she might explode. Sometimes she rested on her favorite rock by the stream that was in a green enclosure of dogwood bushes, all overhung with wild grapevines, like a secret room. The rock was carved with the crude figure of a man, his head and body deep and solid, his arms and legs but tracings, knees bent, as if he were running.

Pink could see life more clearly from her rock than from any other place. She thought about Momma and Jack, and each of them seemed equally mad and impossible. They were glued together by poverty and – worse still – by private and unseemly needs that rose from the depths of their natures. It made Pink angry to the point of being mad herself. She thought, *I will not be like that. I simply won't. I will never get snared like Momma.*

When she was ready to leave, she would gather the willow rods, notching them at the joints for easy breakage, before making her way back to school to hand them to her teacher.

A year after Momma remarried, Pink walked through the woods with Jack, noticing that they seemed to have a mellowing effect on him, too. The air was sweet and warm, and they went slowly, with a pleasant sense of indolence. Birds sang to their hearts' content; lush and fragrant wildflowers grew all around. Pink thought of picking a bunch, but they were sure to wilt along the way. Jack reached past her to pluck a handful of blackberries from a bush and his hand brushed her breast. A bolt of sensation flashed from her breast to the place between her legs, as if they were connected by an invisible thread. She felt hot with shame and excitement, disgusted with herself. Jack was her mother's husband and she hated him.

Back on the road, they passed a group of workmen who had just come upon a number of Native American graves on the hillside. They were clearing the skeletons out indifferently, their shovels rising and falling in the rich earth.

Jack's eyes were flashing. He had a hatred of Native Americans, claiming that it stemmed from having fought against them in the war. He picked up a shovel and cleaved through a skeleton's spine without wincing – the sound hurt Pink's teeth. Its jaw was more pointed than the others, the edge of it sloping gently toward the ear, and she thought that it must have belonged to a woman. Jack piled up the bones at the path's edge and threw stones at them, encouraged by the workmen yelling, 'Hit 'em harder!' and, 'You missed one, over there!' until the bones lay in fine, chalky fragments.

'There. Now they'll have a hard time getting together on Resurrection Day,' Jack said, filling the air with a gurgling laugh that smelled of stale beer and the plug of tobacco he was chewing. The laborers laughed along with him.

Pink felt chilled right down to the bone. She knew that the skeletons' spirits could never find rest, as Native Americans believed that destroying their remains would prevent them from entering the afterlife. She was fearful of the spirits, tethered to this earth and seeking revenge, and she identified with them too, because as a woman, she was only one notch higher in the social system than the red-skinned man. She willed the spirits to unleash their full vengeance on Jack and the workmen.

She tried to make sense of their behaviour. She knew that men fought wars, but this was different, done in cold blood; it was base, vicious and senseless. It changed her perspective – never again would she look at men in the same way. She would always know what they were capable of.

Gradually, the situation at home got worse. Raised voices came more often from Momma and Jack's room at night, and sometimes the sound of breaking glass. First Kate and then Henry would creep into Pink's bed, where they huddled together, their eyes squeezed shut, fingers jammed into their ears to try and block out the ugly sounds. Pink did her best to comfort them, though she was frozen inside. She longed to grow up and get away from home, yet her coming of age was still years away. She didn't know how to survive the wait, as each day felt endless.

The stories she told Henry and Kate were a respite, giving them another world to step into; a world they could keep control of. Whenever Pink had time, she would set down these tales in Poppa's notebook, channelling her anguish about their situation and her thwarted ambitions into writing. It was a release that never failed her.

Presently, Jack's harsh words turned into blows and their mother had bruises on her arms, and her eyes were red-rimmed from crying. On New Year's Eve, when Pink was sixteen, Momma took the children to a church party at the Odd Fellows Hall on Main Street. Jack didn't want them to go, but Momma said to him, 'I need a break. I've got to have some space. I'm sorry.' She told the children to get their coats and shepherded them out the door, with Jack calling after them, 'You'll be sorry for this. I'm telling you.' Pink was scared, but she forgot about Jack when they arrived at the hall.

She thought it the prettiest room she had ever seen. Candles glimmered everywhere. There were flags and bunting on the walls, red-and-white checked cloths, and bottles of beer and wine on the tables. People were talking and laughing, and others were singing songs. Pink sat with her brothers and sister – what was happening at home made them wary of outsiders. It felt like being stranded on an island, watching everyone else getting on with their lives on the mainland. But she allowed herself to drop her guard enough to enjoy the meal.

Suddenly Jack burst through the doors, drunk as a coot and waving a pistol. A stunned silence fell. Pink felt as if all the oxygen had been sucked from the room. Jack weaved toward Momma, ranting that he would kill her even if she were the last woman on earth. The crowd came to life, with men hurrying to herd their families away from the crazy man, while Albert, helped by the butcher and the blacksmith, rushed forward to subdue Jack.

Sweat was pouring off Pink and her heart fluttered and thumped against her ribcage as she sat with her arms around her younger siblings, watching Jack flail in the blacksmith's strong grip. She wondered at how short Jack looked – it was only at home that he loomed larger than life. Momma ran for the door, sobbing wildly, yelling for the children to follow her.

They scrambled to their feet and shot out of the building, forgetting their coats. It was so cold that Pink's breath made clouds of steam, but she felt hot pounding down the street after Momma, with Albert and Charles just ahead. She had Kate and Henry by the hand, tugging them along. They were too scared to complain, though they struggled to keep pace. They caught up with Momma outside Millie and John King's home. She hugged her children one after another; they were all out of breath. 'I'm sorry. I'm so sorry,' she kept saying as John opened the door.

Momma said, 'Forgive me for disturbing you at this time of night—' as he stood and looked down at her, surprised. Millie appeared, took Mary Jane in her arms and steered them all inside. She was kind and efficient, offering cookies with hot milk, and making up pallets on the floor. 'Let's just get you comfortable,' she said to Momma. 'You can tell me what happened tomorrow.'

They stayed with the Kings while Jack cooled off and the town gossip died down. Their house was a refuge and Pink wanted to live there for ever, but she knew that it was only a matter of time before Jack and Momma made up again. Why couldn't Momma stop this terrible cycle of abuse and reconciliation? It was dreadful to see so clearly what her mother could not – she felt a helpless anger and a violent sense of injustice. Sure enough, Jack and Momma were back together within a week and, for a couple of months, things were better. But then the old argument about the housekeeping money erupted over dinner.

Jack went wild, cursing and howling until his face turned dark red and saliva shot from his mouth. Mary Jane was a liar and a damned whore; her children were miserable bastards. He smashed chairs and slammed into the plaster walls until they cracked. Then he swept Momma's newly ironed clothes off a chair, stamped on them and flung them out into the wet backyard.

Something in Momma snapped. She began to weep and beat her head against the wall, screaming at him in a voice they had never heard before. Seeing her pretty mother lose hold of herself – her face red and twisted, her nose all slimy with snot – was worse for Pink than anything she had yet witnessed. She felt half-crazed with pity, rage and helplessness. It even shocked Jack, who stopped yelling and said, 'Okay. Okay, sweetheart, I'm sorry.' He bent over, hands on his thighs, drawing deep, ragged breaths. 'Just stop crying, will you? It makes you look ugly.'

Momma wiped her eyes and nose, and Jack caught his breath, and they turned their attention back to their supper. Jack began to carve the meat, but the smallness of the joint set him set him off again. He grabbed the bone and hurled it at Momma. It grazed her on the temple, drawing blood. She picked it up off the floor and flung it back but missed. He jumped up, whipped his pistol out of his pocket and lunged at her ferociously. Without thinking, Pink and Albert leapt to their feet and formed a human wall to shield their mother while she escaped out the front door. Albert and Charles followed, with Pink and the younger ones hard on their heels. The neighbors were standing at their windows, watching. They did not stop running till they reached the Kings' house. It was exactly like running for their lives from the Odd Fellows Hall, and Pink felt trapped in a nightmare she couldn't wake up from.

Jack nailed the doors and windows of the family home shut, using a ladder to an upper window to get in and out. It was a full week before Momma could gain entry to remove their furniture. Pink and the older boys went with her to help. Jack was in Scott's Saloon – on their way, they'd seen him hunched over a pint – and they were sure he wouldn't be back any time soon.

Pink stood at the threshold, unable to absorb what she was seeing. Furniture broken and overturned, their possessions in disarray, empty bottles everywhere. They stumbled through the rooms, Pink breathing shallowly so as to absorb as little as possible of the rank air. The boys seemed stunned. Pink fully expected her mother to fall apart, but Momma only straightened her spine and said, 'Well! That's that, then.' They got to work, salvaging what they could and set off for the Kings' house, weighed down by belongings.

The sun was low in a clear sky, throwing peach-colored light onto buildings, making gray roofs glow. With a jolt of fear, Pink saw Jack walking toward them, home earlier than expected. She wanted to run, but she was carrying too much. He glared at them with angry, reddened eyes.

'What the hell do you think you're doing?' he yelled at Momma.

Pink shrank into herself, wishing the ground would open up and swallow her right down, but Momma simply crossed the street to avoid him, continuing on her way with a resolute set to her shoulders and her head held high.

Jack's face was a blend of incredulity and rage. 'You, madam, are fucking insane!' he screamed after her.

They carried on walking, not once looking back, though Pink could feel his hot eyes boring into her. The worst thing about it – worse even than the roaring shame, the neighbors hurrying past with pursed lips and averted eyes – was that Jack had not been wrong. Momma had been out of her mind to stay with him for so long.

The next day, Momma set about renting another home and moving her family into it. Jack, realizing that the game was up, skipped town. On 14 October 1878, she sued for divorce in the full, gossipy gaze of all Apollo. It was one of only fifteen divorce actions in the county that year and one of only five brought by the wife. Half of Pink was proud of her mother for finally summoning the courage to take this step, but the other half longed to fit in, to be normal, not to be gossiped about, and this part writhed in shame.

She and Albert had to testify in court, an unadorned room with wood-panelled walls, high windows and rows of benches. Pink thought about all the hours Poppa had spent here, dispensing justice in his calm, rational way, and it brought her a little comfort. Momma's face was tight with pain and worry; she sat with her arm linked through Millie's. Several of the townsfolk were here, which didn't surprise Pink. She knew that in a place as small as Apollo, boredom lent lustre to a scandal. She saw Mr Davis, who had been her teacher during that first difficult year of Momma's marriage to Jack. The atmosphere was unwholesome.

Albert was first to take the witness stand. His movements were rigid and controlled, but his voice kept cracking. 'Our stepfather cursed our mother, called her bitch and whore, and threatened her with a loaded gun,' he told the judge, an old, white-haired man, who listened carefully but hardly spoke. 'Jack tore the house apart. He tried to extort money from my mother many times and never provided her with any kind of living.'

When Albert stood down, it was Pink's turn. Her stomach churned and her knees shook as she climbed the four steps to the stand.

'I am seventeen years old. I was living at home during the years of my mother's marriage to Jack Ford. He was generally drunk the whole time,' she began unsteadily, looking the judge in the eye. His impassive expression unsettled her, as she couldn't tell if she was saying the right thing or plunging her family into more obloquy. She tried to pretend that she was simply presenting her research to Poppa after scouting one of his cases. *Give me the facts,* he would say. *Cut the feelings, I want hard, cold facts.* She took a breath and her voice came stronger.

'When drunk, Jack is very cross, and he is cross when sober. My mother always cooked and cleaned for him, and did his laundry. Momma bought and paid for his clothes out of her own money and was never ugly to him, no matter how he treated her. She was driven to tears very often. He threatened to do her harm and Momma was afraid of him. The first time he took hold of her in an angry manner, he tried to choke her and his thumbnails made marks on her throat.'

When she came to the end, the judge thanked her, saying, 'You did well. I know how hard it was.' Pink nodded gratefully but found she could not speak. She signed the court transcript 'Pinkey E. J. Cochran', her heart pounding so hard that she thought she might vomit or pass out. It had cost her such effort to pull out the details of their personal lives for inspection, like the contents of a grubby purse.

The judge left the bench to consider the case and they waited tensely. Finally he returned, and Pink held her breath. He took his place in her father's old chair, steepling his fingers.

'The case is clear-cut,' he said. 'There is strong evidence. The defendant did not appear to contest it. Therefore, I consent to grant the divorce.'

Momma started to weep with relief and Millie put her arms around her. Albert let out a rough breath. For Pink, it felt like yanking out a knife that had been stuck in her throat. But the gasps and murmurs starting up from the townsfolk confirmed what she already knew: their disgrace was sealed. Divorce was a stain they could never escape.

Four

PINK EMERGED FROM THE station with Momma and the younger children. They halted on the sidewalk, gazing in awe at the streets of Pittsburgh. 'What's *that*?' 'Look over there!' the little ones kept crying.

Everywhere Pink looked, there were people and buildings. Horses clattered past, vehicles rumbled, drivers shouted and honked their horns. Furnaces spewed smoke into the sky, with showers of soot raining down at odd moments. The air stank of smoke and sulfur, a dry, bitter tang that scorched Pink's nose and lingered in the back of her throat. Pittsburgh had shucked off its frontier-village ways since the end of the Civil War and, with a good share of its money made out of the war, had grown into an inventively progressive manufacturing city. Albert and Charles had migrated here in search of work six months after the divorce, and Pink had welcomed her mother's decision to follow them three months later. Pittsburgh was crowded, noisy, vibrant and anonymous. It was exactly the fresh start they needed.

They settled in Allegheny City, an unincorporated suburb of Pittsburgh, in a small, soot-stained house that was identical to all the other houses on the narrow street, with a backyard crisscrossed by railroad tracks. Momma took in boarders to make ends meet, a succession of young women working in menial, badly paid jobs.

Momma bemoaned the fact that there was no money to launch Pink's debut into society, no money to attract suitors for her hand. 'A girl's *supposed* to find the best match she can,' she said, shaking her head sadly. 'She's supposed to go through life with a husband by her side.'

Pink lifted her brows, surprised that her mother's opinion of marriage had not changed, despite the disaster with Jack.

'Why, I don't want to get married!' she exclaimed. 'I thought you knew that?'

'What foolishness is this, Pink? All pretty girls get married, of course they do.'

Pink shook her head. 'No, not me. I don't want to be a wife. I won't be under anyone's thumb.' What she wanted to add, what she did not add, was: *Don't you realize that the scenes I witnessed between you and Jack Ford put me off marriage for life?*

Instead of looking for a husband, Pink directed all her energies into the business of earning a living. For the next few years she worked as a kitchen girl, housekeeper and nanny – hard physical work that left her body exhausted and her heart longing for something larger.

Albert and Charles had found steady positions as clerk and manager of a rubber company, and they earned far more money than Pink did. She was twenty years old now, and her sense of this injustice grew with every week that passed. There were woefully few options open to women who felt trammelled by their roles and their circumstances. Then she saw an editorial in the *Pittsburgh Dispatch* that made her blood boil. It was titled 'What Girls are Good For' and it was a diatribe against working women:

> Women who have an insatiable desire to rush into the
> breaches under the guise of defending their rights,
> but which is in reality an effort to wrest from a man

certain prerogatives bequeathed him by heaven, are usually to a degree disgusting to womanly women and manly men. There is no greater abnormality than a woman in breeches, unless it is a man in petticoats.

Pink put down the newspaper, anger blazing through her. She took a piece of their best notepaper, thinking how unhappy Momma would be if she knew the use it was about to be put to. But the only thing Pink knew how to do was write and so she picked up her pen and let it fly, fired by all the disappointments and struggles she had endured.

Dear Sir,

I read your editorial with interest. While everyone in this land of free speech is entitled to express their views, there are perhaps some aspects of a woman's life you have omitted.

You see, girls have brains and ability, and are good for something else besides cooking and cleaning and hatching babies. What is more, you have overlooked women who must earn their bread, such as my mother and myself. You assume that women all have a choice in life, when the plain fact is that most of them don't. There are hardly any occupations open to women, and those few do not pay well. Women need work – real jobs paying real wages.

She signed her letter 'Lonely Orphan Girl' because she sometimes felt that way, despite Momma, despite her siblings. She sent it off quickly, feeling better for having vented her anger. At the very least he would read her response. It might even make him question his views. A few days later she opened the paper and was amazed to see a notice inviting the anonymous letter writer to come forward:

> If 'Lonely Orphan Girl' cares to send her name
> and address to this office as a sign of good faith, the
> Dispatch shall confer a favor.

As she read, Pink filled with a calm, confident elation. A brainwave struck: perhaps she could write for the paper? She stood up and began to pace the short length of the bedroom. Sunlight fell through the window, illuminating the peeling paint on the walls and the shallow fireplace with half the tiles missing. She wanted bigger things. She wanted her writing to be out there, to be heard, and she was sure that she could adjust her knack for storytelling into turning out hard news. Her dream of being a lawyer began to loosen its hold, as she saw afresh that the realities of training were beyond her reach. Reporting was a more achievable way of earning her living. Besides, her experience of life had taught her that it was full of complicated truths, and she thought that journalism would give her greater scope to express them than law.

The next day, she turned up at the *Dispatch* office in person, bypassing the formalities. She was breathless from climbing four flights of stairs, and shaking with fear and excitement. She wore her Sunday best, a brown cashmere dress with a velvet trim and fluted sleeves, high-button shoes, and her mother's sealskin jacket and matching hat. On her left thumb was a silver ring engraved with forget-me-nots and roses – a gift from her father that she believed brought luck.

She hovered at the threshold of the newsroom, thinking that she had never seen such a vibrant and intriguing place. The walls were decorated with huge pictures of the paper's best front pages. Giant cylinders in the corners spat out spooled ribbons of printed news-sheet. Men in rolled-up shirtsleeves sat at desks, typing, smoking, talking – they gave an impression of buoyant energy and confidence. Office boys darted in and out with messages and copy. Papers were everywhere, heaped on desks and piled all over the floor. The air smelled of printer's ink and tobacco smoke. A few of the men looked at her curiously, but no one came forward to help. She stopped an office boy and asked him where she might find the editor.

The boy pointed to Madden, who was sitting in a corner office with windows set in the door, so he could keep an eye on what was happening in the newsroom. Pink felt relief. She had expected to find an old, cross man with a bushy beard, who would look over the top of his spectacles and snap out, 'What d'ye want?' Instead, she saw a mild-faced person of compact build, whose brown eyes registered astonishment when she knocked on his door and sailed in, saying, 'Good day, Mr Madden. My name is Pink Cochran, but you know me as "Lonely Orphan Girl".'

He shook the hand she offered; his grip was firm and dry.

'You're probably wondering why I came,' she carried on, trying to control the tremor in her voice. 'Well, sir, you mentioned doing me a favor, and I came to tell you what I'd like. I very much want the chance to be a reporter for the *Dispatch*.'

He stared at her. She could guess what he was thinking: *Women don't report the news.*

'Sit down, Miss.'

She had only just begun to put up her hair, and it was threatening to fall down around her shoulders. Her bustle wobbled as she moved to the chair he held out for her, for she hadn't had much practice wearing it and it was an awkward thing to manage, like having a second backside pinned onto one's real one.

Once seated, she felt less at a disadvantage. She gave her lucky thumb ring a twist. Beneath her feet, she could feel the vibrations of the great printing presses from the floor below, which both soothed and exhilarated her. The realization settled in her that she had finally found her place in life.

'I'm sorry you made a wasted journey, Miss Cochran,' Madden was saying, 'because I'll have to turn you down. I—'

'Wait a minute! Before you say anything else, please listen to me. I *can* write. I would make a good reporter.'

'I'm afraid that you are far too young. And even if you were older, I don't employ women.'

'Why not?'

He sighed. 'Well, for one thing, chasing hard news is a tough game. City newsmen travel alone at night into slums, morgues and gambling dens. They fraternize with cops and crooks. They witness accidents, strikes, riots and fights. I cannot with delicacy ask a woman to do that.'

'But I know I can do it.'

She watched a succession of feelings pass over his face. 'I'll admit to being curious about why you'd even want to try,' he said.

She frowned at him, then tried to smile. 'I know it's hard, dirty work, but it's the only thing that interests me. I must earn a living, you see. My mother and I need the money.' She could feel waves of red suffuse her face and she steeled herself to go on. 'My brothers are just start-ing out in business here; I can't ask them to support me. You saw that I can write. Give me a chance. Let me write an article for you. If you decide that it's good enough to print, then let me write more. I can do it as well as anyone on your paper.' She sat on the edge of her seat, gripping her purse tightly. 'I have ideas.'

'What sort of ideas?' He lit a cigarette, took a deep drag and exhaled. They both watched the plume of blue smoke rise.

'Well, Mr Madden, I've gone into every corner of Pittsburgh. I've looked all over – and found stories everywhere. The other day I went to explore the slums. I came upon a family of six children that day, sleeping in one room. Their father was killed in a factory accident last month – he got caught in one of the machines and it chewed him to pieces – and their mother had died giving birth to the littlest one. They had no one to look after them, except some kind neighbors, who were taking it in turns to feed them. The oldest was eleven and she watched over her brothers and sisters day and night. Wouldn't that make a story?'

She leaned forward. 'I've noticed that the most of your readers are working people. They don't just want to find out about society parties, or what's happening in the White House or on Wall Street. They want to read about their own experience – their work and home lives, and what they *think*!'

'It's the job of a paper to report about big lives, not small ones,' Madden explained, flicking ash into an empty coffee cup. 'People buy the *Dispatch* to read about the wealthy, the famous, the influential.'

'That may well be true, Mr Madden. But isn't there room for both kinds of stories?'

His eyes met hers and he looked away. Pink's heart fell, as if there was no end to falling. After all her efforts, she was still nowhere.

She rose to leave.

'Sit down,' he said. He mashed out the cigarette and crossed his arms. 'I'll say this for you, Miss Cochran, you sure are determined. And you can write. All right, then – here's my deal. I want you to do one feature for me. Turn the letter you wrote me into a rebuttal piece about "the women's sphere". If it's any good, I'll give you a job.'

The world tilted and settled back on its axis in this changed formation. 'I can't thank you enough!' she exclaimed.

'No need for thanks,' he said gruffly. 'Write a good article and the job is yours. In any case, you deserve a chance with your ideas.'

Pink stayed up all night to write her rebuttal piece. She worked in the kitchen, a long, low-ceilinged room with a red-tiled floor, warmed by a coal-fired range. Trains thundered past on their way to every corner of the country, making the crockery on the dresser shudder. She chewed her pen and thought back to her thwarted legal ambitions, remembering how much harder she had applied herself to learning than her brothers. But the opportunity Poppa had given her was always going to be an exception, easily lost. Life was unfair for women. She decided to begin the article by suggesting that girls should be treated the same way as boys, that the same opportunities should be opened to them.

> How many wealthy and great men can be pointed out who started in the depths, but where are the many women? Let a youth start as errand boy and he will work his way up until he is one of the firm. Girls are just as smart, and a great deal quicker to learn; why, then, can they not do the same?
>
> Here would be a good field for believers in women's rights. Let them forgo their lecturing and writing and go to work; more work and less talk. Take some girls that have the ability, procure for them situations, start them on their way, and by so doing accomplish more than by years of talking.

She wrote without conscious planning or thought, simply following her pen as fast as her hand could move it across the page. Writing brought her closer to her father, for she was using everything he had taught her. In her mind, Poppa had split into two different people: one warm, shrewd, paternal; the other irresponsible and foolish. As she worked, she felt that the wise Poppa was still with her, that he had never gone out of her life, and it brought her the deepest peace.

By the time she had finished, the blue-gray light of dawn was filtering through the windows and the trains had stopped running. She boiled herself up some tea and settled back at the table to reread what she'd written, warming her cramped, ink-stained hands around the mug. She knew that it was good. Parts were more than good.

She rested for a few hours, then dressed and took her manuscript to the *Dispatch*'s office on Fifth Street. But as soon as she'd dropped it off, her confidence melted away, like sugar in warm water. She began the walk toward home – it was raining and she turned up the collar of her coat to stop the chilly drops from trickling disagreeably down the back of her neck. Carriages made a slurring sound as they passed; their wheels threw up water in a solid, scummy arc that she did her best to dodge. She wasn't a writer at all; she was an imposter with ideas above her ability. She'd got lucky once, but what on earth had made her think that she could pull it off on a regular basis? Probably Madden would hate the article; he wouldn't print it; he would refuse to have anything more to do with her. So far, she hadn't told her family and the loneliness of bearing an unshareable secret only compounded the agony of waiting for feedback.

A week later a check for five dollars arrived from Madden, along with a request for a second article on a subject of her choice. She hurried out to buy the *Dispatch* and found her piece, 'The Girl Puzzle', placed prominently on the second page. The byline read 'Lonely Orphan Girl'.

Seeing her words printed out for the whole of Pittsburgh to read made her feel richer and happier than ever before. The words looked different in print – more authoritative – and for the first time, she had an intimation of just how powerful they might be.

She wasted no time in setting to work on the new article. The topic she picked was something else she knew about: divorce.

The dispute about whether people should or shouldn't be permitted to divorce had been fought from pulpits and in senates and law courts for years. But Pink had not simply picked an interesting topic; it was also an intensely personal one. She still suffered the occasional nightmare or flashback to Jack's violence; still felt scarred deep inside, with most of her heart sealed off. Living with him had left its imprint.

She picked up her pen and the words poured out. She wrote that the divorce laws needed to be changed, and then she went a step further. There ought to be regulations, she argued, like those in existence in Bavaria, forbidding people to marry in the first place if they owed taxes, or if their laziness, bad habits or poverty were likely to create an unhappy home.

After another excruciating wait, her piece appeared under the headline, 'Mad Marriages'. It was followed by a note from Madden: Miss Cochran had fulfilled her share of the bargain. Would she care to come into the office at her earliest convenience to talk?

'Well, Miss Cochran, your writing is certainly controversial enough,' Madden began, when they were once again sitting opposite each other in his office at the *Dispatch*. 'Readers have been responding in droves.'

Pink licked dry lips. 'Agreeing or disagreeing?'

'Both.' He fished a cigarette out of his back pocket and lit up. 'Some of them are convinced that "Lonely Orphan Girl" *must* be a man. Few ladies would dare mention divorce, much less write about it as strongly as you did.' He shot her an amused look and said, 'The piece needed editing – you're not one for style. But what you have to say, you say right out. It's sharp, fresh and honest. You're pushing social boundaries and, what's more, your words are a direct appeal. "Put yourself in their shoes," you seem to say. There's some spark in you that sets you apart from the rest.'

He blew smoke toward the ceiling. 'Remember when you told me that you needed to earn a living?'

'Yes,' she replied, coloring faintly.

'Well, I understand that. See, I came up the hard way too. I cut school in Canada to work secretly in a printing office. I used to sharpen pencils, run errands and deliver the finished copy. All the time I was watching things and learning. Then I came to Pittsburgh to take my first job in a composing room. I worked my way through the positions of reporter, copy-desk man and telegraph editor, before becoming editor of this paper.' He sat forward, rubbing his face. 'What I'm trying to say is that the job is yours if you want it. And I'm not hiring you to write the sort of fashion, cookery and handy household tips that women normally cover. I'm taking you on as a bona fide news reporter. You can start on Monday at a salary of five dollars a week.'

Joy was blazing through her. 'I'll take it, Mr Madden. Thank you, sir.'

He grinned at her. 'Welcome to the team, Miss Cochran. I'm sure that you will be a credit to the *Dispatch*.' He reached out to shake her hand.

'First thing is you'll need a pen name,' he said. 'You probably know that it's customary for ladies who write for newspapers to do so without making their identities known. I can't keep using "Orphan Girl". How about, say, Charles Nash? It has a distinguished ring to it. Or, let me think... Isaiah Johnson?'

Pink shook her head. 'I am happy to use a pen name,' she said, 'but not a man's name.'

'What do you want to be called, then?' Madden sounded impatient and Pink knew she better come up with something fast.

One of the office boys walked past, humming a song by Stephen Foster, the popular Pittsburgh composer:

Nelly Bly, Nelly Bly,
Bring de broom along,
We'll sweep de kitchen clean, my lub,
And hab a little song.

Pink didn't wait for him to finish. 'Nelly Bly – how's that? It's short and easy, and people are already familiar with it from the song.' Adding to herself, *and I will indeed sweep the kitchen clean.*

Madden tried it out. 'Nelly Bly. Nelly Bly. Yes, I like it. Nice and catchy, can't be mispronounced. It will stay in their minds from one article to the next. Here.' He pushed his blotting pad toward her. 'Sign your new name. See how it feels.'

She wrote it out with a flourish. As she did so, something fell into place deep inside her, and she knew that at the grand age of twenty, she was becoming the person she was meant to be.

The first time her pen name was printed in the paper, it was misspelled Nellie. So that became her name.

There was a storm in the family, as she expected. They were in the kitchen having breakfast when she broke the news. The kettle was steaming on the range and Momma stood in front of it, frying eggs. Her children sat at the table.

'You are not going to make a public display of yourself! I won't have it!' Albert declared, thumping his fist on the table, which made the crockery jump. His red-brown hair was carefully slicked back and he wore a red necktie. His face was turning red, and Pink wondered how her daredevil brother could have turned into a young man who only cared about appearances.

He said, 'There are only three occasions when it's acceptable for a lady's name to appear in the newspapers. When she is born, when she gets married, and when she *dies*.' He shot her a look that made her feel she was some kind of aberration.

Momma set the dish of eggs on the table. 'Really, Pink, I wish you'd discussed it with us before you wrote the articles,' she said, in her pert but anxious way. She picked a piece of lint off her black skirt and flicked it away. Since the divorce, she had worn nothing but black, and Pink was unsure if she was grieving for the end of her marriage or reverting to being Widow Cochran in order to erase every trace of Jack.

'Newspaper offices are awful places,' said Charles, shaking his head. 'They're full of rough men swearing and spitting tobacco. As for the work... well, it's going to give you brain strain. Exhaustion and burnout.' He glanced at Albert for approval.

Pink was cutting pieces of bread and buttering them for everyone. 'I must earn a living,' she insisted quietly. 'I don't want to be a housekeeper or nanny any longer – those are only polite names for high-class servants. And I am paid dollars for writing articles.'

'God*damnit*, Mother. Put your foot down. Stop her right now, before she makes a laughing stock of us,' Albert commanded, slicing into his egg. They all watched the yolk bleed out onto the plate.

Momma walked to the window and stood gazing at the railway, lost in thought. Pink's pulse quickened in apprehension. A train passed by with a mournful shriek, then another. At last, Momma turned to face Albert and Charles.

'Boys,' she said, 'listen to me.'

'We're listening,' said Albert. All the children had remained at the table.

'I know that, deep down, you're scared of having Pink on your hands and being obliged to take care of her,' Momma said firmly. 'So stop putting obstacles in her way when she wants to be independent.'

Albert got a bit of bread lodged in his throat and started coughing. Pink shot her mother a surprised but grateful look. Momma's lack of support for her legal ambitions had hurt her deeply, but it made this turnaround all the sweeter. Perhaps Momma's experience with Jack had taught her that a woman must stand on her own two feet?

'Well. All right, sweetheart,' Momma said to her. 'I raised you to shine and it looks like you're going to do exactly that. Now go make us proud.'

Pink jumped up and hugged her. 'Thank you, Momma. I will do my best.'

Her mother's bones felt thin and stiff in her arms, like the skeleton of a bird. Releasing her, she turned back to the table. 'Oh, there's just one more thing. . . from now on, I'd like you all to call me Nellie, not Pink.'

Five

NELLIE CHOSE HER TOPIC for her first series of articles and put it to Madden: working women.

'I want to write about the woman in the street and how hard her life is,' she told him. 'I'd like to go into the factories and investigate conditions. I believe they're among the worst in the country. So are the slums, and most people have no idea how awful they are.'

Madden was watching her closely. 'What's your angle?' he asked.

'To tell the public the truth. To show them the facts about the poor, about the immigrants who come over here and aren't taken care of – good people who could make good citizens. But they're all packed in together, scared and unassimilated.'

'I see. And after you've told the story? What then?'

She leaned forward in her chair. 'If people knew, I think they would be outraged. I want to shock them into pushing for change, shock the government into actually *doing* something.'

As she said this, she understood why she was drawn to journalism. It was storytelling with a difference. It involved delving into complexity, bringing gray areas of morality to light; and it was backed up by collating evidence and finding justice. Journalism reconciled the contributions of both her parents.

But Madden was frowning. He said, 'It's admirable, but you're going to hit obstacles. Don't you see that?'

Nellie felt a stab of dismay. 'What kind of obstacles?'

'Well, for one thing there will be landlords who don't want the public knowing the facts about their slum properties.'

Silence. She held her breath, praying he wouldn't refuse her.

'Look, this paper has never been cowardly,' he said at last. 'The people of Pittsburgh deserve to know the truth. Who knows, this might be the first step in lobbying for a lot of reform.' He drew a hand across his eyes. 'All right then, Nellie, I'm going to say yes. Go out and find the material for your "real experience" stories. I'll get an artist to go with you.'

She felt an explosion of relief. 'Thank you, sir. I promise you won't regret it.'

He raised his brows and said, 'Just be careful, all right? A man's life isn't safe on some of our streets, even in broad daylight. A lady is at even greater risk. You must be vigilant.'

She laughed at him. 'If women aren't safe on the streets on honest business, it's high time they can be. I plan on setting the trend.'

For her first article, Nellie decided to apply a fresh lens to working women's lives: she would write about what they did after hours. She caused a stir showing up at the gates of Allen's Clothing Factory in her pretty dress and bonnet. Boys whistled, women glared, men made lewd remarks. But Nellie kept her composure, ignoring them, and presently, girls and women in brown uniforms began to stream out of the building, walking in small groups. Nellie stopped one after another and asked if they would mind answering a few questions, but they looked at her strangely, pursing their lips and shaking their heads. 'I've so little leisure time, I'd rather not spend it with a stranger,' said a woman whose hands cradled her stomach, as if she were in pain. Finally, a girl with dark, braided hair wound elaborately around her head agreed to talk. She was thin and pale, with a cold sore at the corner of her mouth that must have made speaking painful.

She told Nellie that just about their only relief from the long days of drudgery was the activity known as 'man mashing'. Many a working girl met a man on the streetcars or in a bar, got drunk and accompanied him home, only to repeat the risky routine the next weekend. More often than not, these girls would end up in a home for fallen women.

'Why do you risk your reputation like this?' Nellie asked, concerned.

'Risk my reputation? I never had one to risk,' the girl said, with a short laugh.

'What do you mean?'

'I work twelve-hour shifts, six days a week, for a pittance,' she said. 'At the end of the day, I'm sick of it all and longing for something new. I hardly care if it's good or bad – anything to break the monotony.'

'Couldn't you find a safer form of pleasure?'

The girl shrugged. 'What do you suggest?' she said bitterly. 'I have no books. I can't go to places of amusement because I don't have the clothes or money. No one cares what becomes of me.' She stared ahead, her mouth trembling.

Nellie knew all about desperation, and her heart ached for the girl. She pressed a couple of dollars into her hand and went home to write her story.

If no amusement is offered these girls, they will seek it and accept the first thing that comes along. There's no excuse for girls with pleasant homes and kind friends, no excuse for the men who can seek amusement elsewhere. But for the poor working girl without friends or money, with the monotonous grind of hard work, who shall condemn and who shall defend?

For her next articles, Nellie tramped for miles through some of Pittsburgh's most deprived areas to interview women workers in eight factories, where they assembled everything from cigars to bottles to barbed wire. She'd learned to wear old clothes – the interviews went more easily if she did not stand out.

They told her about the frightful conditions of cold, damp and dirt; the long hours of standing; the wire and broken glass that cut their hands to shreds while rats ran between their feet, looking for anything edible. They weren't allowed to eat or drink while they worked, not even a sip of water, and there was only one toilet for both sexes to use on two floors. It was no good complaining to the manager, for dissent was simply ignored. And for their trouble, they were often despised and shamed. 'I've always been told that factory girls are the worst girls on earth,' a worker with thoughtful brown eyes told Nellie. 'But you can be a lady just as well in a factory as in a parlor.'

When Nellie had finished her research about working women, she turned her attention to the slums. Anger and outrage grew in her as she walked through narrow, unpaved streets, past blocks of shabby tenements and decrepit old houses with broken windows. There were no trees or flowers, only weeds pushing through the mud. Washing was slung from window ledges, gutters ran with filthy water, and dogs – all ribs and fur worn down to inflamed skin – dug in rotting trash heaps, where small ragged children also played. Conditions were worse than anything Nellie had dreamt of. Whole families in one room, eating, drinking, sleeping, working, dressing and undressing, without privacy or dignity. Fire-trap tenements that were hives of disease, their halls full of rats and garbage. Homeless people sleeping in doorways, too ground down to care for their own safety. Children who had never been to school, and others of ten or twelve who were sent to work in the mills because if they didn't earn a wage, their families would starve.

These children broke her heart. They were trained to work, virtually from birth. They were old before their time, their bodies stunted and twisted by heavy labor and long hours. They knew almost nobody who went to school or had enough to eat. Members of their families were out of work and leading chaotic lives, whole segments of their community. They were born with no hope; they didn't stand any kind of chance in life.

Nellie's articles ran as a series every Sunday, with its own logo emblazoned with the headline, 'Our Workshop Girls: Women's Labor in Pittsburgh'. They were accompanied by pictures of women with their feet bundled in rags against the bitter cold of the cement floors. The articles were personal, emotional, giving intimate glimpses into the lives and feelings of female workers. Something was brewing in Nellie. She had a fight to make and a voice with which to make it heard.

The reaction was mixed. The *Dispatch* sold out. Working people flocked to buy it because this was their story and Nellie Bly their champion. Madden was pleased – the paper's circulation was exploding.

But factory owners were livid. Condemnation of Nellie's 'immoral' articles rang out from church pulpits;

how dare she meddle in worldly affairs instead of sticking to the domestic realm, as a woman should? Her mailbox was filled with letters that ranged from threats to marriage proposals. The 'Nellie Bly' articles became a regular feature, her identity the subject of much speculation.

'Women gossip about you while they're sewing,' Madden told her gleefully. 'Businessmen quarrel over lunch. I even heard about a couple of inebriated gentlemen who were dragged off to the cells to cool down, still slurring: "She's a woman!" "Nah, I tell you it's a man using the name!"'

Nellie chuckled.

'The mystery is part of the game and we're going to play it up as fully as we can,' he said.

A newsroom was something of a boys' club, Nellie discovered. Her fellow journalists were a rough lot, unused to having a woman in their midst. They tolerated her presence rather than welcomed it, and they alternated between familiarity and sarcasm. Madden was her stalwart champion, but she had to endure a good deal of teasing from the others.

'You going to run off with some fine young swell and dump us, now that you've made a name for yourself?' one of them might ask, to the accompaniment of boisterous laughter.

She didn't want any of them getting to know her. 'I'd never leave my handsome beaux of the press,' she would reply sweetly, holding her own, giving as good as she got.

Letters continued to flood in to the paper. The ones Nellie treasured most were from working-class women and girls. One young woman proposed that Nellie set up a reading room so that she could go there in the evenings, instead of visiting the bars and taverns. 'If we had more people like Nellie Bly to think of something for the good of working girls, it would be better for us,' she wrote.

Shortly before the series ended, Nellie went to see Madden with an idea for her next story. She would write about the health of workers: the noxious gases they inhaled at home and in workshops, the polluted air of the streets, the long hours and insufficient rest. It was no wonder that diseases were tearing through whole communities. She was sure that Madden would like it, but walking into his office, she saw that he was reading a letter and there was a deep crease between his brows.

'What's up?' she asked.

He waved the letter at her. 'I just received this from the director of Pears Soap. They're one of our biggest advertisers.'

She swallowed uneasily. 'What does it say?'

Madden shifted in his seat. 'Unless I kill your articles, they will withdraw all advertising from the *Dispatch*.'

'*What?*'

'You heard me. I've been getting similar letters from other big businessmen. The fact is, I'm under huge pressure about you and it's mounting week by week.'

Stunned, Nellie sank into a chair. 'I... I don't get it,' she stammered.

'They don't want the public knowing the truth about conditions in their factories. I warned you this could happen.'

She tried to smile. 'You're not going to listen to them, are you?'

'I don't have a choice,' he snapped. Then, more gently, 'You might be a pioneering reporter, but the paper cannot afford to lose its advertisers.' Briefly, he closed his eyes. 'I am very sorry, but your stories must stop – at least until this has died down.'

Nellie couldn't answer. She was seething with anger and resentment, and felt horribly diminished.

'I'll tell you what,' Madden said at last. 'We'll try your hand at something else.'

'Something else' turned out to be a theater opening of a new play, *Dr Jekyll and Mr Hyde*. Nellie covered theater, opera, concerts, lectures and art exhibits. She wrote about tree grafts obtained from garden nurseries, a minister with a collection of 50,000 butterflies, and ladies' hair care. And she hated it.

Her family was relieved and proud. Writing about the arts was considered a literary achievement, worlds apart from seeing her pen name linked to factory girls and slums.

Nellie angled to create a more interesting niche for herself on the staff, but in vain. Madden was well and truly spooked by the threatened withdrawal of advertising, and he wasn't going to budge any time soon. The women's page slush she was writing was dull and confining; it sucked the life out of her. She missed the buzz of living by her wits – of having to produce something new and sharp every day, continually honing her perceptions. It was like being let out of prison, getting a sweet taste of freedom and life, and promptly being walled back up again.

The idea of moving to New York came to Nellie one sleepless night, as her mother and Kate snored softly in the room they shared, and the trains passed by with long, haunted wails.

Why should she stay in Pittsburgh? New York was the nation's publishing capital, with the biggest papers, the greatest papers in the country. New York was gathering the whole world to itself. Why shouldn't she try her luck there?

She shifted uncomfortably – there was a broken spring in the middle of the mattress that was hard to avoid. She couldn't go on writing genteel pieces about the latest lecture by Mark Twain, or the forthcoming concert by the Pittsburgh Symphony Orchestra. More to the point, she couldn't abandon those in need. Abandoning them also meant diminishing herself and her own ambitions.

Surely the men who ran New York's newspapers were audacious enough to take a chance with her? It wasn't as if she were completely unknown to them. She had a reputation, and determination to succeed in spades.

Her thoughts didn't stop racing till the trains had ceased and the dawn light was seeping through the curtains. It gradually revealed the shabbiness of the room – the worn furniture, the crazy paving of cracks running across the ceiling. None of the houses she had lived in since the spacious old farmhouse of her childhood had felt like home. Now her professional home was the only home that mattered to her.

She yawned and her body began to shape itself into the curve she would sleep in. As she drifted off, she admitted one last thought: that writing serious articles was the only way she could keep going. Without it, she sensed the shifting, heavy darkness of her earlier years would close in on her again.

By morning, it was clear that her only option was to quit the *Dispatch*. It was a matter of self-preservation. Three days later, she simply didn't show up for work. She left a note for them to find:

I am off to New York. Look out for me.

BLY

Six

ELLIE STEPPED OFF THE train at Grand
Central Station. The station building was vast
and high-ceilinged, and the air smelled of
smoke. There was a crowd of people on the platform, all
bustling about and talking in loud voices, and trunks and
boxes being unloaded, and baggage carts on the move.
The tumult made Pittsburgh seem sleepy. Nellie had five
dollars in her pocket; she felt excited, a little afraid, but
determined. She was wearing gloves, high-heeled shoes
and a wide-brimmed hat with a big gilt arrow at the side,
tied under the chin and tilted forward at a rakish angle.

She had discarded her modest little bonnets and
embraced the newly fashionable hats with their dashing
trims and veils floating out behind them. Although female
reporters were still rare, there was no harm in having a
trademark look, and her hats were eye-catching. She had
realized that dress was a great weapon in the hands of
a woman, making her more successful at whatever she
undertook. Her sex had so few weapons at their disposal,
they had to use every one available.

Nellie's brothers had not objected to the New York plan.
If their sister insisted on continuing with her newspaper
career, it was better that she did so in a different city. Her
mother had been more reluctant, but her will had never

been a match for Nellie's. And ever since Jack, there had been something hollowed-out in her, like a tree blasted by lightning. She had given way, agreeing to let Nellie go on condition that she found respectable lodgings. Also, that Momma would follow with the younger children as soon as Nellie had secured a steady job. Even so, saying good-bye had been hard. From the time of Poppa's collapse, partings had made Nellie anxious.

She rented a tiny furnished room on West 96th Street, where many of the roads weren't yet paved. Her solitary window offered a view of the alley at the back of the building, lined with trash barrels. Every now and then goats would wander through, snacking on garbage and weeds. She unpacked her notebooks and her few belongings, and set out to get a line on the metropolis.

It was very hot – the hottest summer in memory. Those whose did not have to venture outside stayed quietly behind drawn shutters. Sweating pedestrians carried their coats and fanned their faces with their hats. Every day brought new reports of people taking ill and dying of the dreadful, oppressive weather.

Even blanketed in heat, New York was a tumult of noise and surging movement and crowds. Nellie never knew what kind of speech she was going to hear, for immigrants were pouring into the city; there were strange outfits and strange foods; signs in German, Italian and Yiddish. The streets teemed with vehicles of all descriptions – from lumbering wooden delivery carts drawn by enormous horses, to private broughams and carriages with their sleek thoroughbreds, to carts pushed by human hands – all honking and barging and clattering over the rough cobblestones, throwing up clouds of humid dust. Dust coated everything. The air smelled of kerosene, smoke and horse manure rotting in the hot sun. Crossing the street meant charting a course between swarms of black flies. Over the rumble of traffic and the bells of the omnibuses rang the cries of vendors announcing their wares: the vegetable women, the milkmen, who poured their milk with cream still marbled on the top from huge barrels straight into the jugs of housemaids, the hawkers of brooms and dusters, buttons and scarves, the chimney sweeps, the men pushing wheelbarrows full of cakes of ice, who would chip off bits for a penny, and, lately, the newsboys shouting their headlines on street corners.

There were marvellous sights to see. The Statue of Liberty, less than a year old. The Brooklyn Bridge, the longest suspension bridge in the world. The shiny department stores, the lofty churches, the fashionable and elegant brownstones. At night the streets were lit by the new electric lamps: bright white moons throwing down their beautiful, strange light, casting shadows on the sidewalks that seemed like dancing creatures. But she also explored tenement wastelands that were as bad as anything she had seen in Pittsburgh. She walked through the Tenderloin and the Bowery, past concert saloons and bars, past whorehouses, where painted male prostitutes dressed in chemises relaxed on the front steps ahead of their night's work. They called out greetings to Nellie in falsetto voices and she wished them good day in return, trying for nonchalance, though she had never seen their like. It was as if New York was two distinct cities existing alongside each other: one full of strength, grace and energy, the other marred by poverty, overcrowding, degeneracy and disease. One particular encounter haunted her: a woman in a dirty dress and shawl, huddled in a doorway, nursing a nearly empty bottle of whiskey.

'Have you any change for me, dear?' she asked Nellie in a slurred voice. 'I'm down on my luck.' She had cloudy, unfocused eyes and fishnets of smashed capillaries on her cheeks.

Nellie dug in her purse and gave her a dollar that she could ill afford.

'Bless you,' said the woman, waving the bottle in benediction.

'Please buy something to eat with it and not more whiskey?' Nellie pleaded, kicking herself for not thinking to do that in the first place.

'I'll try my best, but the drink's so hard to resist,' the woman said, half closing her eyes. 'There's no use lying about it. Whiskey is my comfort and my curse. It's robbed me of everything.' She coughed – a scraping sound that seemed to tear at her chest. 'Drink put my sister in the asylum.'

'I am sorry. What happened?' Compassion and a newspaperwoman's instinct for a story were rising in Nellie. Then she remembered that she had nowhere to place a story and desolation rolled through her.

The woman slumped against the wall. 'She saw her oldest pulled under the wheels of an omnibus, and took to drink to forget. But she drank so much, she got dreadful hallucinations, and they took her away to Blackwell's Island.' A tear trickled down her cheek. 'It's a brutal place.'

Nellie shivered, remembering her own childhood hallucinations and how they had brought her to the brink of madness. 'How awful for you both,' she said, with feeling. 'I didn't know there was an asylum on the Island. See, I'm new to New York. Would you mind telling me what it's like?'

The woman shuddered. 'Terrible things happen there. Rats run across the wards in broad daylight. I heard of a patient who hit her cellmate on the head with a chamber pot, cracking her skull. I heard of nurses beating patients and starving them. I can't stand to think of my sister in that place...' She broke off, unable to continue.

'It sounds horrifying!' said Nellie, shocked yet fascinated. She stopped herself saying she could imagine how the woman felt. She couldn't. 'Do you hear from your sister?' she asked instead.

The woman swallowed a mouthful of whiskey. 'Not once since she was sent there. I don't expect to now.' She wiped her mouth with the back of her hand. 'What kills me is that she wasn't mad – only desperate.'

'I'm so sorry,' Nellie said, appalled.

'All I want is enough drink to forget.' The woman drained the bottle, tilting it high to catch the last drops of liquid.

Once Nellie had got her bearings, she embarked on an epic daily trek downtown, speeding giddily south on the Ninth Avenue Elevated railway, and then walking east. But she didn't mind it one bit. The heedless, uncrushable aliveness of New York stimulated and thrilled her, and besides, she had always loved to walk. She loved the solid rhythm of her footfalls on the sidewalk, the frisson of rubbing shoulders with strangers as she took in the sights, smells and sounds. It was an adventure, a meditation. Somehow, when her legs began to move, she found her thoughts flowing. *Solvitur ambulando,* the ancients were fond of saying. To solve a problem, walk around.

Her destination was Park Row, also known as Newspaper Row, a street slanting north-east from lower Broadway, with newspaper offices running down one side near City Hall. Looking at their imposing facades for the first time, the bold logos of the *New York Sun*, *World* and *Journal* glittering in the sunlight, it was all she could do not to cheer aloud. She knew that she had found her true home.

But as June stretched into July, and July into September, Nellie besieged the newspaper offices of Park Row in vain. Her Pittsburgh portfolio meant little to the guards at the doors of the city's top periodicals. They turned away aspiring reporters every day, they told her. More to the point, no right-minded editor would employ a woman on his paper. That was the unanimous verdict and she could not get past it. It began to seem that the cramped room on West 96th Street might be home for ever. To keep body and soul together, she started writing freelance articles for the Pittsburgh *Dispatch* – women's features, mostly – the very subjects she had fled Pittsburgh to escape.

One muggy and starless night, Nellie rested on the fire escape of her building. All around her, people were sitting on their stoops or fire escapes, hoping in vain for a breath of wind that would make sleep possible. Someone was singing and strumming a guitar, and strains of 'Leaning on the Everlasting Arms' reached Nellie.

At first the man sang by himself, but presently some of the others took it up. And the effect spread until, within minutes, the whole block was ringing with sound. There was something unearthly about the way the melody grew until it soared into the air, absorbing the heat and the misery.

> What a fellowship, what a joy divine
> Leaning on the everlasting arms.
> What a blessedness, what a peace is mine
> Leaning on the everlasting arms.

It comforted Nellie, lulling her into a sort of waking dream, and memories of her time at the Pittsburgh *Dispatch* began to run through her mind. The look of surprise on Madden's face the first time he had seen her in the newsroom. The sweet feeling of signing her new pen name on his blotter. She saw now how brave and unconventional he had been to give her free rein with her articles, but even he had been unable to stand up against public opinion and the sway of the money brought in by advertisers. That he had kept her on his staff was more than most other editors would have done.

Why had she ever left the *Dispatch*? If she had known how tough New York was going to be, she doubted she would have done it. She would have stayed and tried harder to create a fulfilling role for herself. She wondered despondently if she would ever make her mark on New York. It was looking less likely by the day. But then an idea landed, making her sit upright.

What if she were to interview the city's most influential editors about whether a woman reporter could succeed in New York? She could do it on behalf of the *Dispatch*. The more she mulled it over, the cleverer it seemed. It would be a way of getting the opinions of the men who had the power to hire and fire. Better yet, it would make her known to them. Scrambling to her feet, she hurried inside and wrote short, businesslike requests for interviews, citing her *Dispatch* credentials. She sent them out first thing the next morning. A harrowing wait for replies followed, but they came back within a week.

Some said that they had never felt compelled to consider the topic and saw no reason to change now, but there were enough acceptances to provide material for her article. When the time came, she dressed with care, choosing a lace-trimmed green dress and her hat with the gilt arrow.

The first paper she visited was the *Sun*. A clerk escorted her up the spiral staircase and through the newsroom, where the air was fuggy with tobacco smoke. She paused for a moment to soak up the familiar atmosphere and it exhilarated her. The men had taken off their jackets because of the heat and their shirts had patches of sweat under the arms. She was the only woman present and some of them stared at her as she passed. She did her best to ignore them, but it gave her a hot, uncomfortable feeling. The clerk knocked on the office door of Charles Dana, the editor, and a voice inside barked, 'Enter!'

Mr Dana was an imposing man with a rippling white beard and a penetrating gaze behind gold-rimmed glasses. A stuffed owl sat on his desk, staring at Nellie with the identical expression. Mr Dana motioned her to a chair and they exchanged pleasantries, but he soon said, 'Shall we get down to business?'

Nellie could feel sweat collecting into drips down her back, gluing her dress to her skin, but she sat forward and asked, 'Do you object to women entering newspaper life, sir?'

He gave a short laugh. 'No, of course not! If they are bright, they can do the work as well as men can. But they're not regarded with editorial favor in New York.'

'Really? Why is that?'

He took off his glasses and began polishing them. 'Well, for one thing a woman might be ever so clever in getting news and putting it into words, but we wouldn't feel comfortable about calling her out at one in the morning to report a fire or a crime, and we wouldn't hesitate with a man.' He cleared his throat. 'Another thing – as a sex, women are less accurate than men because they have a tendency to exaggerate. Newspapers can't afford that. Its articles must be one hundred percent factual.'

Nellie felt a flare of indignation. 'I disagree, sir,' she said hotly. 'In my experience, women are game for anything. As for accuracy—'

He raised a hand to cut her off, and she saw from his expression that arguing would be futile. So she changed tack, asking, 'How do women get jobs as reporters in this city?'

She thought there was a gleam in his eye as he answered, 'I really cannot say.'

The interview was at an end. Nellie thanked Mr Dana and continued along Park Row. Her next interview was with Mr Coates of the *Mail and Express*, who said women were invaluable. He added, 'The way they dress and their constitution rules out hard reporting, but they're ideally suited to covering stories on society, fashion and the arts.'

'Women are more ambitious and more energetic than men,' declared Robert G. Morris, editor of the *Telegram*. Nellie felt relief, but then he said, 'Mind you, I can't imagine sending a woman to cover the police or criminal courts.'

She raised her brows. 'Why not?'

'The officials there would give her as little information as possible to get rid of her. And that's where a man gets the best of her.'

Nellie felt more depressed and discouraged with every meeting. Back in her room, she sat at the small oilcloth-covered table, pondering the words of these men and wondering how best to write her piece. She decided that she would simply summarize their views. 'We have more women now than we want... Women are no good anyway.'

The finished article, 'Women Journalists', was reprinted in New York and Boston, and received praise in *The Journalist*, a national trade magazine. Nellie was elated and hopeful, but no job offers came from it. She was back to square one and, much worse, she was nearly broke.

She would have taken any job, but the *World* was where she really wanted to work. In the four years since Joseph Pulitzer had bought the ailing newspaper from robber-baron financier Jay Gould, he had transformed it into the most successful, most imitated paper in the country, its appeal spanning nationalities and social classes. It was read as far afield as the Tennessee Mountains and the Mississippi Valleys, and while it had its critics, it had a thousandfold more friends.

Nellie bought a copy every day, admiring the pioneering use of headlines with bold, large print to separate them from the rest of the type, the combination of lurid sensation with first-class reporting of hard news, the snappy editorial page. The paper not only had the latest scoops: it had principles. Reform was its mission, and it set out to skewer corruption, both nationally and internationally. It was more than a publication: it was a dynamo, its trail-blazing, unorthodox methods irresistible. Nellie drank in its columns with her morning coffee, wanting desperately to be part of it. One day, she saw an editorial demanding an investigation of alleged brutality and neglect of patients at the Blackwell's Island Asylum. Evidently, the asylum was a hot topic. With a pang, she thought of the woman with the bottle of whiskey, and wondered how she was.

Colonel John A. Cockerill, the managing editor, had shut down her interview request about women journalists, saying that the *World* did not employ females. She wrote to him again, offering as a stunt to go up in a hot-air balloon sponsored by the paper in St Louis. Cockerill answered the letter, thanking her for her interest, but expressing his regret. The assignment was far too dangerous for a lady.

As she read his words, she could feel her hope and courage draining away. What more could she do? It seemed that the position she craved would never be hers. She went for a walk in Central Park, trying to think and regather herself. It was still unbearably hot. The sun, obscured by high cloud, cast a hazy glare, smudging the outlines of the surrounding buildings. Trees hung limp and dust-green. Men and women strolled slowly; a blind beggar played the violin. There was cracked dirt under Nellie's feet, yellowing grass all around. The air was so heavy and motionless, it was like moving in soup. Soon she was feeling sticky and wilted, and it was hard to breathe. She arrived at a stone terrace, with broad staircases leading down to it on either side. She descended the steps and there in the center stood a huge fountain topped by an angel, her wings outstretched, gazing down on the citizens of New York with a stern and sorrowful expression. For an instant it seemed that Nellie had found the city's Angel of Justice, the being that saw every crime and iniquity, every inequality, every unjustness. Nellie walked hurriedly past until she found an empty bench by the opaque, green-brown lake that smelled of frogspawn and rotting waterweed. She sat down to rest, and watched clouds of midges moving over the water and a handful of boys trying to race miniature sailboats.

She was beginning to realize that she needed a sensational story with which to entice the *World* – a story that would set the whole country agog. She didn't care where it came from. She wanted a sensation, and she wanted it fast.

A group of urchins approached her. 'Can you spare a few cents, lady? We're awful hungry,' one of them begged. He had a shock of coarse black hair and a narrow, astute face.

'No. Sorry. No way. I'm not doing too well myself.'

'Please? You look like such a nice, kind lady.'

They crowded round her, shoving large bits of card-board in her face.

She batted them off. She said 'no' over and over. Drops of sweat ran down her back and thighs, under her dress. Eventually the boys realized they weren't getting anywhere and moved off in search of another victim.

She was utterly drained. She felt she could topple right over, or gust into the air like a discarded sheet of news-paper. The dank smell of the lake was thick in her nostrils. You're going to be all right, she told herself, but she did not believe it. Without her mission of uncovering stories, she was a lost soul.

She heard the tinkling bell of an ice-cream cart approaching. That was what she needed to revive her – a cold, sweet strawberry ice. She put her hand in her pocket for her purse. Her stomach lurched.

Her pocket was empty.

The urchins had robbed her. All of her money was gone. She leapt to her feet and scanned the distance, but they had vanished into the trees. While she was swatting away the cardboard, her hands were occupied, and one of them had slid his own into her pocket and lifted her purse. They were probably on the other side of the park by now – it was useless to pursue them. She was trapped, unemployed, destitute.

It was all over. She would have to admit she was beaten and go home. She wept tears of exhaustion, despair and rage.

After she had cried herself out, something at the core of her steadied and hardened. She blew her nose. She threw her shoulders back and took a deep breath. How could she go back to Pittsburgh? There must be a way for her to stay here. Had she really fought hard enough? She would not give in, she simply would not.

The New York job must come now or never. She would make her last and most determined try. She walked back to the boarding house, donned her hat, put her lucky thumb ring on and borrowed ten cents streetcar car fare from her landlady. Then she went downtown, hell-bent on getting in to see Colonel Cockerill.

Nellie got off the trolley at the corner of Park Row and strode resolutely past the offices of the *Sun*, past the *Tribune*, past Baker and Godwin, Printers, and the statue of Benjamin Franklin. She crossed the street to where the *Times* loftily took up the whole triangle apex of two converging streets, but she hardly glanced at it. She was heading for the building with the glittering golden dome – built by Pulitzer to flaunt his success in the face of the other Park Row publishers who had once laughed at him.

She passed through the great archway of the entrance, climbed the steps into the lobby and walked up to the low gate and railing that divided it from the bustling offices beyond.

'Good day,' she greeted the guard. 'My name is Nellie Bly. I am a reporter from the Pittsburgh *Dispatch* and I've come to see Colonel Cockerill.'

'I am sorry, Miss. He's not seeing visitors today,' he told her kindly. He had blue eyes under thick, sandy brows and crinkly sandy hair.

She tossed her head and set her jaw. 'I intend to see Colonel Cockerill,' she said firmly.

He shook his head. 'Even President Cleveland couldn't get in to see the Colonel today. That's his orders.'

'I am going to see him, if I have to stay here the whole day.' Beneath her skirts, her knees had started shaking.

'For Pete's sake, Miss. Surely it's not that urgent? Please – come back another time.'

Despite the heat, and the churning fear and anger inside her, she managed to hold onto her composure. 'If you don't tell Colonel Cockerill that I've come to see him, I shall wait at this gate all day long and all night and all day tomorrow.'

The guard frowned and shook his head. A passing office boy stared at her with unconcealed curiosity. Minutes crawled by. The guard stood a few feet away from her, the baffled look on his face turning to exasperation and finally anger.

Half an hour passed, then an hour.

Word of her presence had spread around the building. Reporters smirked at each other and shook their heads as they walked by. A man from the advertising department came to see what the high jinks were about. Office boys invented errands that would send them through the lobby to get a look at her.

'Please just go, Miss!' the guard burst out. 'You're in everybody's way and I am not going to bother the Colonel. He is trying to meet a tight deadline. Now, shall we do this the easy way, or the hard way?'

She was thirsty and she felt dizzy. There was pressure behind her eyes that threatened to bloom into a full-blown headache at any minute. It was dreadful to be threatened like this, even worse than the too-familiar smiles and insolent stares. Flesh and blood could not stand it. She wanted to run away, but she would not leave without a job.

'What shall I do with her?' the guard entreated a passing reporter.

'For God's sake, O'Connor, turn her out. She's disturbing the whole building.'

'I've tried, sir. She won't listen to reason.'

Newspapermen were gathering, arguing about how to get rid of her.

'Fetch a policeman. She's likely barking mad…'

'Oh, leave her alone. She'll get tired and give it up.'

'What does she want with Cockerill?'

'She says she was a reporter in Pittsburgh.'

'But he hates impromptu callers – especially female ones.'

While they were busy debating, Nellie quietly opened the gate and made her way through the lobby. As she hurried up the stairs, she heard someone yell: 'Stop right there, young lady!'

She did not turn around.

A good-natured voice answered, 'Oh, let her go. If she's that determined… well, hats off to her, *I* say.'

'What will Cockerill—'

'Let him deal with her.'

When Nellie reached the newsroom, a clerk outside Cockerill's office told her that the managing editor didn't take kindly to being disturbed. She saw that there was no point in negotiating. She parked herself in a chair, refusing to budge, and decided to use the opportunity to observe the *World*'s inner workings.

The telegraph instruments clicked away in the corners, and from the floor below came the familiar hiss and grind of the printers. Office boys raced back and forth, newsmen worked away at their desks, and compositors set copy into lead columns. Every now and then, one of the reporters got up to shout into a curious black box on the wall. Nellie had heard about the newly invented telephone, but this was the first time she had seen one. There were placards on the walls proclaiming:

ACCURACY, TERSENESS, ACCURACY!
WHO? WHAT? WHERE? WHEN? WHY?
THE FACTS – THE COLOR – THE FACTS!

Time limped by and still Nellie sat waiting. If she had not been so anxious, she would have enjoyed watching the newsmen at work. As it was, the thought of her troubles was heavy as stone on her mind. If she left here without a job... but that was not an option. She would stay right here until she got one. Perspiration filmed her upper lip and pooled under her arms.

A big, handsome, mustached man was walking down the passage toward her. He looked at her in surprise. A frown crossed his face, stern and forbidding.

'We don't allow visitors in the newsroom, Miss,' he said. 'Are you a friend of one of the reporters? If so, you must wait for him downstairs.'

The clerk who had spoken to her hurried over.

'She's no one's friend, Colonel Cockerill. She's just – well, she behaves just like a madwoman. She's been sitting there for hours and I can't shift her. Will I fetch a cop and have him take her away?'

'No, not just yet.' The man turned to Nellie, his dark eyes boring into hers. 'I am John A. Cockerill, managing editor of this paper. Why are you here?'

Nellie took a breath and said, 'I'm sorry to be a bother, Colonel Cockerill. My name is Nellie Bly. I am a news-paperwoman – and a good one. I came here to see you and I'm not going to leave till we've spoken.'

Tension rippled between them. He was as dashing as an actor, but there was something about him that made Nellie think of a tightly wound spring. She remembered reading that he had once shot and killed a man after a fight over an editorial retraction. Cockerill had claimed that the man, Alonzo Slayback, had turned up at his office and pointed a revolver at him; that it was a case of shoot or be shot. The jury had acquitted him, even though Slayback's friend had testified that he was unarmed and was taking off his coat for a fist fight when Cockerill fired.

'Hmm, Nellie Bly? I've read your letter,' Cockerill said. 'You're the young woman who proposed going up in the St Louis balloon. Mr Pulitzer has already made up his mind about that. The answer is no, I'm afraid. And it's final.'

'All right, sir. I'll drop the idea of the balloon. But I still want to talk to you, about something else entirely.'

'You don't give up easy, do you?' Cockerill looked thoughtful. Then he gestured toward the closed office door.

'Come in here,' he said abruptly.

Nellie got to her feet. Suddenly her legs were trembling, both with the hours of waiting and with the reaction that had set in now that she'd succeeded. She could hardly believe it. All she had to do was convince him that he couldn't manage without her on his staff. Giving her lucky ring an extra twist, she followed him into his office.

Seven

'NELLIE BLY, I'D LIKE you to meet Joseph Pulitzer,' Cockerill said, shutting the office door behind them. 'Joseph, this is Nellie Bly.' Pulitzer shook her hand. 'Oh – so you are Nellie Bly. The hot-air-balloon lady. Pleased to meet you.' He was dressed in black, save for a brick-red string tie. His voice was clear and deep, with eastern European gutturals. He looked to be in his forties; over six feet tall and gaunt, with a leonine head, plentiful gray-black hair and a reddish beard. He had a long, aquiline nose and cloudy gray-blue eyes behind thick pince-nez. Years of pain and invalidism showed on his face, blended with an electric alertness. The combination created a strange kind of magnetism.

Cockerill pushed the dark hair impatiently off his face and held out a chair for Nellie. Pulitzer seated himself on the other side of a huge desk strewn with news-paper cuttings, bundles of proofs, telegrams, cards and notes, while Cockerill perched on the desk's edge. The men appeared to occupy adjoining rooms with an inter-connecting door. The walls were embossed leather, the ceilings were frescoed, and newspapers from all parts of the world lay piled on the floor. Three great windows looked out over Park Row and the old post office. The curtains were half-drawn. Nellie had heard that Pulitzer was going blind and could perceive his surroundings better in muted light.

'So... why are you here?' Cockerill asked.

'I want to write for the *World*,' she answered.

Cockerill gave a short laugh that sounded like a bark. 'Everyone in America wants to write for the *World*.'

'But I can do articles that will sell.'

'You think what the *World* needs is a lady writer?'

Nellie flushed deeply. 'I've worked for the Pittsburgh *Dispatch*,' she said with quiet dignity, taking a packet of clippings from her bag and placing them on the desk. 'I covered most of the news runs and wrote features too. I did a series on conditions for Pittsburgh factory women that attracted a lot of attention.'

As he flicked through the articles, something in Cockerill's face shifted and she knew that she was starting to get through to him. But he wasn't won over yet.

'Name a subject you could write about that the *World* might be interested in,' he shot back. 'Give me one idea.'

Nellie was silent, her mind hard at work. Cockerill glanced at Pulitzer and smiled. *They obviously think I'm mad*, she thought. And then an idea arrived.

'I shall fake madness,' she said clearly. 'I'll get myself committed to the lunatic asylum on Blackwell's Island.'

The men had grown very still; Cockerill shot her an electrifying look. 'Go on,' he said.

'I want to find out how the insane poor are really treated. Then I'll write it up.' She was speaking off the cuff, working it out as she went along. Was she on the right track, or was she crazy herself? She didn't know the answer, so she ploughed on. 'The newspapers are full of stories of asylum abuses. You yourselves ran an editorial in July demanding a proper investigation. The asylum is crying out for independent inquiry. What's more, the subject of ill-treated lunatics is a natural for your paper.'

Pulitzer waved her words away. 'It will never work. We've already sent reporters to the asylum. The doctors and nurses knew they were newspapermen and wouldn't let them past the front door. They didn't lay eyes on a single patient, much less find out how they were treated.'

'That's *exactly* my point,' said Nellie. 'It's why I propose going in disguise. I want to tell this story from the inside – to stand in a madwoman's shoes. I'll see everything she sees and feel what she feels.' She sat up straight and pushed on through the knot of dread in her stomach. 'Some of them are violent, I'll be locked in with monsters. It's dangerous, but I will tell it like it's never been told before.'

'I don't like this idea,' Cockerill said, in an undertone. 'I don't like it at all.'

But they were both attracted by it, she could tell. It gave her the courage to keep talking.

'What about some of the shocking incidents that are being reported from the asylum? The *Sun* just ran a story about that pregnant inmate – what was her name? Oh yes, Meredith Smith. Do you remember? She was put in a straitjacket and thrown into solitary confinement, where she gave birth soon afterward. By herself. In restraints. Just picture it.' Nellie's eyes moved from Pulitzer to Cockerill, catching and holding their attention. 'Meredith's wrists were so swollen from the restraints that the doctor couldn't detect her pulse – or the lack of it. He failed to notice her grave condition, and she died later that day from complications following the birth.' She paused, letting the words sink in. 'Do you recall the asylum's defence? They thought that Meredith's stomach pains were because she was partial to eating grass. And she was so violent that they couldn't avoid putting her in restraints. The straitjacket also stopped her tearing off her clothes and eating them.'

There was a knock at the door. 'Enter!' barked Cockerill.

A young reporter with bushy auburn hair came in and handed a sheet of densely typed paper to Cockerill.

Cockerill scanned it quickly. 'Is this it, Peterson?'

'Uh... yes, sir.'

'All right, fine. Get it typeset – I want it in the next edition. Get a move on.'

The door shut behind the young man and Cockerill turned back to Nellie. 'Sorry about the interruption, Miss Bly. Do go on.'

'I am sure you've read about other incidents that have leaked out.' Nellie said, searching their faces. 'You know as well as I do that a proper investigation of conditions is needed. Urgently.'

Pulitzer cleared his throat. 'I take your point. But the stories I've heard about the asylum are atrocious. A hardened male reporter could be excused for refusing an assignment there. For a young girl to go voluntarily – by herself...'

'Oh, come on,' she urged. 'Your success as a paper is partly down to your appetite for risk.'

'Hmm. That may be. But could you endure living among the insane as one of them?' said Pulitzer, grimacing. 'I'm not sure you have enough bodily strength to get through the ordeal unharmed. It could even be fatal.'

'What do you mean?' asked Nellie.

'Of all the institutions on Blackwell's Island, the lunatic asylum has the highest mortality rate,' Cockerill explained. 'One of the outbreaks of disease that periodically sweep through the Island, like cholera or typhoid, could kill you. Being housed with a berserk inmate might do the same.

Every day spent there is a risk to your safety. Just think about it.'

Thinking about it gave Nellie chills, but the assignment would give her her chance. 'For a good story, I can endure *anything*,' she said quietly.

Silence fell and lengthened. It seemed to throw all her disadvantages back at her: her poverty and her desperation. *A journalist is only as good as her last article*, she thought. She wondered bleakly if she would ever feel secure.

At last, Pulitzer said, 'You know, Miss Bly, the *World* has never let a woman do anything like this before. It might ruffle some feathers.'

'The whole world is changing, Mr Pulitzer. They'll get over it.'

'I suppose it might work,' he mused.

'Oh! It *would*. I know it would!' Nellie burst out. 'And readers would devour it, like their pancakes at breakfast. People love hearing about freaks and lunatics.'

'Let her try it...' said Pulitzer.

Cockerill spoke up. 'If you take this on, you *must* see it through. If you fail, we will all be lampooned. Do you really think you can fool the public, the police and the doctors?'

'I know I can,' said Nellie firmly, though her mouth was so dry she thought she might vomit.

'You must give a factual and accurate account,' he said. 'We're not asking you to go there for the sake of making sensational revelations. Write things up as you find them, good or bad; give praise or blame as you feel it's due and tell the truth at all times.'

'Yes; we don't want any libel suits,' added Pulitzer. 'If the inmates are treated well, say so. If not, put every detail of their wrongs into your story. Impartiality alone can discover the truth.'

'But don't let anyone suspect that you are working for the *World*,' Cockerill cautioned. 'If a reporter on another paper guesses—'

'No one will,' Nellie assured him quickly.

'You must stay there for at least a week. You mustn't tell anyone you are a newspaperwoman. And you must do this strictly on your own – all the steps leading up to your incarceration and everything that follows. We will not help you, not with the doctors or the wardens or anything else. If we like what you write, we'll consider it your first assignment. The job will be yours.'

Excitement and nerves were blazing through Nellie. She tried to thank them, but the words got jumbled up. Tears came into her eyes. She blinked them away furiously.

'In the meantime, you are to keep it secret,' Pulitzer told her.

'I will, I swear.'

Both men nodded, satisfied. Journalists are good at keeping secrets. All too often, they see the consequences of careless talk.

They decided that Nellie should become Nellie Brown. It was a common name. The initials N. B. would match those already sewn on her linen. The paper would be able to keep track of her movements under it.

'I think we've covered everything,' Cockerill said. 'Leave your address at the desk in the lobby as you go out. We'll be in touch about the timing of your stunt. I'll need to clear space for the story and check with our legal department about procedure. We don't want you getting prosecuted for entering a city institution under false pretences.'

He ushered her to the door.

'Do you have enough money?' Pulitzer asked her suddenly. 'Can you wait till we contact you?'

Cockerill looked surprised. But perhaps Pulitzer was remembering the harsh poverty of his youth – the times when a bowl of soup had been his only nourishment for the day.

'Actually, I can't wait,' said Nellie, coloring. She told them the story of her stolen purse. 'I can't even afford my rent!'

Pulitzer took out his wallet and tried to see the notes inside. But his semi-blind eyes could not distinguish one from the other and he gave up. 'Write her a check, John. Make it out for twenty dollars.' Then, to Nellie, 'We will call you. The money is not a loan, by the way. It's an advance on your salary.'

Everything seemed settled now, but for one final question. Neither of them had offered the answer. She had to ask it.

'After I get into the asylum… how will you get me out?'

'I don't know,' Cockerill admitted, after a pause. 'But we will do it.'

She took a breath. 'When?'

'I can't answer that right now. Just play your part and get in.'

After the meeting with Pulitzer and Cockerill, Nellie walked to City Hall Park and sat on a bench, gazing unseeingly at the fountain and the litter on the path in front of her: a lipstick-imprinted handkerchief, a cigar end, a broken bottle. She had to digest what had happened, to let the tumult of thoughts settle in her.

What kind of hell lay ahead of her? Could she really fake madness convincingly enough to pass the doctors' examination? What on earth had made her suggest such a crazy scheme?

She watched a band of pigeons pecking at a crust of white bread, and understood that the asylum had been in the back of her mind since she'd met the woman with the whiskey bottle. Even so, Nellie was frightened of lunatics and lacked the affinity for them that she felt for the poor.

Suddenly the pigeons scattered and burst skyward with a great fluttering of wings. A thin black cat stalked down the path, tail swooshing back and forth, and Nellie's mind flew back to her own experience of losing her reason – her childhood fear of going to bed, the sleepless nights, and seeing shapes come alive in the corners of rooms in daytime. She thought about the time Momma had broken down with Jack, screaming and beating her head against the wall, tears and strands of snot on her face. She had seemed a different creature from the one Nellie knew as her mother. And what about her father, whose mind had vanished completely before he died? A dreadful realization hit Nellie: that her interest in madness – and her fear of it – had been sparked by her own experiences. But the insight only strengthened her desire to tell the lunatics' stories. She would collect enough evidence to get them fair and humane treatment. She wondered if she had the mental and physical strength to survive it.

Then she squared her shoulders and took a breath. She had already been to hell and back with Momma's marriage to Jack. She had known and survived pure terror. Looking inwards, she understood that she was capable of facing the dark side of life head-on, for once you have lost everything, there is nothing left to fear.

Eight

NELLIE KNEW THAT SHE could not take chances simulating a mild form of lunacy. She wasn't at all sure how lunatics behaved, but she knew she would have to do something spectacular to get sent to Blackwell's Island.

She spent the nights leading up to her stunt reading horror stories and ghost stories – Sheridan Le Fanu, Robert Louis Stevenson, Edgar Allan Poe – filling her mind with vengeful ghosts, bodysnatchers and murderous madmen. She recalled her mother's tales of the supernatural and wrote down 'The War of the Ghosts' to bring it back vividly. Every creak of the floorboards, every footstep in the corridor made her jump. The gaslight cast fleeting shadows around the room and she drew her shawl more tightly around her shoulders, fancying that shapes began to move in the corners. In this frame of mind, she spent hours in front of the mirror making grimaces and staring unblinkingly at her own reflection. Distraught expressions look crazy, she decided, so during the day she wandered the streets remembering the painful past and letting it show on her face. The heatwave had given way to fall's chill.

Within a couple weeks of their meeting, a note arrived from Cockerill. 'Everything is cleared. You're to go ahead as soon as you are ready.'

Nellie's mouth was dry and the letter trembled in her hand. But the sooner she started, the sooner she would be out with her story. There was no sense in hanging around. She resolved to lose her mind the very next day.

In her room, she laid out her oldest, shabbiest clothes – a gray flannel dress and a black sailor's hat with a veil – making sure they had no identification marks but the initials 'N. B.'. She took a warm bath and gave her hair a good brushing, as she wasn't sure when she would be able to attend to her toilette again. She went to bed early but struggled to fall asleep. Whenever she closed her eyes, thoughts of what she must do in the morning played and replayed in her head. Was she really a good enough actress to pull it off?

She got up and practiced her role again in front of the mirror. The sight of her own mad reflection in the flickering gaslight unnerved her, and she had to turn up the lamp to rally her courage. When the ache of tiredness was like a stone on her chest, she went back to bed and concentrated on breathing in, breathing out, waiting for her racing heart to steady itself. But it was almost daylight before she fell into a troubled sleep.

By the time she woke up, the sun was high in the sky. She dressed and took a handbag with a few belongings, including a black notebook with silver edges in which she had scribbled a few sentences and some cryptic symbols, her own version of shorthand. She thought it safer to leave her lucky thumb ring behind, though not having it gave her a bad feeling. Glancing around her cramped little room for the last time, it had never seemed so attractive. She shut the door and went down to breakfast, but she couldn't eat, for nerves were making her stomach heave as though she were seasick. She drank a cup of coffee and told her landlady that she might be away for a few days.

Next, she chose a cheap lodging house from a city directory: the Temporary Home for Females at 84 Second Avenue. She arrived there in the early afternoon. A group of old winos watched her from across the street as she climbed the five steps up to the porch. It was just like the dismal houses in Pittsburgh, with the same soot-stained bricks and peeling paint. At least she would fit right in, she thought wryly. She had seventy-three cents in her bag, wrapped in a piece of thin white paper.

She hesitated for a few moments before the battered front door, her hand on the bell. There was still time. She could still turn around and go back, back to Pittsburgh and her old life. Then she straightened her spine and pulled the handle. A chime rang loudly somewhere inside.

Moments later the door was opened by a child with tangled red hair and freckles. 'Whaddya want?' she demanded.

'I would like to see the matron,' Nellie said weakly, closing her eyes.

The girl had begun to work away at a ragged nail with her teeth and paid no attention. 'Go in the parlor. She'll come to you soon,' she said carelessly, and went off down the linoleum-floored hall.

Nellie found the parlor – a narrow, musty space, furnished with a sofa and several mismatched chairs. A worn Bible sat on a table in the middle of the room. Nellie parked herself in a sagging chair and listened to the clock on the mantelpiece ticking away the seconds. Finally a woman came in; thin and harassed-looking, with half-blonde, half-gray hair twisted into a bun.

'I am Mrs Stanard, the matron,' she said. 'What can I do for you?'

'My name is Nellie Brown. I'd like a room here for a few days, if you have space.'

'Where are you from?'

'I've just arrived from Cuba.' She had decided to make this her story, so that there would be no attempt to trace her family.

Mrs Stanard narrowed her eyes. 'A foreigner, are you? You don't look like one. Well, we get all kinds in here.'

'I want to find work in New York,' said Nellie.

'Where's your luggage? We have to be careful, see. If guests don't pay up, we keep their luggage.'

Nellie smiled, trying to please the matron. 'It will be delivered to me as soon as I have an address.'

Mrs Stanard fixed her with a steady, measuring look. 'Where did you live in Cuba?'

Nellie had her answer ready. 'An estate near Havana,' she said and added a few words in Spanish.

Mrs Stanard clearly didn't understand her, but she seemed satisfied. 'Listen, we are busy at the moment. I don't have a single room available,' she said. 'But there's a girl leaving in two days. How about sharing with one of the others till she goes?'

'Yes, I can do that. How much is it?'

'Fifty cents a night.'

Nellie nodded. 'Please take me to my room now. I'm tired.'

She counted out fifty cents and was shown up a threadbare flight of stairs to her room. Mrs Stanard left her, and Nellie lay down on one of the beds to wait. The room was close and dim and so small that the beds nearly filled it. There was a chest of drawers scarred with cigarette burns and rings left by wet glasses, and a washstand with a chipped basin. The walls were roughly plastered, and the window was hung with dingy lace curtains and looked out over a yard that held a couple of trash buckets and a line of laundry flapping in the breeze.

When the dinner bell rang, Nellie went to the dining room in the basement. She slipped into her chair at the long table and quietly forced down the overcooked beef and flabby cabbage. Around her, twelve other women chattered, but her silence went without comment since she was new. Eventually, one of them asked her name.

'Nellie Brown.'

'Your accent is unusual – are you a foreigner?'

'Yes, I am Cuban.' The look Nellie gave them made the whole table fall silent.

The red-haired child cleared away the meal and swirled a grimy mop around, and the women went upstairs to the parlor, where Nellie took up her former chair, surreptitiously watching the others. The light falling from the solitary gas jet made them all look haggard. An older lady kept falling asleep and waking herself up with her own snoring. The majority sat doing nothing, but there were a few who made lace or knitted. Apart from one who was from the country on a day's shopping expedition, they were working women, some of them with children. Nellie thought how harsh their lot was. They worked all day and spent their few hours of leisure in this barren place that called itself a home. Presently, Mrs Stanard came to sit beside her.

'What's wrong, my dear? Have you some sorrow or trouble?' she asked.

'No,' said Nellie, surprised. 'Why do you ask?'

'Oh, I can see it in your face. It tells the story of a great trouble.'

'Yes, well, everything is so sad,' said Nellie haphazardly.

Mrs Stanard patted her arm as she would a child's. 'You mustn't let that worry you. We all have our troubles, but we get over them in good time. What type of work are you looking for?'

Nellie opened her eyes wide and fixed the matron with an unblinking stare. 'Well, really, I don't know. It's all so sad.'

A moment's involuntary recoil. Then: 'Would you like to be a children's nurse, or a housemaid, perhaps?'

Nellie put her handkerchief up to her face to hide a smile and replied in a muffled voice, 'I've never worked before. I don't know how.'

'But you must learn,' urged Mrs Stanard. 'You said that you wanted to work. All the women who stay here have jobs.'

'Do they? Why, they look horrible to me; just like crazy women. I'm afraid of them.' Nellie's voice rose on the last words and a couple of people sitting nearby gave her uneasy looks.

Mrs Stanard shrugged. 'They don't look very nice, I grant you. But they're good, honest working women. I don't take lunatics.'

Nellie pressed her hands against her eyes and began rocking back and forth. 'They all look crazy. I'm scared,' she groaned. 'There are so many crazy people and one can never tell what they'll do.' She let her hands drop and locked eyes with the matron. 'Just think of all the murders committed... *and the police never catch the murderers.*'

Everyone had stopped talking now to stare at her. Mrs Stanard was rigid, her eyes wide with alarm, and Nellie knew that her plan had started to work. The matron stood up hurriedly, saying, 'I'll come back and check on you in a while.' But she avoided Nellie till bedtime, when the child came to tell everyone to go to their rooms.

'Oh, but I'm too scared to sleep! Everyone seems crazy – I'm scared!' Nellie wailed.

'You must go to bed. I don't have guests wandering about at night. House rules,' Mrs Stanard said firmly.

'But can't I sit up on the stairs instead? Please? I promise not to wander.'

'Most certainly not! Everyone in the house would think you were mad. Look, here's your room-mate, Miss Weller.'

Miss Weller was a short, stout woman, with soft, pinkish cheeks. She shook her head, backing away from Nellie. 'I'm not staying with that crazy woman,' she said. 'Not for all the money of the Vanderbilts.'

Mrs Stanard sighed. Her bun was coming undone; tendrils of hair curled around her face, which looked drawn now, with deep circles under the eyes. 'Who will volunteer to share with Miss Brown who, I'm sure, is just tired from her trip?' She looked at each of the boarders in turn, but no one would meet her eyes.

At last, a frail-looking woman, with wings of graying hair coming down from a skilfully twisted topknot and huge dark eyes, stepped forward. 'I'll room with her,' she offered. 'The poor thing.'

'Why, thank you, Mrs Caine.' Mrs Stanard didn't bother hiding her relief. 'And now that's settled, I'll wish you all goodnight.'

The residents trooped upstairs by the light of a wheezy old lamp. Mrs Caine sat beside Nellie on her bed and took down her hair with gentle hands. She tried to persuade her to undress and go to sleep, but Nellie stubbornly refused. A handful of boarders gathered around them.

'Poor loon!' said one, shaking her head.

'Poor loon? Jesus, I'm afraid to stay in the same house as her! She'll murder us all before morning.'

'If they don't get her out soon, I'm moving. I pay fifty cents a night for my room and I got to get some sleep in it.'

Miss Weller was all for sending for a policeman to take Nellie away at once. Goosebumps were rising on Nellie's skin from being stared at and judged. She thought, *It's only after you are in trouble that you realize how little sympathy and kindness there are in the world.*

Eventually the women went to their own rooms, leaving Mrs Caine and Nellie alone. Mrs Caine didn't undress, but lay down on her bed, watchful of Nellie's movements. Nellie had made up her mind to stay awake all night so that she would appear even more haggard and unstable in the morning. She sat at the edge of the bed, staring into space. It threw Mrs Caine into a wretched state of unease. Every few minutes she would prop herself up to look at Nellie.

'How bright your eyes are,' she remarked. 'They're shining unnaturally brightly.' And then she began to quiz Nellie, asking where she had lived, how long she had been in New York, what she had been doing. To every question, Nellie gave the same answer. 'Oh, I've forgotten. Ever since my headache came on, I can't remember a thing.'

'Poor child, poor child,' Mrs Caine said compassionately.

'You are very kind,' said Nellie, feeling a pang of guilt for torturing her. 'I am not much for conversation, I'm afraid, but why don't you tell me about yourself instead? I will try to listen sensibly. Are you from New York? Do you have a husband?'

There was no reply. Finally Mrs Caine said, 'I was married, but my husband died.' She tightened her lips, controlling a tremor. 'He stepped on a rusty nail in the street. It went through the sole of his shoe and lodged in his foot. A surgeon took it out, but he got blood poisoning and, within a week, he was dead.' Tears welled up at the edges of her eyelids and she blinked them away. 'We used to live in Boston, but I came to New York to find work. I was given a job correcting proofs on a medical dictionary, but my health gave way under the task, so now I'm going home to live with my sister.'

Nellie felt terrible. She wanted to comfort Mrs Caine, to whisper that she was not insane at all, that it was only a sham, but she could not afford to let her façade slip. Eventually, Mrs Caine fell asleep. Despite herself, Nellie began to drift in and out of dozing.

She was startled awake by the sound of screams coming from the next room. Disoriented, she wondered if she was already in the insane asylum. Mrs Caine was looking around in fear. She pulled on her dressing gown and went out hurriedly. Nellie could hear her questioning a woman in the next room.

'What's wrong?' Nellie asked, when Mrs Caine returned.

Mrs Caine swallowed. 'Miss Weller had a nightmare. She was dreaming about *you.*'

'Are you sure?' Nellie asked blandly.

'Yes, quite sure. She saw you rushing at her with a knife in your hand and murder in your eyes.'

Mrs Caine got back into bed, agitated but sleepy. Nellie was tired to the bone, but she was determined not to fall asleep again. Midnight chimed – she had six hours to wait for daylight. Time dragged along with excruciating slowness. She gazed at the ceiling, listening to Mrs Caine's snuffly breathing. The noises in the rest of the house and on the avenue petered out, and the silence reminded Nellie of sitting in her father's study as a child, listening to his pen scratching over the page. 'How still you sit,' he would say. 'You're the only one who lets me work in peace,' and she would feel capable and important.

She was jolted back to the present by the sound of a trash can being kicked over, followed by a riotous burst of song – 'Lu, Lu, How I love my Lu!' The racket stopped as abruptly as it had begun.

What would happen to her in the asylum? In her mind's eye the lunatics were reasonless and bestial, raving and shaking the bars of their cages. She was terrified of them, for weren't they the horrors who had always lurked in her imagination? She wondered if she would she have the strength to keep a hold of herself in the face of such uncanniness, things threatening to slide out of control at any moment. What if her own reason slipped, sending her spiralling back to a place she never wanted to revisit?

As morning seeped into the drab rooms of the boarding house, Nellie stretched her stiff limbs and began to rant. 'My trunks are gone! Stolen! I want them back. Somebody *help me!*' She was twitching and rolling her eyes.

Mrs Caine's eyes snapped open in fright. She lay blinking, and then sat up in bed. 'You didn't have any trunks, did you?' she asked anxiously. 'Is there anyone we can send for? Where are your friends?'

'I have no friends, but I do have trunks,' wailed Nellie. 'Where are they? I need them *now!*'

Mrs Caine dressed quickly and helped Nellie get ready. She took her downstairs and tried to press coffee and a bun on her. 'Your trunks will be found in good time,' she soothed, but Nellie's cries only escalated. 'Where's my pistol? Give it to me! I must defend myself against the crazy women!' Spittle flew from her mouth.

Mrs Stanard came in, took one look at her face and asked her to leave.

'No, no, no! No way!' she screeched. 'Not until you fetch my trunks!' She clutched her head and stared blankly. 'Oh, my God. It's back. I can feel it.'

'What is back?'

She shook her head violently. 'The insect. It's in my head. I can feel it pulling the wires just for fun.'

The others had clustered around them, full of excited revulsion. Miss Weller insisted that the police were called right away. Mrs Stanard put on her bonnet and left the house. A churning started up in Nellie's stomach. She was on her way.

Soon Mrs Stanard was back with two policemen. They seemed too big and bulky for the cramped space. 'I want you to take her quietly,' Mrs Stanard said, pointing to Nellie, who was crouched in a chair, her hands moving incessantly, twisting and plucking and clenching.

'If she don't come quietly, I'll drag her through the streets,' shot back the older one, a grizzled man with a worn face.

Nellie pretended to ignore them.

'I have a better idea,' said Mrs Stanard. 'She's fretting about her trunks getting lost. I am sure she will go quietly if you tell her that you're taking her to look for her luggage.'

The other officer – a young Irishman with calm green eyes – turned to Nellie. 'My name is Sergeant Bockert. Will you come with us to find your trunks?' he asked kindly.

Nellie shrank back. 'I don't want to go alone with you. I'm scared.'

Mrs Stanard sighed and rubbed her forehead. 'Oh, all right then. How about I come along with you?' she said, glancing at the policemen for approval. They nodded.

Nellie thanked her, feeling another twinge of guilt for the trouble she was causing. 'But I'll need my hat,' she added.

Mrs Stanard found Nellie's hat and tied her veil, and they left the house, walking across town. The sky was packed with dark-gray cloud masses, and a rising wind buffeted them, stirring up eddies of dust. They passed houses and taverns, stands selling sweet potatoes, onions, russets and plump figs. A butcher in a bloodstained apron drank coffee in the doorway of his shop, purple haunches marbled with fat hanging on great steel hooks above him. Nellie smelled fresh bread from the open door of a bakery and the pungent exhalations from factory smokestacks. People looked at her with scorn or pity. A crowd of ragged children gathered behind them like a parade, making remarks.

'What's she up for?'

'Say, cop, where did you get her?'

'Where did you pull 'er? She's a daisy!'

Nellie was acutely embarrassed, so she hid behind her act and was relieved when they finally arrived at Essex Market Police Court; a gray stone building with thick walls, crenellated at the top like a castle. 'Here's the express office,' Mrs Stanard said brightly. 'We will soon find those trunks of yours.'

There were crowds of people in the courthouse, people of all ages and all nationalities. Some were arguing, others slouched on benches, women were weeping. A handful of police officers in crisp, tightly belted tunics with shining buttons watched them indifferently.

'Have all these people lost their trunks?' Nellie enquired innocently.

'Yes,' said Sergeant Bockert. 'Nearly all of them are looking for trunks.'

'They all seem to be foreigners, too.'

'Mm-hmm, they are foreigners just landed. They have lost their trunks, and it takes up most of our time to help find them.'

Nellie and Mrs Stanard were taken to the back of the building and told to sit on a bench outside a door inscribed 'JUDGE'S CHAMBER'. When it was Nellie's turn, the policemen led them into an austere, dusty room with tall shelves of books and a desk piled high with papers.

Judge Duffy was a silver-haired Irishman with laugh lines around his eyes. He heard the story, looking sympathetically at Nellie over his glasses. Then he said, 'Come forward and lift your veil, Miss.'

'I will not lift my veil,' she replied haughtily.

'It is a rule of the court,' he said. 'If you were the Queen of England, you would have to lift your veil.'

Nellie smiled at him. 'That's much better. I am not the Queen, but I will lift my veil for you.'

As she did so, the judge looked into her eyes and said very kindly and gently, 'My dear child, what is wrong?'

'Nothing's wrong, except that I have lost my trunks and this man,' pointing at Sergeant Bockert, 'promised to bring me where they could be found.'

Judge Duffy turned to Mrs Stanard. 'You say that you don't know anything about her. Did you search her bag for papers?'

Mrs Stanard shrugged. 'There's nothing in her bag but a notebook full of gibberish, and a handkerchief with the initials N. B.'

'Did she have any money?'

'Yes,' interrupted Nellie. 'I paid her for everything and the food was the worst I ever had.'

A chuckle ran through the room, and murmurs of 'She's not so crazy on the food question.'

'Poor child,' said the judge. 'Her looks are refined, and I would stake everything on her being a good girl. I am positive she is somebody's darling.'

More laughter. 'I mean she is some *woman's* darling,' he amended hastily. 'I am sure that someone is searching for her at this very moment. She shows every sign of having been well educated and tenderly reared.' He made a troubled face. 'Well, maybe the newspapers can turn up some relatives.'

Nellie shook her head. 'How can they find my family when I have forgotten their names? And you don't need reporters to help me find my trunks. They are impudent and I don't want to be stared at.' She knew what would happen when the newspaper offices got word of the mystery girl. Legmen would come and question her in droves. Sharp-witted men, hungry to get to the bottom of the puzzle...

She pressed her fingertips to her temples, opened her eyes wide and moaned, 'My head is full of voices.'

'What kind of voices?' Judge Duffy asked worriedly. 'What do they say?'

'Insect voices, hissing and spitting. They keep saying "empty" and "hollow". What was that?' She paused, pretending to listen. 'Now they're saying: "If you don't leave me alone, I'll have to hurt you."'

The others looked alarmed. 'She is clearly suffering from some sort of hallucination,' the judge said. 'In my opinion, in her current state she poses a threat to herself and to others. She must be taken care of.'

'Send her to Blackwell's Island,' suggested the older officer.

'Oh, don't!' cried Mrs Stanard in alarm. 'Don't! She is a lady and it would kill her to be put on the Island.' Nellie was touched, but also felt like shaking her.

'It is possible there has been some foul work here,' Judge Duffy said. 'I believe this child has been drugged and brought to the city, and she is still having visions. Make out the papers and we will send her to Bellevue Hospital for observation. They will decide whether to release her or send her to the Island for further attention. It's my hope that she'll recover quickly and will be able to tell us a startling story.'

The judge asked the policemen to take Nellie to the back office. Presently, another officer came in with a reporter.

It made her nervous – what if the man recognized her? For all she knew, she had encountered him in her search for work. And even if she hadn't come face to face with him, there was nobody in the world who could ferret out a mystery like a reporter. She would rather face a mass of policemen and detectives than one bright specimen of her craft. She turned her face away, muttering, 'I don't want to see any reporters. I won't see any – the judge said I was not to be troubled.'

'Well, there's no insanity in that,' the reporter remarked drily. The men left the room and Nellie's heart contracted with fear. Had her refusal to be interviewed made them realize that she was sane? If she had given the impression of sanity, she must undo it at once.

She jumped up and ran back and forth through the office, Mrs Stanard clinging, terrified, to her arm. Playing crazy was not so hard now – Nellie had been awake all night. Her eyes were dry, her chest felt tight, and her head was hazy with fatigue. She smelled like sweat.

'I don't want to see any doctors!' she yelled. She was dreading being examined by medical men. She wasn't sure that she was capable of fooling experts whose training and experience would tell them the difference between madness and sanity – and clever acting.

Sergeant Bockert led her firmly to a chair and sat down beside her, keeping hold of her arm.

'I won't stay here. There are insects in my head! Why do they bother me with all these people?' she shrieked, rolling her eyes and twitching, and she kept this up until the ambulance arrived to take her to Bellevue.

Nine

ELLIE WAS BUNDLED INTO the ambulance
wagon and they set off, clattering over the
cobblestones. She congratulated herself on passing another hurdle. But she needed to pee and she felt like
throwing up.

'I have to go to the bathroom,' she said to the attendants, but they ignored her and wouldn't speak to her
until they arrived at Bellevue. It was a sprawl of red-brick
buildings at 26th and First Avenue, on the lip of the East
River, and the city's poor and destitute were treated
there.

There was a small, stinking toilet next to the receiving
room and Nellie was able to empty her bladder. Afterward
she was examined by a bald and slope-shouldered doctor,
who looked at her tongue and took her pulse. Her heart
was beating wildly and he seemed to attach great signifi-
cance to that fact. He pulled down her eyelids and said,
'Hmmm.' Then he brought out a light and shone it into
her eyes. Nellie gave him the wide, unblinking stare she
had practiced, and this impressed him too.

'What drugs have you been using?' he asked.

'I have never taken drugs,' she said.

He gave a disbelieving snort. 'The size of your pupils
makes me think that you've taken belladonna.'

Nellie looked at him, aghast. 'That's ridiculous! The only thing wrong with me is that my head is full of insects. You have no right to keep me here against my will. Find my trunks! I want to go home!'

The doctor was making notes. 'Where is home?' he asked.

'Cuba,' she said, keeping her story consistent with the one she had told at the boarding house. 'At least, I *think* it's Cuba...'

'I'll tell you what,' he said, patting her on the shoulder. 'We'll bring you home. Go with this young man,' and he called one of the attendants forward. 'Take her to the pavilion,' he told him in an undertone.

Nellie and her escort started down a long, drab corridor. Her knees and hands were shaking. From the men's ward came the sounds of shouting, snarling and groaning. Suddenly the trial ahead of her seemed too much. She wanted to turn back. Perhaps her own mind wasn't sound to have sought this out? *Think those thoughts and you are lost.* She was nearly crying from exhaustion and alarm.

The attendant noticed the state she was in. 'Those carpenters are making a din,' he said reassuringly. 'They're doing repairs in there. Don't let their noise put you off.'

They had reached huge iron doors fastened by padlocks. He opened the locks and pushed her through, and then they were in the women's ward: a large, bare room that smelled of carbolic acid and floor polish, with afternoon sun coming through the windows. It was furnished with iron cots, lockers and uncomfortable-looking willow chairs. The floor was worn away in places and full of splinters in others. Near the entrance was a pretty sitting room for the staff.

A flint-eyed nurse in a starched cap came up and conferred quietly with the attendant. Then she turned to

Nellie and said, 'I am Miss Scott, the head nurse. You must take off your hat.'

'I am waiting for the boat,' Nellie replied calmly. 'I would like to keep my hat on.'

'Oh, for Christ's sake,' snapped Miss Scott. Her scorn shook Nellie. Miss Scott pulled out Nellie's hatpins and yanked the hat off her head. 'You're not going on any boat, sugar,' she said, over Nellie's protests. 'You are not well. You're in the Bellevue Insane Pavilion. Get yourself settled and a doctor will be in to see you.'

Nellie let out a puff of breath. 'Yes, ma'am.'

The attendant and nurse left, and Nellie looked around her. There were three other women in the ward, sitting despondently on their cots, and only one of them greeted her.

'What's your name?' Nellie asked.

'Anne Neville.' She had a snub nose and freckled skin. Sunlight glinted off her glasses.

'I'm Nellie Brown. I was sent here because I've forgotten everything and there are voices in my head.'

Anne eyed her warily. 'Oh, I am sorry to hear that. I hope the doctors can make you well again.'

Nellie rolled her eyes. 'Why are you here?'

'Well, see, I was a chambermaid, but my health gave way through overwork. My nephew sent me to a Sisters' Hospital to be treated. He always takes care of me – he's a dear young man. But then he lost his job and couldn't pay my bill, and I was transferred here. It's not half as nice and the food is nauseating.'

'But why are you in this ward? It's the Insane Pavilion, you know.'

'Yes, I do know.' Anne was picking at the skin around her fingernails. 'What scares me most is… this is the holding pen for the asylum on Blackwell's Island.'

117

'So I gathered,' said Nellie, a chill rippling up her spine. 'But if you've only had a physical breakdown, you don't belong in either place.'

'Yes, but what can I do about it?' Anne asked, shrugging helplessly. 'The doctors refuse to listen and it's useless to say anything to the nurses.'

Nellie was appalled – Anne seemed as sane as she was. After a while, she tried to talk to the girl on the next cot. The girl gave her a wide, wet smile that revealed bright red gums, and erupted into gibberish. When the food came – boiled corned beef and potatoes, without seasoning and stone cold – the girl put her head in her bowl and ate like a ravenous, savage animal, mumbling and smacking her lips.

The third woman would not even speak to Nellie. Her eyes were dead. She just shook her head and whispered, 'I'll never get well. Never. It's hopeless, hopeless...'

After the meal, Nellie sank onto her cot and tried to rest. She was so tired it struck her like a fever, yet sleep eluded her. Whenever she closed her eyes, images started playing and replaying inside her head: the lodging house, the court, the plight of her fellow patients. It was too much to take in; she simply could not process everything.

In the late afternoon, a teenage boy came in with his mother, a German woman called Louise Schanz. Louise did not look at all insane to Nellie, only lost. She was tearful when the boy left, but a nurse brought her some shirts to mend and it seemed to take her mind off her troubles. She sewed quickly and skilfully, with stitches so fine they were hardly visible.

It was almost dark by the time a doctor appeared on his rounds. He had light brown hair and a florid face. There was a scatter of dandruff on his shoulders, Nellie noticed, as he sat down beside her. He felt her pulse, examined her tongue and made her stretch out her fingers, watching her intently the whole time.

'I've seen that face before,' he said to Miss Scott, who was assisting him. And Nellie knew that she must act at once, before he formulated any suspicions.

'You know me?' she said quickly. 'Tell them who I am, then. Get me out of here.'

'Where are you from?' he asked.

'But I thought you knew! From Cuba, of course.'

'Have you ever been married, or had a lover?'

'Certainly not!'

He smiled with his lips held together and said, 'You can tell me the truth. Are you a woman of the town?'

His tone was more offensive than the words. But she ignored his inference.

'Of what town?' she asked innocently. 'Havana is a long way from here.'

'I think you know what I'm saying. Are you a *street* woman?'

Nellie was so angry she almost dropped her disguise. 'I do not understand you,' she said in a strangled voice.

'Do you let men provide for you?'

She longed to slap him. Instead, she tossed her head and said, 'Oh, of course. My father always provided for me. He would pay you well if he were here.'

At that, the doctor brought the examination to a close, but she heard him remark to Miss Scott, 'Her mind is wrecked. It's as full of holes as a piece of lace. She needs to be put where she'll be taken care of.' And Nellie realized that she had been deemed insane by a second medical expert. Her regard for doctors shrank. Surely it was impossible to tell whether a patient was sane or not from such a superficial consultation? Yet these so-called experts were making diagnoses with complete confidence. Perhaps they were fooled by her simply because they could not conceive of any woman acting insane if she weren't? She resolved to remember every detail of their conversation for her article. Planning it helped contain some of her anger and confusion.

Shortly afterward, a reporter with shrewd gray eyes appeared and asked to interview the girl who had turned up in court with no memory. Nellie guessed that she had attracted attention because she was young, well-spoken and neatly dressed. 'I am curious about her,' he told Miss Scott. 'I've a hunch there's a good story, if only I can get to the bottom of it.'

Nellie threw a blanket over her head to conceal her features on the pretext of being cold, and perhaps mad. Under the blanket was refuge; a break from being watched. It was the closest thing to having her own room and she was in no hurry to emerge.

'You can't see her. She's positively demented,' Miss Scott told the reporter and Nellie breathed out in relief.

Darkness fell and one of the nurses lighted a gas jet. Another patient was brought in, a girl of Nellie's age, registered as Miss Tillie Maynard. Her pale eyelashes framed guileless green eyes in a heart-shaped face. Her hair was so fair it was almost white and cropped short. Nellie knew this as a sign of someone who had had a bad fever. 'My nerves were strained by my recent illness, and my friends brought me here to recover,' she told Nellie in a low, confiding voice. Nellie wondered if her friends knew that they'd dropped her at the Insane Pavilion. Clearly Tillie had no idea where she was and, looking at her shaking hands, Nellie did not have the heart to tell her.

At six o'clock, they were given a cup of tea and a piece of bread. At six-fifteen Miss Scott announced that she wanted to leave and sent them all to bed. She ordered Nellie to strip off and hand over her clothes, and she made them into a bundle labelled 'Brown' and took it away. Then she gave her the same kind of garment worn by the others, a threadbare cotton-flannel gown.

Nellie got into bed and pulled the thin blanket up to her chin. There was no heat. Stingingly cold air blew through the cracked window. She heard the iron doors bang shut and the click of the padlocks being fastened.

It was difficult to sleep. Nellie lay on her back with her arms rigid by her sides, staring up at the ceiling. Tillie twisted and moaned; the night nurses clomped up and down in their stout shoes. Someone in the male ward was screaming. At dawn the attendants began noisily beating eggs for breakfast. The sound made Nellie realize how hungry she was.

At six o'clock a nurse wrenched the covers from Nellie's bed and threw her bundle of clothes at her. 'Get up and get dressed,' she commanded. 'This is your big day. You're leaving for the Island at one-thirty.'

Nellie had almost reached her goal. A feeling of nausea tightened her stomach and her skin pimpled. But she reminded herself that she was a reporter. What mattered was the story and she could face anything for its sake.

Breakfast was a greasy soup, which they were told was chicken broth. Evidently the eggs were for the staff. Afterward Miss Scott decided Nellie's fingernails were 'sharps' and cut them down to the quick, while the other nurses remarked that Nellie was quite the mystery girl and wondered if a lover had cast her forth on the world and destroyed her mind. Nellie noticed that the staff kept to themselves as much as possible, as if they feared the madness was catching.

Tillie begged to know why she had been brought to this ward and Miss Scott answered in surprise, 'Why, have you only just found out that you're in the Insane Pavilion?'

'Yes – my friends said they were sending me to a convalescent ward. I want to get out of this place at once.'

'Is that so? Well, you won't get out in a hurry,' said Miss Scott, with a narrow-mouthed smile. Tillie's eyes filled with tears and Nellie gave her a hug, feeling terrible for her.

Reporters arrived all morning and she marvelled at how untiring they were in their efforts to find a new story, turning up again and again at police courts, hospitals and other such institutions. But although they were eager, they also seemed worn out from the strain of living on their nerves, always hoping that the next moment would turn up some thrilling scoop. A few of them knew her by sight and, to her relief, she was placed off limits before they could get close enough to recognize her. As the time for departure neared, she grew increasingly agitated, convinced that each new arrival would find her out.

At last, she was given a moth-eaten shawl, and her hat and gloves. By this time, her nerves were so unstrung she could hardly put them on. With Tillie and Louise, she was half led, half dragged to a waiting ambulance and the door was bolted behind them. Nellie sank into her seat thankfully. She had done it – she was on her way to the Island. But as the ambulance moved off, her triumph gave way to fear and she wondered what new horrors awaited her.

The ambulance attendant was sitting next to her, his breath reeking of whiskey. Before long he was making sheep's eyes at her and he asked, with a sly grin, if she had a sweetheart. Nellie said she did not, and furthermore, she had no intention of getting one.

'What a pity,' he said. 'A pretty girl like you ought to have a fellow,' and he put his arm around her, drawing her close. 'You might as well enjoy this while you can. There's no chance of getting it where *you're* going.'

Revulsion gave her strength and she shoved him away, her heart pounding.

The man stared at her, then frowned. 'Hoity-toity, ain't we?' he sneered. 'Well, my lady, the Island will soon knock it out of you.'

At the wharf, a crowd assembled around the wagon and a police escort was fetched to allow Nellie and the others to alight. The policemen shuttled them out, shouting at the people to stand back and give them room, or someone would get hurt. Nellie felt the weight of dozens of pairs of eyes. The chaos made her anxious: the strange bodies pushing toward them, the shouts, the lurching wheels and clashing hooves. Tall buildings loomed above them, bisected by crooked alleyways. Piles of trash lay in drifts on the sidewalk. Nellie could smell the fish market across the street, tangy and rotting.

The women were escorted through an archway that had 'Public Charities and Corrections' inscribed over its portals, and across a gangplank to the Blackwell's Island barge. The water looked dark and cold, the current swift. Nellie found herself in a filthy, stuffy cabin with a bunk that stank so badly of shit and vomit that she had to take shallow breaths till she got used to it. They sat on a long, narrow bench, and Tillie was deposited on the bunk, pale and trembling. The sullen-faced guards began to strap her down.

'Is that necessary?' Nellie asked, horrified. 'Tillie has no more strength than a baby.'

'If you know what's good for you, you'll mind your own business,' the bigger one snapped, yanking Tillie's bonds tighter. A feeling of having lost control came over Nellie; an unsettling feeling, like she didn't exist. The barge pulled away from shore, pitching sharply, and she began to shake.

Ten

THE FINAL APPROACH TO the asylum was lined by low stone outbuildings. A pocket of warm air rolled out of an open door, smelling so strongly of rotten meat that Nellie held her breath, hoping it wasn't the kitchen. Next to it, a sign read: 'VISITORS ARE NOT ALLOWED ON THIS ROAD'. An unnecessary prohibition, she thought, as any visitor walking the road once, especially on a warm day, would not want to come back. At last the ambulance came to a stop.

The nurse, Miss Grupe, herded them out and into a narrow vestibule. She was fair-skinned and fine-boned, with light brown hair, blue eyes and lips that puckered into hard lines when she compressed them. She locked the doors behind them, and a high, broken wail echoed around the building. Nellie shivered and gritted her teeth. She was going to sleep with madwomen, eat with them, be considered one of them. Anything could happen, anything at all. But she reminded herself that she was different from the other inmates: it was only a matter of time before she returned to freedom across the East River. To keep herself strong, she imagined her story in news-print, with her own byline.

They sat on hard benches lining the walls. A majestic spiral staircase rose from the ground floor, with several doors leading off each landing. A wave of vertigo swept through Nellie as she took it all in. She rested her head against the wall but recoiled in horror when she saw that it was stained with what looked like mucus and blood. Looking more closely, she realized that the marks were drawings and writing: heads of men, women and children; names and initials and prayers.

One by one, the new patients were brought to see the doctor. When he examined Louise, the German woman Nellie had arrived with, they heard peals of laughter coming from his office.

'What's going on?' Nellie asked Tillie, who was sitting closer to the entrance, listening in.

'The doctor is asking the nurse to speak German,' Tillie answered in a half-whisper. 'With a name like Grupe she likely has German parents. But she's insisting she don't know a word.'

Nellie edged toward the door and heard Louise speaking, her voice broken by sobs. She was begging in halting English to know where she was and pleading for an interpreter, but the doctor and nurse were talking intently and took no notice of her. It made Nellie feel cold and sick.

Tillie pressed her hands to the sides of her head and said, 'It's so unfair! I mean, it's easy to get an interpreter. How can they lock her up in an asylum without even giving her a chance to be understood?'

When it was Nellie's turn, Nurse Grupe took her bag and rifled through it, pulling out her notebook. 'What's this? You won't be needing it in here, Miss, er...' she consulted her notes '...Brown. It doesn't say here where you're from.'

'I can't remember. I... I forget things. I need my book. It helps me remember.'

The nurse pursed her lips a moment and said, 'Do you think we can afford to supply you with notebooks and pencils? This isn't a charity. You'll be thankful for what you get.'

Losing her book made Nellie panicky. She didn't know what she was going to do if she couldn't write. She sensed that Nurse Grupe knew it, took pleasure from it, opening the notebook and reading a few sentences aloud. 'Pithiness! Do more with less!' 'Check your copy!' The nurse shrugged. 'What kind of crazy nonsense is this?' and she tossed the book and handbag into a crate that was piled high with the inmates' belongings.

The doctor's room was small and smelled strongly of ammonia. There were glass-fronted cabinets full of medicine bottles, a weighing scale and a cot. Nellie was ordered to sit at a desk opposite a plump, smooth-skinned man with a high forehead and prominent blue eyes, who introduced himself as Dr Kinier. Nellie straightened her back, trying to act less mad.

'Is she clean? Free of lice?' he asked Nurse Grupe.

'Yes, I think so.'

'What color are her hair and eyes?' he asked, not bothering to look for himself.

'Her hair is reddish brown and she has gray eyes.'

'My eyes are hazel,' Nellie corrected, but the doctor was writing notes and ignored her.

'What is your name?' he asked, still not looking at her.

'Nellie Brown,' she replied easily.

'How old are you?'

'Twenty-three last May.'

He turned to Nurse Grupe and asked, 'When is your next day off?'

'Next Saturday,' she said, coloring faintly.

'Will I see you in town?'

'Mm-hmm. If you play your cards right.' And they both laughed.

The doctor took Nellie's pulse, made her stick out her tongue, shone a light in her eyes and, with the nurse's help, weighed and measured her. He never missed an opportunity to touch Nurse Grupe's hand. He showed far more interest in her than he did in Nellie.

At the end of the examination, he wrote Nellie's fate in a big book. She tried to see what it said, but his handwriting was a careless scrawl, impossible to read upside down.

'I am not sick and I don't want to stay here,' she declared, looking him straight in the eye. 'No one has a right to shut me up.'

His eyes flicked up to meet hers, then went back to his writing. 'You are suffering from dementia. Delusions of persecution,' he said curtly. He finished his notes and sat back, crossing his arms. 'Your delusion is complete and all the more dangerous in that you speak just like someone who is sane. You will stay here until we judge you are well enough to come out. By that stage, you will no longer be a risk to others, or to yourself. Now, time is running on. Next patient, please.'

The new inmates followed the nurse up a corridor to Hall Six, an austere, utilitarian room, in sharp contrast to the ornate beauty of the Octagon. It smelled of carbolic acid, with a waft of human waste. The floor was covered with brown linoleum, and the walls were plainly wainscoted and bare except for a couple of lithographs. One depicted Fritz Emmet, the actor; the others were of minstrels singing and playing banjos. A large, barred window gave light. At the other end of the room, iron doors were secured by a padlock. There was an old upright piano in the corner and, in the center, some nurses sitting at a round table.

They wore brown-and-white striped uniforms and white aprons, with bunches of keys dangling from a cord around their waists.

There were about forty inmates, sitting or crouching on yellow benches along the walls. Some were wild-eyed and absent; others were restless, babbling to themselves. A young girl sat curled into a ball, her feet on the bench and her knees drawn up, hands covering her head as though to ward off blows. Those who were conscious of their surroundings were examining the fresh arrivals with hungry curiosity. They were told to sit down and the patients obligingly made room for them. The benches were bolted to the floor so that they couldn't be shifted or tipped over. Nellie found herself seated between a stone-faced woman, whose eyes were not quite open and not quite shut, and a curly-haired girl with a dimpled chin, who introduced herself as Sofia Fierro.

After looking Nellie up and down, she said, 'What are you in for? You don't look mad at all.'

'Well, Dr Kinier says I have dementia.'

'Dementia?' repeated Sofia, tucking an escaped strand of hair behind her ear. 'Oh, I don't think so. I am a veteran of this place; I know the signs. There's not much the matter with *you*.' She had an Italian accent but spoke English fluently.

The woman was too clever for her own good. 'Why are you here?' Nellie enquired, to distract her.

'My husband put me here.'

'Why?'

Sofia looked abashed. 'I fell in love with one of his friends. And he with me. My husband found us together.'

Nellie tried to mask her surprise. 'You broke your marriage vows, but it doesn't make you mad!' she exclaimed. 'Surely the doctors could see that when they examined you?' She was quickly reassessing her view of the inmates.

There were women who were troubled and women who seemed perfectly sane, but none of them were the monsters she'd been expecting.

Sofia grimaced, her eyes locked on Nellie's. 'Do you think they listened to a word I said? I would be better off if I'd murdered my husband. At least that way I would have had a trial before being sentenced.'

A bell rang. 'Supper time!' one of the nurses shouted.

The patients were lined up in the corridor and made to wait as more and more joined their ranks from other halls. They shivered while they stood there. The windows were open and the draught flowing through them was icy.

Nellie felt faint with hunger, but as she watched the others, her appetite dwindled away. They looked so lost and hopeless. There were vacant faces and tortured faces, some gibbering to themselves, others laughing or crying for no reason. One was counting the moles on her arm with ghastly patience, while another was saying in a soft, reedy voice, 'She is always hungry after school, always very hungry, so I'm going to fix her a sandwich.'

Nellie became aware of a gray-haired inmate prodding her arm. She was barely four feet tall, with a humpback, and she carried one shoulder higher than the other. Her face was round and her features seemed to be melting into fat, except for the mouth, whose underlip protruded loosely. Her limbs twitched intermittently, as if a puppeteer controlled them.

'I'm Miss Gressley. You mustn't mind those other poor creatures,' she said, looking Nellie in the eyes to make sure she would pay attention. 'You see, they are all mad, quite mad.' She nodded several times, her shoulders jerking. 'They can't help themselves.'

Before Nellie could reply, the doors were flung open and they were marched into a long, narrow dining room, smelling of rancid grease. There was a rush for the tables. Large bowls had been set out on them, filled with a pinkish liquid, which they called tea. A piece of bread, cut thick and buttered, and a small saucer containing five prunes were laid by each bowl. The patients sat crammed together on benches without backs, talking in high, clamorous voices, except for a few who were mute. Some couldn't manage cutlery and ate with their hands, like starving animals. Some chewed with their mouths open, tea and masticated bread spraying from their lips. A good portion of what was served landed up on the front of dresses or on the floor. As they went on sipping and swallowing, the nurses walked up and down behind them, shouting at those who didn't eat, shouting at others who ate too fast, hitting one poor woman who spilled her tea on the table.

Opposite Nellie, a woman with a mulberry birthmark on her face put her head down on the table and wept. One of the kinder nurses tried to sit her up and put the bowl to her lips, but she couldn't drink – the tea dribbled out of her mouth and ran down her chest. Further down the table, a heavy-set woman was snatching the bread and prunes from the places near her. Then, while holding her own bowl, she lifted her neighbour's and drained it with loud slurping and smacking noises.

Nellie was torn between horror and pity, but she reminded herself that she had a mission to carry out. She must stay rational and detached, look at everything from all sides and report objectively. She was so absorbed in thought that she didn't notice another patient steal her bread until she looked up and saw the remains of it disappearing into her mouth. Tillie, who was sitting next to her, had observed it too.

'Oh, too bad. Have my piece instead,' she said, holding it out.

Nellie smiled at her. 'That's nice of you, but I want you to eat it all. You must keep up your strength.' And turning to the nurse, she asked for more. A thick slab was flung down on the table. She bit into it, but the butter was off. She took a mouthful of tea, tasted something gritty and metallic, and left the rest.

'Eat a little, all right?' urged Sofia. 'You must eat, or else you'll get sick. To stay healthy, the stomach must be cared for.' Her brown eyes were full of concern.

'What a pity the management doesn't share your view,' Nellie said drily. She realized that the building they had passed on the way here, with the rotten-meat smell blossoming out of it, must be the kitchen.

They were given ten minutes to finish the revolting meal before being told to stand and line up. The doors were unlocked and they were led back to their halls. Hungry, tired and cold, Nellie felt her spirits sink. Were there no activities planned for the patients: only the hall, the brief trip to the dining room, and then back to sit and stagnate? The nurse gave one of the women a needle and thread so that she could sew up a rip in her petticoat. The others watched enviously; it was clear that many of them were desperate for something to do. Nellie wandered to the piano.

'Do you play?' asked Sofia.

'Oh, yes; ever since I was a child.'

'Play something for us? Please?'

Nellie struck a few notes, but they were so out of tune it set her teeth on edge.

'How horrible,' she said, turning to a nurse, Miss McCarten, who had come to stand at her side.

'Should we get one made to order for you?' the nurse asked quite poisonously, and she smiled, showing big yellow teeth like a horse.

132

Ignoring her, Nellie decided to play for the patients – perhaps she could bring them a little comfort. She began with a sonata by Schubert, her cold fingers moving softly over the keyboard, trying to smooth out its irregular touch.

The effect was instantaneous. The women crowded around the piano, their faces lit with such wonder and tenderness, it went through Nellie with a slice. Even the most disturbed of the patients were quiet. When she reached the end of the piece, they begged her for more.

Nellie had noticed Tillie humming along in a sweet contralto and asked if she would join her in a duet. Tillie agreed, shy but pleased. The first song she suggested was 'Home, Sweet Home'.

I gaze on the moon as I tread the drear wild
And feel that my mother now thinks of her child,
As she looks on that moon from our own cottage door
Through the woodbine whose fragrance shall cheer
me no more...

No more from that cottage again will I roam,
Be it ever so humble, there's no place like home.

Tillie's voice was full of sweetness and yearning. The song was sad, yet with a strand of hope caught up in it, and it made Nellie ache for own mother. She mused about how easily Momma might have been deemed insane and put in an institution like this one, but she shoved the thought away at once.

After the music, the women were taken to the bath hall, which had mold-stained walls, several sinks and three large tubs anchored into the rough concrete floor. There was nothing else in the room except a pile of clothes in the corner. Nellie noticed one of the inmates standing beside a filled bathtub, mashing a stained rag around in her hands. Nellie realized what she was in for and her gut clenched in anxiety. The patient was chattering to herself, her face alight with a nasty merriment.

The line of women moved slowly. The same rag was used to wash all of them, even though some of the faces were a mess of boils. Ahead of Nellie, Miss Gressley was reluctant to undress, embarrassed to be seen naked. Nurse Grupe grabbed her by the hair and dragged her into the bath. Nellie caught a glimpse of distorted purple-and-white flesh, and toenails that curled like a bird's.

When Nellie reached the front of the line, she was ordered to take off her clothes. The sight of the bathwater turned her stomach: a thick, oily sludge, with dead lice and bits of waste floating on the surface.

'Please, don't make me get in that,' she begged.

'Get in and don't argue,' Nurse McCarten snapped. 'Everyone must bathe. Do you think we have time to change the water for your ladyships?'

She grabbed Nellie and held her still. With rough, practiced movements, Nurse Grupe yanked her dress over her head and turned out her pockets, then stripped off her underclothes and pulled the hairpins from her hair.

Hunched and shivering, she was manhandled into the tub. The water was so cold it made her gasp, seeming to flay her skin. Pain shot up behind her eyes and made her head ache. She began to protest again, but it was useless. She pleaded that at least the other patients be made to go away.

'Do you think you're made any different from the rest of us?' Nurse Grupe asked scornfully. 'You think they haven't seen a girl in her birthday suit before?'

The inmate took a dirty sliver of soap from the wash-stand and rubbed it all over Nellie, into her face and hair, till she was past seeing or speaking. The woman began to scrub her roughly with the rag, muttering to herself the whole time. It felt like being worked over with sandpaper and seemed to last for hours, though in reality, it was no longer than a minute or two. When it was over, Nellie rose to climb out. Without warning, a bucketful of freezing water was dunked over her head, followed quickly by a second and a third. Panic gripped her; she began to choke. Her lungs burned and her teeth ached, water gushed from her mouth and nose. She could taste soap, hair, the waste from other women. *I am drowning*, flashed in her mind. So this is how drowning feels.

She was dragged, sputtering and humiliated, from the tub. Her limbs shook uncontrollably and seemed to refuse to support the weight of her body. Still wet, she was put into a flannel slip that barely reached her knees, thin and ragged from endless washings. It was labelled in large black letters: 'LUNATIC ASYLUM, B. I. HALL 6'.

By this time Tillie had been undressed. Nellie was dismayed to see how frail and skinny she was – the bones of her shoulder blades seemed sharp enough to pierce her skin. She explained to Nurse McCarten that her head was still sore from her illness and asked that the inmate be made to wash her gently.

'There's not much fear of hurting you,' snapped the nurse. 'Shut up or you'll get it worse.'

Tillie did shut up, her eyes flickering with panic. She tried to cling to Nellie, but the nurses tore her away and put her in the tub, her pale flesh glimmering under the foul water as the madwoman bent over her. The brutal scouring began. Tillie sobbed with pain, protesting, plead-ing, twisting to try and escape the ice-cold soaking. But it was no use. Nellie watched in anguish, wishing she could bear the ordeal for Tillie. When the nurses saw that Tillie was too chilled and weak to dry herself, they were rougher than ever, exasperated at having to do the extra work. She was handed a flannel slip and Nellie couldn't contain herself any longer.

'Don't you see how ill she is?' she burst out. 'She'll get pneumonia in that thin slip! For the love of God, can't you give her a warm nightgown?'

'We don't have nightgowns here,' said Nurse Grupe. 'This isn't a charity.'

'But the city pays to keep up the asylum. And it pays people like you to be kind!'

All the nurses had stopped their work now to stare at her. The head nurse, Miss O'Grady, came up close. She was a tall, well-built woman with thick, springy black hair drawn into a tight bun and dark, deeply set eyes.

'You better stop hoping for kindness – you won't get it here,' she said in a loud, flat-toned voice. 'Am I clear?'

Nellie nodded. She had stopped shaking, become numb.

'I see you're a troublemaker,' said Nurse O'Grady. 'Don't make me have to tell you again.'

'Don't try to help,' came a soft whisper from the line of women, when the nurse had turned away. Nellie searched their faces, but the light was too dim to see who had spoken.

The voice came again: 'You'll only be punished. You don't want to end up in the Lodge.'

'What's the Lodge?'

'It's the building with the high steps and the bars all around. It's where they send the worst cases, the violent ones. You're in danger if you end up there.'

That night, the women slept eight to a room in dormitories that led off Hall Six. The doors were bolted and the nurses took away the oil lamps, leaving them in darkness. Nellie's straw-filled pallet smelled of sweat and stale piss. It was made up with a sheet over an oilcloth, covered by a mildewed blanket that was too short for her. Her wet hair soaked the pillow, her thin slip offering no comfort against the chill. However tightly she curled in on herself, she could not get warm. Cold seemed to wither her skin, to sink down into her bones.

Exhausted as she was, sleep would not come. She could hear the telltale scuttling and scratching of rats inside the walls. From other parts of the building came unholy noises – wild sobbing and screams, running feet, the ringing of bells. In the next bed was Cathy, whose husband had put her there because she could not keep a child in her womb, and on the other side was Hester, easily seventy years old and blind, who wept from the cold and begged God to take her home. Early on in the night, Nellie had slipped out of bed to try and comfort Hester, but she'd only succeeded in making her more agitated, and a night nurse had told her to stop it at once and get back to bed.

Nellie must have fallen into a brief doze. She woke with a start to find Sofia bending over her, just visible in the darkness, her curly hair tumbling around her shoulders.

'I can't sleep. Want to keep me company?' Sofia whispered.

'Sure,' said Nellie, jumping at the chance to get to know Sofia, as she was impressed by her quick wits. She also needed material for her story.

She got out of bed, wrapping her blanket around her shoulders, and they sat on the floor, leaning against Nellie's bed.

'Your accent has a lovely rising lilt,' Sofia began, pulling her fingers through her hair. 'I'm guessing you're from West Pennsylvania?'

'Yes, that's right.' Since arriving at the asylum, Nellie had dropped the pretence of being Cuban.

'I have an aunt who settled in Pittsburgh.'

'Oh, really?' said Nellie, trying to rub gooseflesh from her arms. 'I lived there for a time, but I prefer New York. What about you? Your English is great, by the way.'

Sofia grinned. 'Thank you. I studied hard when I arrived in this country. I was born in Naples. It's a beautiful city, but we lived in a rough area and I don't miss it.'

She put her hand in her pocket and drew out an orange. Nellie wondered where she'd got it. Sofia broke the skin with her thumbnail and the smell brought saliva to Nellie's mouth in a painful rush. As Sofia peeled the fruit and divided it into segments, Nellie thought she could have wolfed it down in a single bite. She tried not to reach too eagerly for the pieces she was offered, not wanting to appear weak so soon. 'This is good,' she said, with her mouth full. 'Thank you.'

Sofia was eating slowly; she seemed thoughtful. 'It is good,' she said, 'but I would far rather have a cigarette. Or a kiss.'

Nellie guessed that Sofia was referring to her lover. 'I wouldn't know about that. Never been kissed,' she confessed, glad it was too dark for Sofia to see her blushes.

'Why are you here?' Sofia asked suddenly.

Nellie had decided to evade questions like this for as long as possible. 'I'll tell you another time,' she said, licking the last drops of juice from her fingers.

'Why not now?'

Nellie hesitated. 'I'm tired,' she said, which was true enough.

They heard a loud thudding coming through the ceiling.

'What on earth is that?' asked Nellie, alarmed, but also relieved by the distraction.

'Another loon throwing a fit,' Sofia said offhandedly, as Nellie wondered if the noise was an inmate's head pummelling the floor.

'Shut up, you two. I'm trying to get some rest,' someone called from across the room.

'Sorry, we'll stop now,' Sofia said. Then, to Nellie, 'We'd better get back to bed. They'll be doing checks soon, anyway.'

Nurses came in and out at regular intervals to inspect the patients, shining a lantern in their faces. Even if Nellie had been able to sleep, the loud talking and heavy footsteps that signalled their approach, followed by the unlocking of the big door, would have woken her. As the night wore on, she began to feel lonely. She missed her mother, who had no idea where she was. To comfort herself, she called up her good memories of childhood. Walking through Owens' Wood with the warm fragrance of the trees all around and the leaves swaying overhead. Sitting on Momma's lap as she listened to her stories; discussing her future with Poppa. How differently things had turned out! Her last thought before falling into a fitful sleep was: *What would Poppa think if he could see me now?*

Eleven

NELLIE WOKE TO AN ice-gray dawn creeping through the high, barred window. She could see the shapes of the other women in the beds around her, hear them sighing and muttering to themselves. The air smelled of stale breath and the full chamber pot in the corner. Nellie huddled under the thin blanket; her skin goosefleshed with cold, her hair still wet from last night's bath. She heard a heavy tread in the hall, the jangle of keys, the click of a lock being opened.

Nurse O'Grady stood in the doorway. 'Time to get up,' she ordered, flinging the window open, while another nurse threw some clothing at Nellie and told her to put it on.

'Where are my own clothes?' Nellie asked.

'You'll take what you get and shut up,' came the reply.

Nellie blinked, got out of bed and picked up the stained white calico dress and coarse black underskirt. A stench of mildew rose from their folds and she felt a surge of nausea as she pulled them over her aching body.

While the nurses dressed those women who couldn't tend to themselves, Nellie stole a moment to go to the window. The early-morning mist was beginning to burn off the river. Manhattan shimmered beyond it. The rising sun was striking the windows, making them glitter as if small flames were leaping in them. You'll be back there soon, she reassured herself.

Nurse O'Grady's hand clamped down on her shoulder. 'Get into the hall. Go on, shoo. There'll be no idle gawking here.'

Nellie struggled as the woman pushed her toward the door. 'You have no right to manhandle me.'

For a moment, Nurse O'Grady's grip loosened. She narrowed her eyes. 'Your opinion counts for nothing in here. The quicker you get that, the better it will be for you.'

She gave Nellie a hard shove and she fell. A heavy boot landed on her coccyx, pain flashing up her spine.

'I'll be keeping my eye on you. Got that?'

Nellie nodded, clamping her bottom lip between her teeth to stop tears falling. She would not give the nurse the satisfaction of seeing her crumple.

Once they were dressed, the forty-five patients of Hall Six visited the bathroom, where they washed and were given two towels to share. The woman in front of Nellie had weeping sores on her face; the skin in between eruptions was the color of raw steak. Nellie took the towel but didn't use it, drying her face and hands with her underskirt instead. Afterward, Nellie's hair, matted and damp from the night before, was brutally combed by Nurse McCarten. The nurse moved slowly and sighed as she went about her work, as if it took great effort.

'Please stop,' Nellie begged. 'Some of the women's heads are infested. I saw lice in their hair.'

'Full of airs and graces, ain't you?' sneered Nurse McCarten, baring her big teeth. 'What makes you think you're any better than the rest? You're all just alike in here.'

Nellie gave up and endured in silence. She asked for her hairpins, but was refused. 'We plait your ladyships' hair so you can't tear it out by the roots.'

'Oh, but I would never do such a thing!'

'There's enough who try,' said Nurse McCarten, sighing, and she tugged Nellie's hair into a single plait and tied it with a red cotton rag.

They were told to go to breakfast and were once again made to wait in the cold corridor for the dining-hall doors to be opened. Nellie found herself next to Louise, who was talking earnestly in German to a young girl. Louise's relief at being able to communicate with someone was palpable. There were a number of foreign patients, whose English was poor. Nellie was sure that the majority of them were sane and they had ended up on the Island because they could not make themselves understood. Ahead of her, she recognized Tillie by her shorn fair hair, and went to join her. Tillie's skin was drawn tight over her cheekbones and her eyes seemed to have sunk into their sockets.

'How did you sleep?' Nellie asked.

'Honestly, I had an atrocious night. I almost froze and then the noise kept me awake. My nerves were so unstrung before I came here, I fear I shan't be able to stand the strain.' She let out a sharp, sudden laugh.

Nellie did her best to cheer Tillie up. She put an arm around her shoulders and hummed the opening bars of 'Home, Sweet Home', encouraging Tillie to sing along with her. Nellie broke off to ask a passing nurse if they could have more clothing to keep out the cold. The nurse stared at her with lifted eyebrows and a tight mouth, and told her to shut up. The patients had as much as they intended to give them.

Breakfast was a bowl of cold tea, a slice of buttered bread and a saucer of oatmeal with molasses. Nellie's

143

stomach ached with hunger, but the food would not go down. She asked for unbuttered bread and was given a hunk that was hard and blackened. Remembering Sofia's words about eating to stay healthy, she gnawed on it till it was soft enough to swallow. As the first mouthful went down, something scuttled out of the bread in her hand and dropped onto her plate. She gagged and spat – it was a spider! A chunk of vomit filled her mouth as she watched it run over the table and vanish into a large crack in the woodwork. Her appetite was gone.

After breakfast, it was compulsory to use the toilets, whether they needed to or not. The inmates stood in long lines for ten cubicles without doors, set over a long trough filled with water. A plug was supposed to be pulled in order to drain the water into the river, but this clearly wasn't done often enough, and the stink almost turned Nellie's stomach inside out. There was no toilet paper. If a woman wanted paper, she had to ask Nurse Grupe, who decided how much was needed.

Those who were capable of work were then given a variety of household tasks, from tending the gardens to sewing, doing laundry, making beds and cleaning the nurse's rooms. Nellie soon realized that the patients did every chore the nurses considered beneath them. She was given the job of polishing the floor with an acrid-smelling brown paste.

A bell rang, and they were told to put on shawls and hats for a walk. There was a skirmish for the hats, which were conical and made of white straw, reminding Nellie, incongruously, of the ones worn by bathers at Coney Island. Once the hats were on, Nellie could hardly see anyone's faces. They were led out of Hall Six, down the stairs and along a corridor that took them past the kitchen where the food for the doctors and nurses was prepared.

Peering in the half-open door, Nellie saw melons, grapes, fresh bread and beef. Her mouth watered. The doctors and nurses had the best of everything, while the patients were slowly being starved. They went through another door and found themselves outside.

Forming lines as far as the eye could see, hundreds of inmates were shuffling around the lawns or leaning against the walls of the building. Women dragged along in straitjackets, women talking to themselves and screaming, women with faltering steps and glassy eyes who looked like they were drugged.

'It takes some getting used to,' said Sofia, glancing at Nellie's face.

Nellie couldn't answer, too distraught by the sheer scale of the misery in front of her. It was unimaginable – a world of suffering that the outside world knew nothing of. For several moments she struggled for detachment, reminding herself that it was her job to tell the world about it.

Slipping her arm through Nellie's, Sofia led her down a pathway that ran south, toward the convict-built sea wall. The leaves were already turning red and gold, as if they were on fire. Overhead, a flock of geese flew in a shifting V and Sofia said, 'They're heading south for winter.' They passed a low pavilion with a motto emblazoned on the side: 'WHILE I LIVE I HOPE'.

'It's absurd,' Nellie remarked. 'They should rather put "SHE WHO ENTERS HERE ABANDONS ALL HOPE" in big letters above the asylum gates.'

They were looking out at the choppy brown river. The low sky resembled a sheet of metal, and a cold wind shuddered among the trees. To the north they could see the lighthouse, and to the south the almshouse and the prison, large, rectangular buildings made from the same cold stone as the asylum. They listened to the slap and suck of waves as they hit the shore, the bray of a boat horn, a couple of mud-hens making noises like gear being stripped. Nellie breathed in brine and oil from the river, the sweet dankness of rotting vegetation. Across the water, Manhattan was tantalizingly close. She could see people going about their business – a fisherman unwinding a net on the quay, a woman tugging her dog away from a lamp post and hurrying it along.

'Has anyone ever escaped this place?' Nellie asked.

'Some have tried.'

'How?'

'Swimming across. We call them river-runners.'

'And?'

'Drowned.' Sofia sighed and rubbed the side of her mouth. 'Don't even think about trying it.'

'Oh, I won't. Never fear.'

Sofia gave Nellie a measuring look. 'Perhaps the river-runners didn't realize how strong the currents are,' she said. 'I don't know. Maybe they just wanted to end it all.'

Manhattan was a quarter of a mile at most, Nellie figured. Any good swimmer, unaware of the currents and the patrol boats that circled the Island, would look across and think: *I could certainly manage that.* But even if an inmate succeeded in dodging the boats, even if she plunged into the river and struck out half underwater, unnoticed, she would still be weakened by starvation and dazed with the drugs she was given. Perhaps a different woman, sick of being roughed up by the attendants, sick of the cold and the baths and inedible food, would see death in those tumultuous waters as a blessed release. For a moment Nellie imagined wading in and slipping under the surface. What would it feel like? Would she struggle against the current, her instinct for survival kicking in despite herself? Or would she surrender gratefully, sinking down through drifts of muck and sulfur, her skirts billowing behind her like sails till she came to rest on the silty riverbed, with shoals of fish swimming indifferently past?

A long line of women was approaching, yoked together like beasts by a rope that was attached to their waists by sturdy leather belts. A sharp, curdled smell rose from them. At the end of the rope was a brightly colored wagon, like a circus chariot. Two women sat inside it – one nursing a sore foot, the other screaming: 'You beat me and I won't forget it! You want to kill me!' in between sobs and shrieks.

'Who are they?' Nellie breathed.

'They are the violent patients from the Lodge. They're too dangerous to walk on their own.'

'Good Lord,' murmured Nellie, fascinated yet torn. If monsters existed at all in the asylum, they had to be right here in front of her. She gazed at the violents, unable to decide if they were ghouls or very sick women.

Some of them were shrieking, some were jerking, others were staggering or gibbering or sobbing. She saw one woman whose every breath was a scream, and every scream a prayer for mercy. 'Oh Lord, Oh Lord,' were the only words that Nellie could make out, but it seemed as if the woman was tortured by some unbearable memory. Another, with matted red hair and a face peppered with freckles, saw Nellie looking at her and turned as far as she could to hold her eyes. She smiled. It was the most chilling and vindictive smile Nellie had ever received, and it filled her with fear and revulsion. The inmate put a finger to her lips and shook her head before a tug on the rope dragged her forward.

The worst hours were yet to come. After the walk, Nellie's group was taken back to Hall Six and made to sit on the benches in silence. There was nothing to look at, just the walls with their few lithographs, and the window that was barred on the inside. Those who tried to talk were scolded and ordered to shut up by the nurses. Those who slumped, or changed position, or tried to walk in order to relieve their stiffness, were told to sit up straight and keep still.

Time crept by. Nellie couldn't tell how much time. There were no clocks. She watched Nurse Grupe filling out some charts, chewing on her bottom lip in concentration. She counted how many noises she could hear – the scream of a gull overhead, the wheeze of pipes, the murmur of the nurses talking among themselves. She glanced at the sad and hopeless faces around her, and wondered how they could stand being shut up like this, year in and year out, with nothing to do but brood on whatever tormented them. No wonder they got worse instead of better.

The iron doors swung open and heads swivelled. A tall man in a dark suit with glistening black hair walked in. The nurses stood up.

'Good afternoon, Superintendent Dent,' they greeted him.

'Good afternoon, ladies,' he said.

He walked through the hall, occasionally asking, 'How do you do?' or 'How are you today?' His voice was as cold as the hall and the patients meekly answered, 'Fine,' and, 'Thank you, sir,' without any mention of their sufferings.

'Why doesn't anyone tell him how wretched we are, with the cold and insufficient clothing?' Nellie whispered to Sofia.

'Because the nurses would beat us if we did. And anyhow, if Dent acknowledged that he believed us, it would look as though he treated us wrong on purpose. As things stand, he gets along very nicely without committing himself.'

Nurse Grupe scowled at Sofia and she stopped speaking. The superintendent went out.

Nellie's stomach rumbled; she was light-headed from hunger. As more minutes crept by, she could feel her whole body getting stiff. Aches pulsed up her back. She was seized by a powerful urge to stand and stamp her feet, to shout as loudly as she could. She fought it down and felt the beginnings of panic fluttering in her chest. Her heart started thumping as if she'd been running; her skin pimpled with cold, though her armpits were slick with sweat. She shut her eyes and struggled against it.

What drove her to get into the dark places of the world and dig out the truth? This time, she had let it carry her too far. She was suffering from some kind of fit... dropping, dissolving into a mad fit. Here was where the madness lay – in being imprisoned in this space, trapped and caged like an animal. The thought made her more frightened still. Just then, two of the nurses brought Hester in, the blind woman who had begged the night before for God to take her home. They were dragging her backwards, a nurse on either side of her, hooking her under the arms. They threw her onto one of the benches, next to Sofia.

'Oh, what are you doing with me?' Hester cried. 'I am cold, so cold! Why can't I stay in bed, or have a shawl?'

Nurse O'Grady struck her across the cheek. This was followed by half a dozen blows to her head. 'There now, that should settle your brains,' the nurse said with a short, harsh laugh.

'Why did you do that?' cried Hester, turning her milky, unfocused gaze in the direction of the nurse's voice. She had a livid welt on her cheek and one of her eyes was swollen almost shut. 'What have I done?'

'Just shut your mouth.'

Hester began to rock back and forth, moaning softly. Sofia shushed her gently and rubbed the old woman's hands, which were purple from the cold. After a few minutes, Hester stood up and tried to feel her way out of the hall. The attendants jerked her back to the bench, where she sat slumped and motionless. When she stood up again, they let her walk. They laughed when she tripped over the other women's feet or bumped against edges of the bench. At last, Hester gave up and tried to lie down on the floor, but they yanked her upright again.

'Won't you please give me a pillow and pull the covers over me? I'm frozen,' she begged.

Nurse Grupe went over to Hester and sat down on top of her.

'What are you doing? Oh, that hurts!'

Vainly, Hester tried to twist away from under her. The nurse ran her chilly hands over Hester's face and down inside the fabric of her dress. When the old woman screamed, Nurse Grupe laughed and did it again, lips parted, eyes bright. Nellie saw that she was enjoying herself and her mind flashed back to Jack grinning as he snapped the female skeleton's spine in two. A cold turmoil rose in her.

Once Nurse Grupe had finished amusing herself, Hester was carried away to another ward, and they did not see her again.

Twelve

O N HER SECOND MORNING, Nellie was brought to see the doctor. She found not Dr Kinier, but a tall, fresh-looking man with fair, curly hair and the air of a gentleman.

He held out his hand, his grip was warm. 'It's good to meet you,' he said, gesturing her to the chair opposite his desk. 'I am Dr Ingram, the assistant superintendent. How are you feeling?'

'Oh, I feel all right,' she replied, surprised to be treated an equal after the usual brutal handling.

'But you are sick, you know.' He spoke in a reasonable, reassuring way.

'Well, I'd be a good deal better if we were given more clothes. It's awful cold in here.'

'You're right – it is unseasonably cold for October. I'm going to speak to the nurses about getting you some warm garments.'

Crossing to her side of the desk, he picked up her wrist and took her pulse. He felt her temples, as well as behind her ears and along her jawline – his touch was gentle. He went back to his chair and began to ask questions.

'Your admitting report said you hear voices in your head. Can you tell me more about them? What exactly do they say?'

Nellie looked at him quickly, then looked away. 'I haven't heard any recently,' she said.

'That's good,' he smiled. 'It sounds like the asylum is having a calming effect on you already.' He was making notes as she spoke, writing down everything she said.

His pen paused and he raised his eyes to meet hers. 'Why don't we begin at the beginning? Would you say your childhood was a happy one?'

Nellie hadn't expected this and it threw her. Should she invent a fictitious early life? Or was it better to talk about her real life because she was less likely to make mistakes? She decided to go with the truth, despite never having spoken of it to anyone before.

'We were happy until my father died. But then, my mother remarried. My stepfather was... violent.' Saying it triggered the familiar twinge of anxiety in her stomach.

Now the doctor sat up straight. 'Violent? In what way?' he asked. 'You can be perfectly open with me. You needn't hold anything back.'

It was impossible to tell him. She had not talked very much since her father died, not about anything personal, the way other girls talked. It struck her that she was far more comfortable telling other people's stories than her own. She didn't know how to be confiding, so she gave Dr Ingram a blank, staring look.

'You have nothing to be afraid of,' he said.

She shook her head, pressing the back of her hand against her mouth.

Dr Ingram watched her for a moment, silent and pensive. Then he brightened. 'Maybe you will find it easier to talk when you know me better,' he suggested. 'It takes time to build trust, but I am a patient man. So, since you're finding it difficult to talk about your life, why don't I tell you about mine?'

'Yes, I would like that.'

He sat back and crossed his arms. 'I qualified seven years ago and I've been working at the asylum for the past two years. My medical speciality isn't bodies, but minds. I treat diseases of the brain and nerves. You see, I am fascinated by the nervous system because it's both material and ethereal. It holds the key to the human psyche – the angels and the demons in us all.'

'The angels and the demons,' she mused. 'Yes.'

'To get to the point, I think I can help you through a talking cure. We are going to meet like this every day. If you will try to talk to me, I will try to listen.' He paused, giving her a searching glance. 'Do you understand? Is there anything you want to ask me?'

Nellie pulled at a loose thread on her skirt and said, 'I don't see how talking can cure me.'

'Well, look at it this way. Mental wounds can create madness and it's clear that you have been wounded. If we can uncover those hurts together during the course of our conversations, perhaps I can heal them.'

'Oh, I think I get it,' she answered levelly, though his words had thrown her into turmoil. She had never told her own story – her father's death, her mother and Jack – and it seemed unthinkable that she should do so now, especially to a stranger.

'Are you willing to try?' he asked.

She forced herself to answer: 'Sure, if you are.'

He smiled. 'That's the spirit. Good girl.'

At the end of the examination, he sat back and made a steeple of his fingers. 'So, I regard your case as hopeful. Very hopeful,' he said. 'Physically, you're as sound as a bell. Your psyche has been damaged, but I am confident we can restore you to good mental health.'

He called Nurse O'Grady and told her to give the patients extra clothing, adding, 'The cold is almost unbearable and you'll have pneumonia cases if you are not careful.'

'Yes, doctor,' she said meekly, but her face curdled.

The nurse took Nellie back to the hall, her fingertips digging into the soft flesh of Nellie's upper arm so hard that pains ran right the way through her.

'We know all about you,' Nurse O'Grady said, as they made their way down the long corridor. 'There's an article just come out in the *Mail*. Says you were thrown in the bin for having a head full of voices and no memory. They believe your brain got scrambled like an egg after your lover dropped you. So don't go thinking you're any better than the rest.'

So that was what the newspapers were saying. It was an odd, exposed feeling to be the story, rather than the reporter writing it. But she saw that the interest in her was an advantage. Her article would have all the more impact for it. The other papers would look foolish, which would increase the *World*'s stature. She was desperately curious to read the *Mail*, but there wasn't time to think about it now.

'I'm not requesting warm things just for myself. It's for every—'

'I knew you were trouble from the moment I laid eyes on you,' Nurse O'Grady interrupted. 'Always complaining, always wanting things done differently. One more word from you and I'll make you regret the day you were born.' She spoke with a quiet hostility that made the hairs on Nellie's arms rise.

Later that morning, Nurse McCarten called Nellie to the sitting room at the end of the hall, where she found a man and a woman standing by the window. They were in their fifties, neatly dressed, their clothes carefully mended and shiny with wear. At the sight of Nellie, the woman's face sagged and the man exhaled roughly and shook his head. 'No, no, that's not our girl,' he said, laying his hand comfortingly on his wife's shoulder as tears trickled down her cheeks.

Nellie realized that they must have read the article in the *Mail* and come to Blackwell's Island hoping she was their missing daughter. She felt a great wave of sadness for them, for what were the chances of finding a missing person in this city of lost souls? They got up to leave and Nellie followed them to the door, but Nurse McCarten said, 'Stay right where you are, Brown. There's more folk to see you. You're quite the celebrity, it seems.'

Nellie sat down on the small settee with her hands folded in her lap. It was a welcome relief from the hard benches, but the interest in her was worrying. She hoped that nothing would happen to blow her cover.

Before long, another man and woman were ushered in. Compared to the first couple, their clothes were sumptuous. The woman was handsome, if daubed in too much powder and paint, and the man had a gold watch chain and snuffbox, and lush, dark side whiskers. They quickly established that Nellie wasn't their lost sister, but they were in no hurry to leave.

'What's the food like?' the man asked.

'It's simple and barely sufficient,' said Nellie.

'Ah – yes,' he said. 'I've read that a rich diet can stimulate insanity.'

'You are *so* well-read! I'm amazed by the things you know,' the woman exclaimed coquettishly. She turned to Nellie. 'Is there anywhere you can walk if you want to?'

'Yes, we are taken to the grounds once a day.'

'How do you spend the rest of the time?'

'Walled up behind deadbolt locks, with nothing to do but dwell on our madness,' said Nellie, who was tiring of this.

The woman shuddered pleasurably. 'Gee, can you picture it?' she asked her companion.

Nellie was beginning to wonder if their missing sister even existed, for they seemed to be here purely for the spectacle, entertaining themselves with a free freak show.

'I don't know how you stand being shut away in this place. It makes my flesh creep,' the man said to Nellie, putting a pinch of snuff on his hand and sniffing it up loudly.

'You must have nerves of steel,' the woman added.

'It's not as if I have a choice,' answered Nellie, and the woman tittered.

They hung on her words with relish. They wanted to stare at her, to drink her madness in like a fine wine, until the nurse said, 'If she's not the right girl, you can't stay here, you know,' and showed them firmly to the door.

Tumultuous clouds drove swiftly across the sky when the inmates went for their walk, and the wind went rushing through the trees and whipped the river into peaks. In the distance they could hear the convicts singing as they worked, the clink of their hammers breaking rocks.

Nellie walked with Tillie, whose sweet nature and dependence reminded her of Kate. She felt protective of her and grieved to see how quickly she had gone downhill in only two days. Tillie shivered with cold all the time and had stopped eating. Her eyes were deep-set and anxious. She seemed confused, so Nellie encouraged her to sing songs to keep her mind active. A gust of wind sent fallen leaves rolling along the path toward them, and Tillie broke off from a rendition of 'Beautiful Dreamer' to pick up a rust-red maple leaf. 'Oh! Oh, look! It's so pretty!' she cried, her face alight with pleasure.

'I love maples,' said Nellie wistfully. 'Where I grew up it was mostly pines. The air always smelled of pine needles. I often wish I hadn't been so keen to leave it behind...'

'You're lucky that you were raised with hills and trees,' Tillie said, her teeth chattering. 'I grew up in a tenement and what I mostly remember smelling was smoke from the factories and other people's trash.' She gave a wry smile.

'Do you have a big family?' Nellie asked.

'Yes; I have two brothers and three sisters. I'm the oldest. We lost my mother last year.'

'I'm awful sorry,' said Nellie, taking her arm.

'Yes. Well. She died of tuberculosis. My father did everything in his power to keep her alive and comfortable, but he just didn't have the money to find her the best doctors or the right medicine. She wasted away before our eyes, till we couldn't handle her care any more.' A single tear hung on Tillie's eyelashes, then crept down her cheek. 'Father sent her to the workhouse infirmary to die. It just about broke him... He turned to drink and lost his job. I had to go into service to help keep everyone.'

Nellie squeezed her arm. 'You've had a bad time.'

Tillie nodded and sucked in a shuddery breath. 'Wondering how they're managing without me is driving me half out of my mind with worry.'

'What have you got there?' a passing nurse snapped. 'Drop it and keep walking,' and she knocked the leaf out of Tillie's hand.

Tillie looked stricken, but was fortunately distracted by Miss Gressley, who had seen what had happened and hurried over to them.

'Oh, my word! How mean the nurses are,' she said, with feeling. 'Not that they're proper nurses, any more than you or me. Most of them never even saw the inside of a hospital, let alone had any training.' And without giving them the chance to reply, she began to chatter about the cold weather. At times, a sort of talking fit took Miss Gressley – Nellie supposed it to be another symptom of her disease. Her eyes rolled and her face pulsed as torrents of speech fell from her lips.

'How long have you been here?' Tillie enquired when she paused for breath.

Miss Gressley considered this, her lower lip thrust out. 'Oh, I have lost track of time, but I believe it to be more than twenty years,' she said finally. 'Yes, I think so. Yes.'

'What put you here?' asked Nellie, shocked, wondering how anyone could survive the asylum that long. 'Have you ever had a home of your own?'

'I came because I lost all my money. You see, the lawyers took my home and everything I owned, and it made me ill.' She gave a fluttering sigh. 'If I hadn't been so harshly treated here, I should have got well long ago. Now I can't get well and I don't want to. There's no place for me in the outside world.'

A bell clanged near the old boathouse and a squabble of gulls burst skywards with hoarse cries. High waves slapped against the stones. The day's ferry was arriving at the Island. They watched her dock and the cargo being unloaded.

Suddenly, Miss Gressley shrank back, a look of terror twisting her features.

'What is it?' Nellie asked, in surprise.

Miss Gressley pointed to a dark heap of caskets that were being carried onto the forward deck. 'Coffins,' she whispered. 'They're bound for paupers' graves on Hart

Island, where they're buried with no more ceremony than an animal has.' She shuddered. 'One of these days – and it won't be far from now… one of these days when the ferry goes across the river, I will be part of that cargo.'

After the first hour of sitting that afternoon, Nellie felt panic gathering inside her again. Her heart began to beat unpleasantly. Sweat pearled on her upper lip and she was shaking. She wanted to get up, as Hester had done, and run right out of the hall, but she still had hours to get through.

If she was going to hold onto her sanity, she had to work out how to manage the endless sitting. She tried to pray to God to protect her and keep her sound in mind, but the words clotted on her tongue. It did not surprise her, for her understanding of God was weak and shaky. If he was as paternal, all-knowing, and just as he was supposed to be, how come he had let her family suffer so horribly? She had long felt that God was more remote from her than from other people; she wasn't even sure he existed. Perhaps there was no God to pray to, no Heaven or even Hell, but only ice-cold emptiness. And even supposing he did exist and was noting Nellie's lack of faith in him, she did not fear him as she should, for hadn't he already brought catastrophe down on them?

Religion would not help her. She would have to rely on herself. If she concentrated hard enough, she could seal off Hall Six behind a sort of wall in her head, while keeping the rest of her mind occupied with something other than the present. Something pleasurable. It was a trick she'd learned during the bad times with Jack.

She turned her thoughts to her mother. In her mind, Momma was disjointed, as if she were not one woman, but several – happy and miserable, foolish and wise. *Focus.*

Search for a single memory and hold it up for inspection. One of the good ones...

She saw herself sitting on her mother's lap, listening to her tell stories. She recalled the feelings of terror and safety inside the circle of Momma's arms, as they both surrendered to the spell of her words. Nellie came back to the present to find tears flowing down her cheeks. They were tears, not of sorrow, but of awe that nothing was left behind for ever, that everything could be recovered, that time was not linear, but circular. Overlapping. Inside her head, she still owned all her memories. As long as she held onto this knowledge, she would survive the asylum.

'Put Nellie Brown into a room alone tonight,' Nurse O'Grady ordered at bedtime. 'Give her a chance to reflect on her high and mighty ways. I've found it's best done in solitude and darkness.' Smirking, she turned to Nellie. 'That'll teach you to complain to the doctors, my lady.'

Nurse McCarten led Nellie to a small cell with a tiny, high, barred window that was next to the toilets. It had no furniture, except for an empty wooden pail that served as a chamber pot, and a straw pallet on the floor covered with a dirty blanket. The walls were scratched and gouged, as though someone had attacked them with fingernails or teeth. A thick stink of sewage hung in the air. They heard the scraping of tiny nails over the cement floor and the nurse's lantern caught the flash of a disappearing tail.

'A nice room, ain't it?' said Nurse McCarten. Her lips curled back, showing rows of teeth. 'I hope you like it.' And with that she lumbered out, bolting the cell from the outside, leaving Nellie in darkness.

Nellie went to lie down on the pallet. She tried not to gag from the stench, telling herself that she'd get used to it. She listened to the nurse stomp down the hall in her heavy boots, locking each dormitory separately. After a few minutes, she thought she heard an insect crawl up the wall and fall onto the mattress with a thud. The night-time shrieks and sobbing of the lunatics started up and panic seized her – a clutching darkness closing in. Perhaps madness had already taken root in her and was blossoming inside her skull. She felt her breath come shorter.

She must try to keep calm. *Don't think of rats and bugs and madness. Lord, don't think of being shut in with them.* It would be impossible to sleep. She took deep breaths, willing herself to be that dispassionate journalist bearing witness. But she could not detach herself and the failure made her still more agitated.

Why was the asylum so fraught with danger and suffering? The inmates were kept in conditions too harsh for animals. What if fire broke out? There were 1,600 patients in the building. Escape would be impossible. They were locked one to ten to a room, with all the windows barred. What's more, there was no firehouse on the Island; they would have to wait for the firemen to arrive by boat. By then it would be too late. The jailors of nurses would never think of releasing their charges. They wouldn't risk the flames and their own lives while they unlocked the hundreds of doors for a horde of madwomen. The patients would burn to death amid scenes of unequalled horror.

Nellie got up and went to the window. She had to stand on tiptoe to see out. Fog had settled low on the riverbank, turning the boats into ghostly shapes. The gas lamps on the dockside wore luminous haloes, while on the far side of the water, Manhattan was an embroidery of light.

It was like looking at an enchanted castle from afar.

Still, the sight of the outside world calmed her. If she was not destroyed by fire, pneumonia or the nurses' cruelty before deliverance came, she knew that she was on to the scoop of a lifetime. She would expose the myths about Blackwell's Island and bring about the reforms it so badly needed.

A cold thought stopped her in her tracks. Once a man or woman got into an asylum, they rarely came out again. She had never heard of anyone who had come out. She remembered asking Cockerill how and when she would be released, and he had said he didn't know. Foreboding crept through her and she shivered. What if the *World* failed to get her out?

Thirteen

NELLIE FELL ASLEEP JUST as morning was beginning to dawn and, within only a few moments, she heard the scrape of a key in the lock and the cell door being opened.

Nurse Kelly stood on the threshold; a short, gray-haired woman, with placid blue eyes and a voice made husky from tobacco. 'Time to get up,' she announced, coming in and handing Nellie her clothes. She wrinkled her nose as the smell hit her. 'What a wretched room this is,' she sighed. 'I've always hated putting our ladies here. Ah, well. You're to see the doctor when you're dressed, and after that, you can join the others for breakfast.'

'Thank you, Nurse,' said Nellie meekly. From here on, she resolved to behave as sanely as possible. She would not give them reason to detain her for a single minute longer than it took to get her story. Half an hour later, she was sitting opposite Dr Ingram. Her eyes were prickly from lack of sleep and her chest felt tight.

'Well,' he said. 'Well, Nellie. You're looking a bit peaky today. Are you ill? It doesn't look like you got the warm clothes I requested. I'll follow up with that.'

The kindness in his voice made her want to cry. She dug her fingernails into her palm to stop tears falling and wondered whether to tell him about last night's ordeal.

But it would only bring more punishment from Nurse O'Grady.

'Oh, I'm all right,' she said, in a voice that sounded croaky from disuse. She cleared her throat. 'Last night I started worrying about would happen if there was a fire, and it spoiled my sleep. That is all that's wrong with me.'

'Tell me what you were thinking.'

She began to describe her concerns.

'The nurses are expected to open the doors,' he said.

'Yes, but you know perfectly well they wouldn't wait to do that. The patients would all burn to death.'

He was unable to contradict her.

'Why don't you have the system changed?' Nellie asked.

'What can I do?' he replied, shrugging. 'I offer suggestions until my brain is tired, but what good does it do?' There was another moment of silence. 'You have strong empathy... what would you do?' he asked.

'Well, in the first place, I should insist on them having central locks put in,' she said decisively. 'I have seen in some places that by turning a crank at the end of the hall, you can lock or unlock every door on the one side. Then there would be some chance of escape. At the moment, with every door being locked separately, there is none.'

A cloud of worry passed over his face. 'Nellie Brown, what institution have you been an inmate of before you came here?'

'None,' she answered truthfully. 'I have never been confined in an institution, until this one.'

'Well then – where did you see the locks you have described?'

She had seen them on an assignment to the new Western Penitentiary in Pittsburgh, but she didn't dare tell him. 'I have seen them in a place I was in,' she said vaguely. Blushing, she added quickly, 'I mean, as a visitor.'

'There is only one place I know of where they have those locks and that is at Sing Sing Prison. The inference is conclusive.' He looked at her steadily, his eyebrows raised in reproach.

Nellie's heart sank. He thought her a felon and was disgusted with her. Then she asked herself why she should care. Was it any worse than being thought a lunatic?

'Oh! You've got it all wrong,' she said, hating the way her voice cracked with embarrassment. 'I've never been an inmate of Sing Sing, or even visited it.' She forced a chuckle.

He didn't reply; his expression was still wary. They heard a flurry of wind, and rain started falling in gray sheets, slapping against the window.

Nellie plunged into the breach. 'You want to know about my early life?'

'Yes,' he said, 'Yes, I do,' and at once, he was restored to himself; attentive and sympathetic. An image of Poppa's gaping mouth and empty eyes appeared in her head. Memories of his collapse and of Momma's disastrous remarriage started coming of their own accord...

At first, the strangeness of speaking about what had been locked inside her for so long made her throat ache. But as she warmed up, she experienced relief in telling her side of the story for the first time. Dr Ingram's eyes never left her face, except to jot down notes. He listened to her in a way she hadn't known before; a way that made her feel *seen*.

At last she paused for breath. She could scarcely believe she spoken so much. It was unnerving, and yet it was liberating too. She felt opened up, like one of Momma's chicken pot pies, and not even cut into, but perfectly cooked, so that the crust split by itself and the insides came bubbling out.

'Thank you for trusting me,' Dr Ingram said. 'I can see how traumatic it must have been for you. These things aren't easy to talk about, but you have done very well.'

He gave her a smile so warm that she felt a change in her body – a sweet, liquid sensation, as if her insides were melting. It was a moment of pure intoxication, utterly surprising, and she couldn't think of a reply. Her mouth opened and closed. She felt her face go hot.

He checked his watch. 'I'm afraid we have run out of time. I have other patients waiting to be seen. But I look forward to continuing this conversation with you tomorrow. Good day, Nellie.'

Back in Hall Six, Nellie's thoughts kept returning to Dr Ingram. She recalled the dusting of freckles across the bridge of his nose; the gentle, tingling pressure of his touch. A flicker of feeling tugged at her belly, like electricity. Oh, but it was hopeless! He thought her a madwoman, flotsam on the subhuman tide that washed up routinely on Blackwell's Island. If only she could tell him the truth. But she could not break her cover, there was too much at stake.

Superintendent Dent came in and began his usual cursory enquiries of the patients. Every now and then his mouth squeezed upward into something he must have intended for a smile. Sofia begged him to bring her a newspaper or a book to read, but Dent passed speechlessly on, seeming not to hear a word. Then Tillie got up and addressed him with something of the confidence she'd shown while singing with Nellie at the piano.

'If you know anything at all, you should be able to tell that I am perfectly sane.'

The superintendent's brow lowered. 'If you were sane, you wouldn't be here.'

'Why don't you test me?' Tillie answered, laying a hand on his arm, and it seemed as if she wasn't going to let go till he agreed.

'We know all we want to on that score,' he said, and shook her off without offering her one chance to prove her sanity. The nurses came up and dragged her back to the bench, and when Superintendent Dent had gone, Nurse Grupe said, 'When you learn that the doctors won't notice you, you will quit running up to them.'

Tillie began to sob, hiccupping and shaking. Nellie felt racked with outrage and with pity. She longed to put her arms around Tillie, but she didn't dare stir from her seat.

Supper that night was a bowl of soup, a piece of bread, one cold boiled potato and a chunk of tough, stringy beef with blobs of yellow fat on it. There were no knives or forks – the patients had to pick up the meat and pull at it with their teeth, which made them look like savages. The toothless, or those with poor teeth, could not eat it. Tillie retched at the first bite and had to rush, overcome, from the table. On her return, she received a scolding from Miss Grupe.

'But the meat is rotten. You can't expect us to eat it,' Tillie protested.

Crease lines had formed around Miss Grupe's mouth. 'Well, *really*,' she spat. 'You wouldn't have beef for supper if you were at home. If you ask me, what you're given is too good for charity patients.'

Nellie watched their exchange, feeling weak with hunger. Pains were starting up in her stomach, but she forced herself to chew her way through a slice of bread. As the evening wore on, her stomach ache intensified. It felt like hands wringing her intestines and she feared that the asylum diet had ruined her digestion for good. It was impossible to sleep. She'd been put back in the dormitory and the muttering of the other patients seemed familiar and almost soothing after her solitary confinement. Even the dreams that burst from them in sobs and screams made her feel less alone in her suffering.

How could she be a detached reporter when the asylum was making her ill? She wondered how much longer she could hold out. The newspapermen had to come for her soon, they simply *had* to. Who else could she turn to? Her thoughts went to Dr Ingram; she had a hunch that he might eventually work out she was sane. Perhaps he would come through for her if the *World* failed to?

The night nurses came in at intervals to check on the patients. One of them shone a lantern in Nellie's face and noticed that her eyes were open.

'Holy Mary!' she said to her companion. 'I don't think this one has slept a wink since she arrived.'

'Chemical restraint?' the other nurse suggested. 'We don't want her getting overwrought.'

'Yes. Yes, I think so.'

They left, returning a few minutes later with a dose of medicine in a glass, which they urged Nellie to drink to help her sleep. The stuff smelled acrid, like the drug she'd been given for her childhood insomnia that she now knew was laudanum. Nellie refused to take it. She had noticed the nurses' fondness for stuffing the troublesome patients full of drugs to make their own jobs easier. Certain patients were rendered unconscious and kept that way for hours, or even days at a time.

One of the nurses made a *tsk* noise and they went out. Nellie hoped that that was the end of it and she would be left in peace for the night. But her hopes proved vain, as they soon came back with Dr Kinier, the doctor who had examined Nellie on her arrival.

'What's this I hear about you being stubborn?' he enquired. He spoke very loudly, as if Nellie were deaf. 'You must be a good girl and take your medicine.'

'But I don't want it,' she said. She was determined not to lose her wits, not even for a few hours.

'For Pete's sake, choke it down so the rest of us can get some sleep,' came a weary voice from the corner of the room.

'Silence!' Dr Kinier thundered. There were shadows under his eyes and the skin around them was deeply creased. Briefly, Nellie wondered if his romance with Nurse Grupe was going badly.

'You must sleep,' he said, turning back to her. 'Sleep is nature's healer, especially in mental diseases.'

'But I don't like taking drugs.'

Dr Kinier let out a harsh sigh. 'I have wasted too much time with you already. If you don't drink it right now, I will put it into your arm with a needle.'

Nellie's mind flew back and forth – she was trapped. Then an idea came to her. If he injected her with the drug, she would not be able to get rid of it. But if she swallowed it, there was one hope.

'Oh, all right. I'll take it if you insist,' she sighed and a thin, triumphant smile stretched the doctor's lips. They all watched her drink it down. It was bitter and the taste lingered in her throat.

As soon as Dr Kinier and the nurses had gone, Nellie got out of bed, stuck two fingers down her throat as far as they would go, and vomited the contents of her stomach into the chamber pot. She lay down feeling shaky and spent, hoping she would be able to sleep. At least her stomach ache had eased. But it appeared that the drug had got into her system after all, for a sort of warm fog drifted across her mind, and the shape of her body under the blanket seemed shifting and strange – at one moment grotesquely elongated, the next as tiny as an infant's.

She began to feel thirsty. She knew that there was no point in asking the nurses for a drink. She had seen patients wild for water from the effect of the drugs, and the nurses refusing to give it to them. She had heard one woman beg for a whole night for a single drop and it was denied. Nellie's skin burned and her mouth felt gluey. She imagined a glass of cool water slipping over her parched lips and tongue, yet it brought torment, not relief.

She fell into a strange, trance-like state in which she didn't know if she was asleep or awake. There was a babel of voices in her ears, though she couldn't make out what they were saying. Now and then she recognized the subdued tones of her mother and Kate; at other times, she heard those who meant her harm – Nurse O'Grady, Dr Kinier, Jack Ford. They were all talking about her, and though she could not distinguish the words, she knew that they were denunciations.

A memory began to unspool behind her closed eyelids, of Jack throwing stones at the Native American skeletons until their bones were dust. Jack cleaving through the female skeleton's spine without wincing. Over and over again, she saw the spine snapping, the skull flying off, the ugly merriment in Jack's eyes. She knew that the skeleton could not reassemble, would never reach the afterlife, was damned for ever, and there was nothing she could do about it.

Then a shimmer of hummingbirds flew through the windows, their feathers a vivid blend of blue and green, with flashes of yellow or pink. They brought her an intense, glowing happiness. Her mind cleared and her heart seemed to expand, becoming light and buoyant, throwing off the dreadfulness of the asylum and making her past

170

struggles seem like naught. Hardly daring to breathe, she watched the birds hovering in place just above her bed or settling on the blanket, their eyes like polished beads, their wings glittering and making a faint thrumming sound. But all too soon they faded away, leaving her with a gaping sense of loss.

As though it was the inevitable corollary of such enchantment, she began to fall down, down to a place of darkness, in which she hadn't the strength to move or think. A dank horror seemed to be settling over her – formless and altogether ghastly. And she realized that this shadow had been with her since her father died; invisible, entwined, threatening to rise up and overwhelm her. She *knew* it, in her deepest self, in her bones and blood. It was a despair so deep and black that once she sank into it, she might never find her way out.

Fourteen

IT WAS NELLIE'S FOURTH day in the asylum and she was having another session with Dr Ingram. He smelled of peppermint and soap. It was a comforting smell and, suddenly, she longed to reveal her true self to him. She squashed the desire sternly. After everything she had been through, how could she even think of jeopardizing her story?

'Have you been dreaming recently?' he asked.

'Everyone dreams, or I assume they do.'

'Yes, Nellie, but I am interested in *your* dreams. What did you dream last night?' He was leaning forward, as if expecting some great revelation.

She thought about her drug-induced visions and felt no inclination to share them with him, for they made her ashamed. Besides, she had so little to call her own in the asylum, she needed to keep something back for herself. So she said, 'I don't remember. It's all scrambled in my mind.'

He looked disappointed and she felt compelled to add, 'Well, maybe I dreamt about my stepfather. Yes, I'm almost certain I did. It's too confused to tell you, but I can talk more about our life with him, if you'd like?'

Dr Ingram perked up considerably. 'Yes,' he said, pen at the ready. 'Yes, I would like that very much.'

173

Nellie paused to gather her thoughts before carrying on from where she had left off last time. But talking about her past was more painful today. She seemed to be back inside it, reliving all the feelings. Dr Ingram listened carefully and wrote everything down, and she realized that he was the first man she'd allowed herself to open up to since Poppa. She welcomed the closeness and she repudiated it too, because of her distrust of men.

After she had told him about Jack nailing up the windows and doors of their home, Dr Ingram asked her to take a break so he could catch up with his notes. He said she was doing very well and he wanted to record her account accurately. So she sat quietly and watched his hand moving across the page. It made her realize how much she missed her own writing.

Finally he said, 'I am sorry I interrupted you. Please go on.'

'Actually, I've finished. There's nothing more to say.'

'It's a harrowing story,' he said, laying down his pen. 'Remember how, at our first meeting, I spoke of mental wounds that could drive a person mad? Well, there's no doubt that the trials you've described were traumatic enough to trigger your insanity. I think we might just have got to the root of your illness.' He looked very pleased.

Nellie gave an awkward wiggle. There was no denying that Momma's second marriage had made her feel broken and isolated; an outcast with an unshareable view of the world, driven to behave in extreme ways. Was that a form of madness? Probably. Although if sanity was accepting the lot of most other women, she didn't think she wanted it. She could hardly believe she had divulged so much to him, but she was not sorry, not at all. It made her feel lighter.

'It may have been what drove me mad,' she said. 'But one thing I know for sure is that it made me feel even more responsible for my mother. She led a frightful life. See, our sex is trained to look at marriage as the highest earthly joy. But really, it's only drudgery, disappointment and suffering.'

'That's rather a harsh view of marriage, though understandable in the circumstances,' said Dr Ingram, with a faint smile.

'On the other hand, it taught me some useful lessons.'

'Such as?'

'Well, I learned that a woman has got to take care of herself,' she said, looking him full in the eyes, 'and that does not include marrying any man.'

Nellie returned to Hall Six to find that Nurse O'Grady had a half-day off. Nurse Kelly was in charge. She clapped her hands together and cried, 'All right, all right, it's time for fresh air! You're getting a special treat today for being good girls – a ride on the Island merry-go-round!'

The announcement was met with cries of pleasure. The women hurried to put on their outdoor garments and they scrambled into a two-abreast line. They walked along the river road, scuffling through drifts of fallen leaves, two nurses at the head of the column and two at the rear. It was the first time Nellie had left the asylum grounds. The road was quiet and, once, a red fox crossed in front of them. The few people they passed – a laborer, a couple of guards from the penitentiary – wouldn't look at them or greet them because they were pariahs. It was as if there was a wall separating them from the rest of the world.

The merry-go-round was at the center of a small, bleak park: gravel paths and windswept lawns cordoned off by low railings. The hand-carved horses were majestic, but their gold, white and blue paint was blistered and peeling. The women chose their mounts and clambered astride. There was a skirmish when two of them wanted to ride the same horse and started shoving each other in a determined sort of frenzy, but it was soon settled by Nurse Grupe with sharp cuffs across the backs of their heads. The organ began to crank out a march and the carousel began to move.

The women must have made a strange sight in their calico dresses, shawls and hats, their hair matted, their eyes wild or unfocused, skirts swelling into the shapes of bells. Most were grabbing onto the brass rings for dear life. One or two thought that they were riding real animals and murmured words of encouragement, or gave reassuring pats to their necks.

There was something dreamy about going round and round; it was hypnotic and dreamy. Out of sight, someone was burning dead leaves; the smell of the bonfire was in Nellie's nostrils. The outside world seemed indescribably beautiful. She closed her eyes, relishing the music, the crisp air on her face, the motion that seemed to be taking her worries and bearing them away. For a few precious minutes she felt free, but all too soon the ride ended, and the women were ordered to dismount and line up for the walk back to the asylum.

On reaching Hall Six, the nurses took one of the inmates, Rachael, to do her hair and change her dress, because she was due a visit from her sister.

'Oh, but I wish they'd change my clothes!' Nellie sighed to Sofia. 'They're so stiff with dirt, it feels like they could walk off my back.' She smelled rancid and feral, like a wild animal. She couldn't believe how fast she had deteriorated in only four days.

'I know what you mean,' agreed Sofia, 'but our dresses aren't changed oftener than once a month, nuh-uh.' She shook her head. 'If a patient has a visitor, the nurses will quickly freshen her up, as you just saw. It keeps up the charade of good management. The ones who can't take care of themselves, like Tammy over there, get into disgusting conditions.' She nodded toward an extremely overweight blonde woman who sat with her eyes fixed on her hands, plaiting and unplaiting her fingers together. Her skirt was patterned with all kinds of stains, crusted, greasy or damp. 'The nurses never look after her, but order us to do it,' Sofia added.

The visitor arrived, bringing in her arms a baby boy who looked at everything with solemn brown eyes, his thumb in his mouth, his tiny fingers clutching the stuff of his mother's dress. The mother cupped Rachael's cheek with her hand and gazed at her so tenderly that Nellie's breath caught in her throat. They were similar in appearance, with auburn hair and the same gap-toothed smiles. They seated themselves in a quiet corner of the hall and started talking intently.

'Looking at their faces, you can't tell which one is sane and which is mad,' Nellie observed to Sofia.

'Right.' Sofia fixed her with thoughtful eyes. 'Rachael's illness isn't at all obvious.'

'What's wrong with her?'

'Well, when she looks at objects, she sees other things inside them.'

'What, you mean like hallucinations?'

'No, not exactly,' Sofia said, smoothing down hair that was escaping from its plait. 'She knows she is looking at a floor or a bedspread. But all patterns have something else lurking behind them, so when she looks at, say, the tiles on her kitchen floor, they come to life. She might see

177

a forest, a swarm of butterflies or a pair of eyes staring right at her! At home, she'd sit and follow patterns for hours, getting so confused and tortured that it drove her to a breakdown.'

They fell silent. Nellie was thinking about her own interest in these mental diseases. She needed the information for her article, but her curiosity seemed to go over and beyond research. There seemed something morbid in it. Perhaps what she really wanted to know was: *What's the difference between that woman and me?... Could that happen to me?... Am I already on my way to it?* After all, what was sanity, except being able to contain the madness inside yourself?

Another inmate tapped gently on the visitor's arm and asked permission to hold the baby. She had been separated from her five young children, she explained, and she missed them so much it hurt.

'I'll be glad if you do,' the mother smiled. 'It will give me a chance to talk to my sister without interruptions.'

The babe was handed over, and the patient walked him up and down the hall, rocking him and crooning nursery rhymes and nonsense, her worn face shining with tenderness. His big dark eyes were fixed on hers, perfectly calm and contented. When it was time for the visitor to leave, the patient's grief was uncontrollable. Her body convulsed with sobs and tears streaked down her cheeks as she begged to keep the infant, for she had begun to imagine that he was hers. 'He's my baby,' she kept crying, in a wild, shaking voice. 'He's my own firstborn.'

'Hush, my dear. Hush,' soothed Nurse Kelly, patting her on the back. 'He's not yours. Your baby is safe at home,' but the woman's cries only escalated.

Nurse Grupe hurried over. 'You're too soft with them, Shannon. It doesn't work,' she said with a great deal of energy. 'Here, I'll deal with this.' And turning to the inmate, she slapped her face several times, the retorts cracking out like gunshots. 'That's quite enough of that,' she scolded.

The inmate subsided at once, though tears continued to roll silently down her cheeks. Looking into her eyes, Nellie saw that there was a grief only beheld in lunatic asylums, a grief so deep and black that its victim was submerged beyond reach, far more wretched than a criminal. It was horrifying to witness such suffering and not be able to help.

The incident disturbed the patients more than Nellie had ever seen them disturbed. They surged this way and that, and a great wailing and chattering broke out, an uprush of sound that seemed to permeate the whole building.

'So, you think your approach works better?' Nellie heard Nurse Kelly say to Nurse Grupe, her eyebrows raised reprovingly.

Nurse Grupe pressed her lips together so tight they almost disappeared. Then she blew hard on her whistle. 'Order! Order this minute!' she yelled 'You'll all go without supper if you don't quit this racket AT ONCE!'

Other nurses hurried in and they slapped and pushed the patients back to the benches, threatening them with the Lodge if they moved or spoke. And this was how they passed the time, in rustling and unhappy silence, until the supper bell rang.

Though the inmates of Hall Six were not supposed to talk or move about, they found opportunities to whisper to one another, and their favorite topic of conversation was food. They would gather in small groups and torture themselves by fantasizing about the first thing they would eat when they got out of the asylum, picturing and tasting each mouthful. Tender steak marbled with fat and oozing juices, hot, comforting piroshkis, luscious oranges and apples, pancakes dripping with syrup. If Nellie had not known that they were famishing, the conversation would have been funny. As it was, it made her desperately sad.

In the evenings, one of the cooks would come to the hall with raisins, grapes, apples and crackers for the staff, which they would snack on while gossiping about fashion, about the physicians and the other nurses. It was agony for the starving patients, forced to sit with nothing to do but watch them eat.

On the fourth evening, Nellie saw Sofia walk past the dish of fruit and slide a small bunch of grapes into her pocket with deft, practiced movements. Realizing the source of her contraband, Nellie smiled to herself. After lights out Sofia came to Nellie, wanting to talk, and once again they sat on the floor beside Nellie's bed, wrapped in their blankets. Sofia brought out the stolen grapes and gave three of them to Nellie, who straightaway bit into one. The juice burst out, flooding her mouth with sweetness. After four days of the asylum's inedible food, the sensation was overwhelming. 'Thank you. You're keeping me going in more ways than you know,' she said.

'I'm happy to hear it,' said Sofia warmly. A shadow passed over her face. 'But honestly, I still feel awful about Clara, the mother who thought the baby was hers. I can't imagine how it must feel being wrenched away from your children. Did you see her eyes?'

'Yes, I did. Nurse Grupe is inhumane and the whole thing was agonizing. I mean, why is Clara even here? She doesn't seem mad at all.'

'Women are kept here for plenty of other reasons than madness,' said Sofia darkly, and Nellie realized that this was a golden opportunity for research. 'Tell me more,' she said.

Sofia drew her fingers through her hair. 'Well, sometimes they send a woman here when she's suffering from hysteria, or from uterine neuralgia,' she began. 'Some come because of religious mania or financial problems, or because of overwork. Others come because they can't get over a broken love affair, or the death of a loved one, or because they've seen something dreadful that they can't heal from.' She popped another grape into her mouth. 'Some women are here because they got married without their parents' consent, or because they refused to marry at all. Some are wives whose husbands have tired of them. And then there are those, like me, who dare to fall in love outside marriage.'

It was too dark to see Sofia's expression, but Nellie heard her swallow. She put an arm around her and waited for her to say more. Sofia leaned her head on Nellie's shoulder, but no words came. Nellie reflected how fortunate she was to have Dr Ingram to talk to – Sofia was assigned to Dr Kinier.

At last Nellie said, 'So, the women you've been telling me about are branded mad simply for rebelling against our system, which keeps women downtrodden?'

'Yes, that's right. Men make up the narratives that put them here.' They heard the clump of heavy boots coming down the hall and Sofia pulled away from her. 'We'd better hurry back to bed.'

They got there moments before the nurses came in. After checks were complete, Nellie curled up under her blanket, shocked by what she'd just learned. No human creature deserved to be treated that way, whether they were mad or not. And she wondered if the women should be in the asylum at all.

Her purpose had changed; it was all about campaigning now. The public had to know the truth and the asylum needed to be shut down.

181

The nurses were fond of teasing patients on rotation.
Lately they had been calling Sofia up to the nurses' station
and saying things like, 'We know you have an eye for a
nice young man. Wouldn't you like to have one in here?'

'Oh, yes, a young man is all right,' Sofia would answer,
refusing to be provoked.

'Well, wouldn't you like us to speak a good word to
some of the doctors for you?'

A wave of laughter rose from the others.

'No, not really,' said Sofia.

'Go on, we know you would. Which one do you fancy?
Dr Kinier? Dr Ingram? Why don't you pick one and make
love to him when he next visits?'

Sofia hesitated, cornered. Her tormentors watched.
Which way would she jump? At last she closed her eyes
and turned away; it looked like she was willing herself
elsewhere. Was she was musing about her lover and
wondering if he still thought of her, or if he had given
up and moved on? The nurses kept taunting her, but she
had shut herself down, become a shell of a person, and
they soon lost interest in the game. Nellie edged closer to
Sofia and gave her cold hand a squeeze. Sofia returned it
weakly.

Later, Nellie overheard Nurse Grupe say to Nurse
O'Grady, 'God, I'm tired.' She bit into a succulent-
looking red apple and the juice ran down her chin.

'Oh, me too,' Nurse O'Grady answered. 'I didn't sleep
well last night. I had awful nightmares.'

'About this place? I'm not surprised.'

Nurse O'Grady grimaced. 'No, actually, I dreamt about
my mother. When I was young, she would claim that she
could read my mind and fathom any lies. It put the fear

of God into me.' She gave a shuddering sigh. 'If Mother decided I was lying – and I'd usually be telling God's truth – she would beat me with a belt till my skin purpled and bled. It wasn't till I was fourteen that I plucked up the courage to test her by telling actual deliberate lies.'

It took Nurse Grupe a moment to work her way through to the core of this. Then she said, 'It sounds tough.'

'Yes. Well. What can you do?' Nurse O'Grady drew in her bottom lip with her front teeth and kept it tucked in, and Nellie had a sudden inkling as to what she might have looked like as a defenceless little girl. But almost immediately, the hardness came back into her face.

'I don't know, but we're all worn out at the moment,' Nurse Grupe said, wiping juice from her lips. 'It seems to me that this lot is getting more troublesome by the day.'

'I'll stand none of their nonsense, and they know it,' Nurse O'Grady tossed back. 'Hit them hard enough, and nine times out of ten they'll not trouble you again.'

'You know, if anyone had told me before I started working here that I would find myself hitting patients, I would have called him mad himself. But now I knock them around as a matter of course.'

'You grow a thick skin,' Nurse O'Grady said, frowning, as though this was something she did not wish to be reminded of.

Fifteen

A S THE DAYS PASSED, Tillie got worse. She was cold all the time and couldn't eat. Day after day she sang to try and maintain her memory, but eventually Nurse O'Grady told her to shut the hell up. After that, Tillie was less and less inclined to speak, despite Nellie's efforts to coax her out of herself. She grew slower and more hesitant in her movements, and she shuffled her feet along the floor when she walked. Her hair was lank. Constant weeping had left her eyes red-rimmed and bleary. She would sit motionless for long periods, not hearing when Nellie spoke to her. It was painful to watch her folding herself up and packing herself away, retreating to some place deep inside.

On the fifth morning, the inmates were sitting on the benches and the hall was so cold that their breath made globules of steam. Tillie's limbs shook and her teeth chattered. Nellie asked the attendants, who were lounging at their table with coats on, for extra clothing for her.

'She has on as much as the rest of you, and she'll get no more,' Nurse Grupe said shortly.

'It's cruel to lock people up and then freeze them,' Nellie retorted, but the nurses ignored her.

Nellie tried to warm Tillie's stiff hands in hers, not knowing how much longer they could stand this. Being half-frozen, day in and day out, was worse torture than being starved. Hunger was a local affliction, but when one was cold, every nerve in the body shrieked its distress. Tillie gave an odd smile that stretched tightly over her teeth. Her whole body stiffened and she reached forward jerkily, as if controlled by a puppeteer. Her back arched and her legs thrashed out, heels slapping the floor. Her eyes rolled back in their sockets and foam started bubbling at her lips.

Fear sparked through Nellie. She caught Tillie in her arms, supporting her as best she could, awkwardly, with one hand under her neck and the other around her waist. 'Easy,' she soothed. 'Hush, my dear. Hush now.'

'Let her fall on the floor. Teach her a lesson,' Nurse O'Grady said roughly.

Nellie shot her a look of incredulous scorn. 'I'll do no such thing! How can you be so heartless?'

Nurse O'Grady glared back. 'I hear another word from you, I'll put you in the Lodge.'

Superintendent Dent came to the door. Asking Sofia to take Tillie, Nellie got up and hurried toward him. 'Please, please help us,' she begged. 'We're suffering cruelly from the cold and it's made Tillie Maynard really ill.' Then without quite knowing how it happened, she found herself pouring out her misery.

'The food you give us is inedible and we're all sick with hunger. The nurses are beasts, unfit to care for vulnerable people.' She spoke rapidly and incoherently, the words tumbling over themselves. 'For the love of God, can't you help us?' She was almost in tears.

The other inmates were staring at Nellie in astonishment. Sofia gave her a discreet thumbs up. Nurse O'Grady glared fiercely and snapped, 'Be quiet!' She turned to Dent. 'She's raving again. She has no idea what she's saying.'

'Oh, but I do. I *do!*' cried Nellie. 'You've got to believe me, Superintendent.'

Dent's face was full of dramatic scepticism, eyebrows raised, lips compressed. He reached for Nellie's wrist to take her pulse.

'No, no, it's not me who needs medical help. You must go to Tillie!'

Tillie was still convulsing in Sofia's arms. Dent walked over and caught her roughly between the eyebrows, pinching until her eyes bulged out and her face turned crimson from the rush of blood to the head. A vein swelled dangerously in her temple and her hands flailed in the air. The inmates held their breath. Finally, she let out a whimper and subsided, limp as an emptied bladder.

'There now, that should settle you down,' Dent said to her, and he walked straight out of the hall, without making his usual rounds.

For the rest of the day, Tillie suffered from terrible headaches and she became so cowed that whenever an attendant passed, she would flinch away. Nellie was in a blaze of outrage and pity, but there was nothing she could do except sit as close as possible to Tillie, trying to bestow comfort through her proximity.

One thing was certain – if Tillie was not crazy, she soon would be. As the interminable sitting crawled by, Nellie inwardly cursed the doctors, the nurses and all public institutions – corrupted worlds in which every value was wrong. She was beginning to feel unwell herself. Waves of dizziness and nausea moved through her, and she thought she might faint. In her mind, she flipped through her store of scenes from the past, searching for one with which to console herself. But all she came up with were bad memories, and so she decided to think about her story instead. She reassured herself that when it finally broke, it would be a sensation

187

like no other. It would make all her suffering worthwhile. Her mind went back and forth, musing about the material she'd collected, wondering what was still missing from her account. For one thing, she didn't know enough about the medical side of madness – about the causes of it and the latest treatments. She wondered how she could find out and the answer came at once. She would interview Dr Ingram.

'Guess what? I was thinking that our conversations are a bit one-sided,' Nellie told him at their next session. She was gazing out at the treetops, but her mind was hard at work.

'What do you mean?' The doctor sounded baffled.

She turned from the window and said brightly, 'Well, you know all about my life. I've never talked to anyone as freely as I talk to you. So, how about giving me a turn to ask *you* some questions?'

Dr Ingram considered this. 'It's not my usual therapeutic practice, not at all,' he said. Then he grinned. 'Look, I suppose it's fair. Because you're doing so well, I am going to say yes. Though if a question is inappropriate, I reserve the right not to answer.'

'Of course,' she agreed, with a stab of gratitude that she could say anything to him, anything at all, and he wouldn't be thrown or put off.

'You have almost returned to full reason,' he said, giving her a look so penetrating that her gut twisted in anxiety in case he had found her out. Relief followed: if Dr Ingram thought she was sound in mind, then she must be. His expression softened; he threw down his pen and sat back in his chair. 'All right then, Nellie. Ask away.'

She took a deep breath. 'Well, I've been wondering what made you choose to work in this grim place. I mean, surely all of the medical establishments would have jumped at hiring you?'

She thought there was a slight flush rising on his cheeks. 'Oh, I came here for the same reason that most of the young physicians come. To learn,' he said. 'Of course, the asylum needs more experienced men. The young ones make dreadful mistakes, and when they have got all the training they need, they move on to better-paid jobs, and another novice is appointed. There have been eighteen different physicians in the asylum in the last two years.'

Eighteen rounds of dreadful mistakes, thought Nellie.

'Another problem is that the asylum is managed by the same people who run the penitentiary and the work-house – the Commissioners of Charities and Correction,' he went on, leaning toward her and resting his elbows on the desk. 'Trying to administer punishment and charity at the same time is an impossible juggling act.' He spoke readily, like someone who had stored up his thoughts for a long time and was relieved to get them out. 'It also means that in people's minds, the criminal, the poor and the insane are all clumped together.'

She rolled her eyes. 'In other words, the mentally ill are dangerous and poor people are only thieves waiting for the chance to commit a crime.'

He looked at her in surprise. 'Exactly, Nellie. How quick you are. But the commissioners' worst decision was to bring convicts into the asylum, to work as nurses and attendants. So you see, the roughest types are sent here to care for the most vulnerable patients.'

Nellie's mind was whizzing – this explained so much about the nurses.

'One night, I heard a patient screaming,' he continued. 'I followed the noise and found her trapped in a room with a worker from the penitentiary, who'd just pinned her down and shaved her hair right off.'

Nellie clapped her hand over her mouth. 'Oh, my Lord!'

'I know. I know. It was lucky I caught her red-handed. She was planning to sell the locks to a wig-maker.' He shook his head sadly. 'She was dismissed on the spot, but I would rather the inmates weren't cared for by prostitutes and thieves.'

'If you were in charge, what would else you do differently?' Nellie asked.

'Well, I would like to see a much kinder and more merciful approach to mental illness. For a start, I would have the term "asylum" replaced by "hospital". And I would ban restraining devices, like straitjackets. They are never necessary and they cause great harm.'

Nellie nodded. 'The asylum seems to me to be more a place of punishment than a place of healing and refuge,' she said softly.

'Yes, and it's all wrong. Insanity is a disease – a complex and many-layered disease that we still don't understand. But I do know this much – that it involves the greatest suffering physicians ever see. And if we treat patients with respect, listen to them, try and understand, we just might reach them.'

'If only there were more doctors like you,' sighed Nellie. 'Modern. Progressive.'

'Thank you, but I only wish it was in my power to do more for the patients.' He gave one of his marvellous smiles, then glanced at his watch. 'My word, I am quite forgetting myself. Time is getting on and there are patients waiting to be seen. We must say goodbye, Nellie.'

After the consultation, Nellie floated back to Hall Six, the horrors of the asylum scarcely touching her. She felt redeemed. *Pull yourself together*, she told herself. *Just because you have never felt this way before. Because you've reached the full age of twenty-three without experiencing this... this lunacy.* For lunacy was plainly what it was; it was only by exerting strict willpower that she could stop herself from skipping down the hall.

The thought kept her occupied all through breakfast, morning chores and the sitting, which was even longer than usual because it was raining again and the patients missed out on their walk. Stiff and sore from not being allowed to move, Nellie was glad to have something to keep her mind busy with. For the first time, she had an inkling of what her mother might have felt, falling in love with Jack Ford. She pulled herself back. There was no way Dr Ingram would reciprocate her feelings, because she was a patient. And if he even felt a particle of the attraction she felt for him, it was impossible, because she would have to confess that they'd got to know each other under false pretences.

Nellie had thought of getting herself committed to the Lodge, but when she saw how brutally the patients were treated on the quiet wards, she decided not to risk her health. And she did not get violent. But she needed to know what happened there for her article.

A woman called Mrs Cotter was brought to Hall Six from the Lodge. Tall and rangy, she had ashen skin and wide-set eyes with yellowish rings beneath them. She didn't seem in the least bit savage or dangerous, so the first chance Nellie got, she asked her what the Lodge was like. Mrs Cotter's jaw tightened and her eyes scanned the distance unseeingly. She seemed to be reliving all the things she had seen there.

'Listen, I was sent to the Lodge for breaking a window in a fit of despair,' she said. 'It's the worst place on the Island. It is dreadfully dirty and the stench there is awful. In summer, flies swarm the place. I often saw patients seize their plates and tumblers, without the slightest provocation, and hurl them in a frenzy so they flew around our faces like huge hailstones. At night, the women sleep on the floor, on straw mattresses, chained or strapped by their wrists to hooks on the ground. All through the night, they groan and rage and strain against their bonds. Sometimes, they wet and shit themselves, and the nurses leave them lying in their filth. The sickest ones smear their heads and faces with it, and even the walls and floors. But they're still human beings and they need help.'

She broke off, sighing. 'But, really – the memory of how I was treated is enough to make me mad. The nurses are big and muscular, and the beatings they gave me were dreadful. For crying, they hit me and jumped on me, injuring me internally so that I will never get over it. Then they tied my hands and feet and threw a sheet under my head, twisting it round my throat to stop me screaming. All trussed up, I was dunked in a bathtub of freezing water. They held me under for such a long time, I thought my last moment had come and lost consciousness.'

Nellie reached for her hand, which looked papery and birdlike, and squeezed it gently.

'At other times, they grabbed me by the ears and beat my head on the floor and against the wall,' Mrs Cotter went on. 'They also tore a hank of my hair out by the roots so it will never grow in again.' She showed Nellie the dent in the back of her head and the pockmarked bald spot where her hair was missing. Nellie nodded, but couldn't find words to reply.

Mrs Cotter cleared her throat and gazed at her unhappily. 'The thing is, I wasn't treated worse than anyone else. Some of the women were gagged or had their whole heads bandaged up to keep them quiet. Others were force-fed so brutally that the spoon handles punctured their mouths. Women were chained to the floor for hours and beaten in their chains. I saw filthy, infected sores brought on by chaining. I saw patients being dragged along the floor by their hair so their eyes bulged out, or hit with broom handles and bunches of keys, leaving their faces cut and bruised for weeks.'

Nellie shook her head. 'What about – well, restraints?' she asked. 'Are they used much?'

'Oh, yes, they're used on troublesome patients all the time. Including me.'

Nellie looked at her in surprise. 'You don't seem in the least bit troublesome.'

'I asked so often to be allowed to go home that they got fed up and put a straitjacket on me.'

'Oh, Lord! That's just too bad. I've never seen a straitjacket up close – what was it like?'

Mrs Cotter clasped her hands together tensely. 'It's made of canvas, with sleeves coming below the hand and sewed up like mitts, and it fastens up the back. I was laced into it so tightly, with my arms crossed on my chest, that I was completely helpless. My left hand was positioned so that one of my fingernails cut into the flesh of another finger and soon, sharp pains began shooting all the way up my arm.

'For the first few hours, I suffered the worst agony I have ever known. Before the night had passed, it had become unbearable. Pains racked not only my arms, but half of my body as well. I cried and screamed so loudly that the attendants must have heard, yet they ignored me. When a nurse eventually came, I begged her to loosen the jacket enough to allow me to take a full breath, but she refused. She seemed to enjoy adding to my torment.

'By midnight, I felt I couldn't stand it any longer without losing my sanity. My mind was twisting and turning in dark tunnels, and it made me think that I might be flung out of kilter with the world... I had fallen off the bed and was forced to stay absolutely helpless where I lay. I couldn't even raise my head.

'After twelve endless hours, they took the jacket off me. Before it was put on, I had been energetic enough to resist the nurses, but by the time I came out of it, I was feeble as a newborn babe. As soon I was freed, every joint in my arms and shoulders seized up in agony. I had lost control over my hands – I couldn't have dressed myself, had I been promised my freedom for doing so.' She shut her eyes, unable to go on. Tears slid from between the lids.

Nellie felt a spasm of impotent rage. 'It kills me to hear this!' she exclaimed. 'How can such cruelty be practiced and nothing said about it? Why doesn't anybody tell the doctors?' She thought about Dr Ingram and how horrified he would be if he knew. He would stamp out the abuses at once.

Mrs Cotter wiped her eyes with the underside of her thumbs. 'The nurses always keep a quiet patient posted at the door to let them know when the doctors are coming. So the doctors never see what goes on. And the nurses hold patients under water and threaten to leave them there to die unless they promise not to tell. Of course we all promise because we know the doctors won't help us and we'll do anything to escape the punishment.'

'I am sorry,' Nellie said. 'Oh, God, I'm so sorry.'

'Yes, well – I haven't told you the worst thing that happened. I can't forget it.' Mrs Cotter swallowed hard. 'One day, a pretty young girl was brought in. She had been sick and she fought about being put in that dirty place. The same evening the nurses beat her, and then they held her naked in a cold bath and threw her on her bed. By that time, she was unconscious. A bubble of blood kept appearing and disappearing in her nose and after a while it stopped. The girl was dead. The doctors said she died of convulsions, and that was all that was done about it.' A sob escaped her lips.

Nellie couldn't answer, for her throat felt thick and tight. This assignment had gone way beyond finding a lurid sensation with which to entice a newspaper. Things had to change and she hoped her article would be the catalyst.

194

Sixteen

NELLIE HAD GATHERED ENOUGH material to write her article. As a final piece of research, she decided to try and secure her release herself, to find out how easy or hard it was. Dr Ingram thought she was sane and she felt confident that he would get her out, if all else failed. She was relieved to have survived the asylum intact, despite one or two close shaves and, soon, she would be free to tell her story. The only things she would regret leaving were her friends and her talking therapy with him. She was feeling more and more connected to him, to the point where she didn't know how she would get by without their conversations.

'You have no right to keep sane people here,' she complained to the nurses. 'I am sane and have always been sane.'

'Is that so?' Nurse O'Grady drawled.

'Yes, and I would like a thorough examination to be freed.'

'I'll be sure to note that down.' The nurse smirked at her.

Nellie kept trying. 'Several of the women here are also sane, but the doctors merely say good morning and refuse to listen to them. Why can't they be properly tested?'

Nurse O'Grady stopped, pretended to consider this.

'They are insane and suffering from delusions,' she said at last. 'Plain and simple.'

The inmates were unusually calm and quiet that afternoon. A fly buzzed against the window; the nurses talked among themselves. The sky was full of lively clouds, the sun breaking through intermittently. An oblong patch of sunlight appeared on the wall with a pattern of bars from the reflected window, dark against the luminous yellow. The patients' eyes were caught by it, held. It was as good as a magic lantern show. The patch began to quiver, as if a breeze were flowing through the hall, and Nellie longed to be striding through Owens' Wood, with sunlight sifting through the leaves and the wind in her hair.

Superintendent Dent and Dr Ingram came in, deep in conversation. Nellie heard Dent say, 'Our budget is tight. There's nothing to spare.'

'Not even to dress the patients properly?'

'Not even for that,' said Dent brusquely, and Dr Ingram tightened his lips, white with anger. They began their routine inspection of the patients. On reaching Nellie, they felt her pulse and asked how she was feeling.

'I feel fine. Just fine,' she assured them. 'Why don't you do more tests on me and tell me if I am sane or insane? Try my heart, my eyes. Watch me stretch out my arm and put my finger on my nose. Ask me any question you like and see how rationally I answer; then decide if I am sane.'

Dent clicked his tongue. 'She is quite raving.'

'But her pulse and eyes are not those of an insane girl,' Dr Ingram said doubtfully.

'In cases like this, such tests fail,' the superintendent told him briskly. 'I have seen it time and again. Nellie Brown is positively demented – I consider her a hopeless case.'

They moved on.

'Well, I call that pretty discouraging,' Tillie whispered, apparently returned from whatever far-off realm she had been inhabiting, though who knew for how long? 'I mean, there's no way out of here. Once one doctor has called you mad, the others follow suit.' A sigh – caught and held. 'And once you're declared insane, all your protests to the contrary, anything you say or do, are called part of that insanity. Crazy people can talk till they're blue in the face. No one listens.'

Nellie was filled with anguish for her friend, shut up with no hope of release, trying to live with dignity under the most degrading circumstances, her reason baffled and threatened at every turn. How could anyone resign herself to this existence and live it to the end? At least it wouldn't be like this for Nellie, as Dr Ingram knew she was sane. If only she could take Tillie with her when she left the Island! Perhaps there was a way of securing Tillie's release, and Sofia's too? She vowed to find it.

As the doctors were about to leave, Dr Ingram's eyes found Nellie's. He looked at her and she looked back, all modesty forgotten. Their mingled gaze felt potent as a drug.

Dr Ingram dropped his eyes first. He gave his head a little shake. 'Nellie Brown's face is the brightest I have ever seen for a lunatic,' he said to Dent, as they carried on their way.

Glancing across the room, Nellie saw Nurse O'Grady staring at her with eyes as sharp as needles, and realized she had intercepted their look. Deep dread filled her as she wondered what the nurse guessed.

'Nellie Brown, you're wanted!' Nurse O'Grady yelled later that day. 'You have a visitor.'

'Oh?' said Nellie, getting stiffly to her feet. 'Who is it?'

'A gentleman looking for a missing loved one. We think it might be you.'

Nellie followed her to the sitting room, feeling apprehensive, as she knew it was too soon for the newspaper to spring her from the asylum. Nurse O'Grady flung open the door and standing by the fireplace was Al McCain, the *Dispatch*'s correspondent in New York; a short, stocky young man with close-cropped hair and eyes that were eager yet wary. They had known one another since she'd started working at the paper.

At the sight of her, his face paled. Nellie's gut clenched in anxiety. She could see her reflection in the mirror above his head (mirrors were forbidden on the wards and it was her first glimpse of herself since being committed). Her hair was matted to her skull and her face was white. Her eyes – raw-edged and swollen from lack of sleep – were popping in surprise. Her cheeks looked hollow and sunken, her neck scrawny. The stained calico dress hung off her like a sack. No wonder Al was shocked.

For a long moment they looked at each other. Nellie's mind was racing. She guessed that he must really be following up on a story. Maybe it was the story the papers had put out about her: the unknown young girl with memory loss and voices in her head, who had been committed to a mental institution. If he betrayed her identity, the abuses at Blackwell's Island would never be exposed.

On the other hand, he could get her released right away. Surely she had seen enough and suffered enough? But there was a voice in her that said she must experience more in order to write the most powerful story possible. She could not ignore that voice. Besides, how could she leave before she'd had the chance to tell Dr Ingram who she really was? She decided that it was safe to stay, because either he or the *World* would get her out.

She shook her head at Al. She would insist that she had never seen him before. With Nurse O'Grady within touching distance, she mouthed, 'Don't give me away.'

Then, turning to the nurse, she said, 'I don't know this man.'

'Do you know her?' Nurse O'Grady asked Al.

'Um, no. This isn't the young lady I came looking for.' His voice was strained.

The nurse was looking suspiciously from one to the other, evidently sensing that something was off. 'If you don't know her, you can't stay here,' she said, and led him to the door.

Suddenly, Nellie was struck with the fear that he would think she had been sent to the asylum by mistake, and would tell her friends and try to get her released. Her heart beat in little palpitating jumps as she waited for Nurse O'Grady to unlock the door, knowing that the time it took would give her the chance to speak. She called, 'One moment, sir.'

He came back to where she was standing and she asked loudly, 'Tell me something, is the sun out today?' Whispering, 'It's all right. I'm after an item. Keep still.'

'No, it's quite overcast,' said Al, with a peculiar emphasis that she knew meant he would keep her secret.

'Thank you,' she said, with feeling.

'What happened?' he whispered. 'What have they done to you? You look terrible.'

'Nothing. They haven't done anything.'

'It's a ghastly place.'

'It's really not that bad,' she lied, conscious of Nurse O'Grady's eyes on her. 'They'll get me out soon.'

When he had gone, Nellie started shaking, realizing how nearly her cover had been blown. She was taken back to the hall, and sat down beside Tillie, who shrank away with a look of sorrowful anger and reproach.

'What's the matter?' asked Nellie, surprised.

'Listen, I know what you're up to. I'm not so blind and foolish as you think.' Tillie gave a twittering, mirthless laugh.

'What? What are you talking about?'

'I think you know very well. You're trying to pass yourself off as me.' Tillie began to sing in a thin, reedy voice. 'When I get sorrow, I'll sit down and cry, and think of my darling, my darling so nigh.'

Dread was creeping through Nellie. 'I don't follow you.'

Tillie bristled. 'Huh. Course you do,' she snapped. 'That man, the one you just saw, is *my* friend. He is looking for me because he wants to take me home. But you're trying to deceive him.'

'Tillie...' Nellie was lost for words. 'Oh, Tillie. Don't be this way.'

'Don't you try to deny it! I know it's true, I *do* know. You want him for yourself.'

'Why ever would I do such a thing? And even if I did, the nurses wouldn't allow it.'

'You're a bitch and a liar,' said Tillie with a change of tone, an edge of viciousness. And Nellie, worried and upset, realized that Tillie had become paranoid and delusional, and trying to reason with her was useless.

The days in the asylum seemed never-ending and the patients welcomed any event that might provide them with some diversion. They watched anxiously for the hour the boat was due, waiting to see if there were new arrivals. Whenever a newcomer was admitted and was ushered into the hall, the patients would exchange expressions of sympathy with each other, and they were keen to show the fresh inmates small marks of attention. Hall Six was the receiving hall, so they saw everyone who entered.

On the seventh afternoon, a girl called Urena Little-Page was brought in. She had a whispery, childish voice, lank blonde hair and a dazzling smile that didn't reach her eyes. Miss Gressley sat beside her, patting her hair and telling her how pretty she was, while Urena flashed her incongruous smile, as if she were a contestant in a beauty pageant.

Urena was docile enough, but the nurses soon found out that she had a tender spot that was the same as with many sensible women – her age. She claimed to be eighteen and would get extremely worked up if contradicted. The nurses teased her mercilessly.

'Urena. Oh, Urena,' sang Nurse O'Grady. 'The doctors say that you are past thirty instead of eighteen.'

'You don't look a day over thirty-five,' added Nurse Grupe, and dug Urena with her elbow. 'No offence meant.'

The other nurses laughed.

'Say, Urena, do give us your beauty secrets. We want to be as well preserved as you are when we reach your age.'

They kept this up until the simple creature began to weep and beat the air with her hands. 'I'm not that old! *I'm not that old!*'

At that, the nurses' amusement began to pall, and they scolded her and told her to be quiet. Urena's sobs grew louder. 'I want to go home! Please send me home! I am so unhappy here. You all treat me badly.'

'Stop your noise! Stop it at once!' Nurse O'Grady shouted, but Urena's crying had risen to a high-pitched wail.

Nurse O'Grady hurried over and slapped Urena hard across the face. This only made the poor girl sob harder, so the nurse wrapped her meaty hands around her neck and began to choke her. Urena's face purpled, her eyes bulged out, and a ghastly rattling sound came from her lips. Then Nurse Grupe and Nurse O'Grady hooked her under the arms and dragged her, kicking and struggling, out to the closet. Before they left, they ordered Sofia to station herself by the door and warn them if a doctor came.

'Quick!' Nellie hissed, when the nurses had gone. 'We must fetch a doctor – tell him what's happening.'

Sofia shook her head. 'It's no use complaining, as the doctors won't help us. They always say it's nothing but our diseased imaginations. And besides, we'll only get a beating for our trouble.'

Distraught, Nellie listened to Urena's panicked screams from the closet turn into smothered ones. When she was brought back to the sitting room, she smelled of sweat and piss, and she was cringing away from the nurses, her eyes dilated with fear. One of her cheeks was a shiny, swollen lump and the crescent-shaped marks of the nurses' thumbnails were clearly visible on her throat.

This punishment seemed to awaken the nurses' desire to administer more. Their eyes roved from patient to patient, seeking out another victim. Tension hung in the air, like the zoo smell of the hall.

Those women who had sufficient wit sat unnaturally still, their shoulders hunched and their eyes fixed downward, trying to disappear into themselves. But Miss Gressley slipped into one of her talking fits, apparently brought on by nerves. Her words came out in splutters and it was hard to decipher them, but she seemed to be railing against the lawyers who had taken her property.

'Shut up!' growled Nurse O'Grady. 'Shut up or I'll shut you up for good.'

Miss Gressley continued to babble, looking helpless and petrified, eyes rolling. Nellie saw that she could no more stop chattering than she could grow a straight spine.

Nurse O'Grady's face darkened. 'I told you to stop! Get away – to the far end of the hall with you. Go on now, *GO!*'

Miss Gressley stood up and did her best to comply, breaking into a trot to keep ahead of Nurse O'Grady, who was closing in on her. As they passed Nellie, the nurse punched Miss Gressley behind the ear. Miss Gressley went down like a bowling pin, her head barely missing the bench.

'Did you see that?' Nurse O'Grady asked Nellie.

'Yes, and I won't forget it.'

'Be sure to report it to Dr Ingram now, won't you?' Nurse O'Grady sneered.

At that moment, a chilling shriek splintered the air. Miss Gressley had scrambled to her feet and was rushing at the nurse with astonishing force, hissing and letting out a flood of insults, trying to pull her down. The bigger woman staggered under the onslaught, but regained her balance and shook Miss Gressley off. They began to fight, panting and swearing, knocking over a table, a hamper of laundry. Miss Gressley seemed possessed of preternatural strength – the tendons of her arms stood out like cords.

Attendants came running, shouting and blowing whistles. They tried to pull them apart, but Miss Gressley kicked out at anyone who came near. Sometimes she gained a slight advantage, but she was no match for the young, burly nurse. Finally, Nurse O'Grady caught hold of Miss Gressley's arms and twisted them until the old lady's face turned purple and a vein bulged in her forehead. Nellie feared that her arms would pop right out of their sockets before she gave in. Suddenly, she went limp and fell to the floor.

Nurse O'Grady kicked her where she lay. 'How dare you attack me?' she screamed, her head trembling with rage. 'I'll have you in the Lodge as soon as I've got my breath. None of your wicked defiance to me!'

She tried to grind the heel of her boot into Miss Gressley's face, but Miss Gressley flinched away. Two nurses grabbed her by the hair and dragged her out of the room. She was taken to the closet and the other inmates heard the thuds of the blows landing, and they heard Miss Gressley begging for mercy until there was no breath left in her to cry out.

Afterward, Miss Gressley dragged herself around the ward, whimpering pitifully. She complained of pain in her side and difficulty breathing, and Nellie suspected that some of her ribs had been fractured. Evidently the nurses knew how to inflict injury in such a way as to leave no external evidence on the body of the victim. The horrendous, calculating violence tore Nellie apart. She had been right to stop Al arranging her release. She must stay here to bear witness, to expose this brutality and bring the culprits to justice.

Seventeen

I T WAS THE SEVENTH time Nellie had sat in this room with Dr Ingram and, as they talked, she felt herself filling with a curious, warm aliveness. She was chatting in circles, asking him about the daily workings of the asylum, getting him to open up about his job. Wanting the information for her story, but also wanting to know him better.

'Asylums are not exactly places of cure,' he was saying. 'They're more like holding pens – removing a woman from the danger she poses to herself and others, and perhaps calming her.' He cleared his throat. 'But one day, many forms of insanity will be properly treatable, including yours. We're getting a handle on diseases of the body like diphtheria and yellow fever, so why shouldn't we do the same for diseases of the mind and the nerves?'

'That's good news,' she smiled. 'How close are you to a cure?'

His forehead puckered into soft furrows. 'Not as close as I'd like. You see, in order for it to happen, we need to look at mental illnesses as rationally as physical ones. And a lot of the received thinking about mental health needs to go out the window.'

'Oh. Such as?'

He sat with lowered eyes, thinking. 'Well, I don't believe that madness is caused by demonic influence and possession, nor by an excess of passion, whether earthly or holy. It's not hereditary. Being female doesn't predispose you to it, and it certainly isn't brought on by leaving the feminine sphere to pursue an unsuitable occupation or profession.'

'Ah, yes – I quite agree. What's the thinking behind that?' she asked, suppressing a chuckle about how far out of the feminine sphere the new, wild-side genre of stunt reporting had taken her.

'Listen, any deviation from the domestic realm is believed to risk uterine derangement, which in turn is thought to lead to mental breakdown,' he said. 'But it's muddle-headed thinking, without any scientific basis. In my view, it's precisely being warned off exercise and freedom of mind that cause the trouble.'

'Yes, exactly.'

He took a breath, lining up his thoughts. 'Another thing: some of the treatments directed at women's reproductive organs – removal of ovaries, electrical charges applied to the uterus and so on – are just plain sadistic. They should all be abolished.'

Nellie looked out over the treetops, thinking of those women brutally mutilated for no good reason, and shuddered.

'I am sorry,' he said. 'Did I speak too bluntly? I forgot my—'

'No, no, not at all. I was just thinking... if women did to men what was being done to them, men had better look out. Someday, the tables could turn.'

A grin flashed across his face. 'Touché, Nellie.' The grin vanished; he looked troubled. 'You seem so well,' he began, picking up his pen and passing it from hand to hand. 'Your case doesn't fit any of the recognized types of insanity. Are you sure you heard voices?'

206

Nellie's mouth went dry – she was not ready to be found out. He waited for an answer.

'I don't know what you mean,' she lied. 'My head was as full of voices as... as a saloon on Saturday night. But I'm a hundred times better, thanks to your talking cure.'

He was looking at her hard. She forced herself to return his gaze. Finally, he gave a small nod and his lips curved upward. 'I am glad to hear it,' he said. 'In fact, I regard you as one of my most successful cases.'

She smiled back in sheer relief. 'You're a brilliant doctor. Tell me, what made you want to go into medicine?'

At first she thought he wasn't going to answer. Then he said, 'My father died of tuberculosis when I was twelve. It's a cruel disease, quite dreadful to watch. It tortured him. By the end, he had to be restrained with ropes tied around the bed.'

'I am sorry,' she said. 'I'm very sorry.'

'Thank you.' He frowned, then tried to smile. 'Seeing him suffer like that made me want to help the sick. My mother worked two jobs to give me the best start she could. Eventually, I won a scholarship to medical school.'

'What an achievement!' she exclaimed. 'Good for you!'

'I don't tell many people, but I feel I can talk to you.'

He looked surprised by what he'd just said and, for a moment, Nellie was tempted to break her cover. *Look here, I'm not who you think I am. This is not what it seems*, she didn't say.

'I know how it feels, losing your father young,' she offered. 'I suppose you could say we have a sort of... shared landscape.'

The smile he gave her caused the tight coil of pain and anger that she carried in her chest to ease. He seemed to know instinctively how to gentle it. Her mind flashed back to the perpetual state of warfare Momma and Jack had lived in, and how determined it had made her to stand on her own two feet. If a girl married poor, she became a housekeeper and a drudge. If she married wealth, she became a sort of pampered pet. Nellie had no intention of becoming a drudge or a pet. But Dr Ingram was different – he spoke to her as an equal. Was a different kind of relationship possible; a relationship in which she had the freedom to be what she wanted?

At that moment, a hair-raising scream came from the floor above, followed by a crash and the sound of running feet. Dr Ingram checked himself. 'Ah, well, I do have other patients to take care of. I'd best wish you good day, Nellie.'

She got to her feet. Walking away from him, back to the cold, mind-numbing monotony of Hall Six, made her feel like she was tearing inside. She forced her legs to move, one step in front of the other.

As she reached the hall, a nurse came in with mail for Miss Gressley. A letter arriving for an inmate was a rare occurrence and it awakened a keen interest. All the patients crowded round her, thirsty for a word from the outside world. And it seemed as if Miss Gressley gently filled as she sat reading it.

'Who is it from?' Sofia asked, unable to tamp down her curiosity any longer.

'My nephew,' Miss Gressley said.

'Oh? How old is he?'

'What's he like?'

'Where does he live?'

'What does he write?'

Miss Gressley let out a breath. 'He has come of age and has inherited a substantial sum of money,' she said solemnly. 'He wants to secure my release. I shall be cared for by a private nurse in my own home.'

Tears started trickling down her cheeks. 'Last time I saw him, he was a pretty infant. You know, there are good people in the world. There are truly good people. It's easy to lose sight of that in here.' She swiped at her eyes with her sleeve.

Glancing at the others, Nellie recognized the look on their faces – envy struggling with hope. Miss Gressley had walked right into a dream. If it could happen for her, it could surely happen for them too?

Miss Gressley's nephew was getting her new house ready for her to move into. In the meantime, she kept to herself, away from the crowd. Whenever the women exercised, she walked alone. During the sitting, she took her place a little apart, keeping as still as her fidgety limbs allowed and refusing to make eye contact with anyone. She didn't want trouble, didn't want anything to go awry and spoil her chances of release. Nurse O'Grady still bore her a grudge and watched her like a hawk.

The nurse's chance came at lunchtime. She gave Miss Gressley a large, heavy tureen and ordered her to carry it to the kitchen. Miss Gressley tried several times to get a grip on the dish, but could not do so because of the twitching of her arms. The more nervous she got, the worse the spasms grew. Nurse O'Grady watched her with loathing.

'What's the matter with you?' she jeered. 'Will you pick it up, or will you wear it out pawing at it?'

Finally, Miss Gressley got the tureen into her hands. But as she hastened to the kitchen, her arms gave a violent, uncontrollable jerk and it flew from her grasp, striking Nurse O'Grady on the forearm.

The nurse gave a shriek. 'Oh, Miss Gressley threw this dish at me. See the bruise!'

The other nurses hurried over and Nurse O'Grady showed them the mark on her arm. When she'd had her fill of sympathy, she went to the table, seized a tall jug of water and dashed it into Miss Gressley's bosom.

The old lady flinched and cried out as icy water hit her skin and ran down between her breasts. A dark stain spread over the front of her dress.

Nurse O'Grady gave her a vindictive smile. 'That'll teach you,' she sneered.

The nurses made Miss Gressley sit all afternoon in the sopping wet garment. They refused to give her a change of clothes, even though the fabric took several hours to dry and she was shaking all over from cold.

The following morning, Miss Gressley didn't appear at breakfast. From the conversation of the nurses, Nellie learned that she was suffering from a high fever. Nurse Grupe ordered an inmate to carry a tray of food to Miss Gressley in bed. It held a bowl of congealed oatmeal and a hunk of bread that was little more than dried dough – a meal that the healthy patients could hardly stomach. Nellie's mind flew to the fine food the doctors and nurses were given every day, and agitation tore through her.

The inmate returned to the dining hall with the tray untouched. Nellie asked if she might sit with Miss Gressley but was curtly refused. Later, Miss Gressley was moved to a room on her own and Dr Ingram was summoned. He was with her for some time and when he came out again, his face was grave. At the sight of him, Nellie's heart gave a small, thrilling jolt, but he strode away without glancing at the other patients.

'It doesn't look good for Miss Gressley, does it?' she breathed to Sofia.

'She wasn't in the best health before this,' Sofia replied, a pleat of worry appearing between her brows.

'I don't know, I really don't. I just hope she doesn't die before her nephew gets here.'

'Oh, come on. Surely the Lord wouldn't be that cruel?'

Nellie clamped her lips and kept quiet, as she didn't have much faith in God's mercy. If it even existed, it wasn't in evidence at the Blackwell's Island Asylum.

'I need you to clean and disinfect Miss Gressley's room,' Nurse Grupe ordered the following day, flicking her fingers impatiently against her palm. 'Get it spotless and ready for a new inmate.'

Nellie felt the ground sliding away from under her. 'Oh, my goodness, has she died?' she whispered to Sofia.

Sofia scratched her head. 'It surely looks like it. I mean, we wouldn't know if she had, because the dead cart comes in the middle of the night.'

Tears were stinging Nellie's eyes. 'Ah. Well. Right.'

'If you're still awake, you can sometimes hear it trundling around. A patient's room-mates don't know what's happened to her, often for months. They are told she's been discharged, when in fact she is rotting in her grave.'

Nellie shuddered. Poor, sweet Miss Gressley, who didn't have a mean bone in her body. Why had God turned away from her?

Just then, Miss Gressley appeared in the doorway. She looked pale and was dressed for the outside world. The inmates crowded around her, buzzing with questions and concern.

'My nephew is coming to take me home,' she said tremulously.

'You must be over the moon,' said Sofia.

'I'm scared to leave. Been here so long, I don't know how to behave in the real world.'

Nellie felt the excitement beneath her words. She vowed to tell Miss Gressley's story as soon as she got out. Miss Gressley hugged each woman in Hall Six goodbye, and Nellie guessed that the others were feeling the same mixture of happiness and envy. They were glad for her, but her departure only underlined their inability to follow. After Miss Gressley had gone, the hall was colder than ever.

'Well, that's that and good riddance,' Nurse O'Grady declared.

There wasn't anything to do, just harsh, idle time to wait through, marked off by meals and sleep. Tillie came to sit beside Nellie, which pleased and surprised her. Ever since Al McCain's visit, her presence had made Tillie angry, and she'd given her a wide berth, reluctant to provoke her further.

Tillie leaned her head on her hands and whispered, 'Sometimes the day drags by so slowly I can hardly stand it. I am in despair over my spoiled life and I'm still not sure how it came to this.'

Nellie put her arms around her, murmuring, 'Don't, my dear, please don't. I am in this with you. We will stand it together.' But she was full of unease. How could Tillie endure this without losing the will to live? If Hell existed in the universe, it was right here. As if it were contagious, Nellie could feel herself going under. The torpor and coercion of the asylum enveloped her like a bad smell, and it was almost impossible to imagine life outside it. There was still no word from the *World*. Pulitzer and Cockerill had promised to get her out, but they hadn't said when, and she cursed her own stupidity in not tying them down to a definite date. Just as disturbingly, Dr Ingram had shown no intent to release her.

How was it possible that she, who had sworn never to depend on any man, was now dependent on men for rescue? What if they failed to get her released soon? What if release never came? She was hanging on by her fingertips. Still holding Tillie, her mind drifted back to Al McCain's visit. It might have been her one chance to escape and she had pushed it away. If only she had known, she would have jumped at it.

Nurse O'Grady's voice cut through her thoughts. 'Stop touching! You two, cut it out at once. No touching.'

'Is that a rule?' Nellie asked, dropping her arms, and the nurse turned on her. 'Yes, it is. And you better remember it.'

Perhaps it was an essential rule, Nellie reflected, in an institution where most of the inmates lacked inhibitions, and where some of them were violent. But wasn't a little physical contact and warmth exactly what they needed to heal? And wasn't the lack of it just one more way in which the asylum made them feel less than human?

'I let Gressley hug you because she was on her way out of here,' the nurse continued. 'Remember, with her gone, I'll have more time to keep my eye on *you*. And I mean to repay you for complaining to Dr Ingram. I always repay my debts, you see.' She shot Nellie a deadly look. 'I suggest you look out for the next bath day.'

Eighteen

'A IN'T YOU THE LUCKY ones? You're getting entertainment tonight. Magic lanterns,' Nurse O'Grady announced before supper. Murmurs of anticipation rippled through the hall.

The bell rang and the patients lined up. The mood was more cheerful than usual, but Nellie didn't feel right in herself. She was suffering from a dull, nauseous feeling that had crept over her so gradually she didn't realize it had taken hold until too late. She still told the doctors she was quite sane and demanded that they test her properly. But she said it so often that the words grew worn out and lost their meaning, like the senseless gibbering she heard around her all day. The sense of foreboding still nagged at her, but it had become part of her suffering in a pattern where one hideous day melded into another.

While the women waited for the dining room doors to open, shivering in the draught from the window, Nellie heard Nurse McCarten ask Nurse O'Grady the date. At the reply, her legs nearly gave way beneath her. To make sure she was right she counted carefully on her fingers. Eight days had passed; for eight days she had been an inmate of this place. *And she had not received a single word or signal from the* World. Chills ran up her spine, contracting her flesh.

Pulitzer and Cockerill couldn't have forgotten her. But perhaps there had been some kind of snag – some legal issue. Perhaps entering the asylum under false pretences was against the law. The men hardly knew her, after all; she wasn't a regular member of their staff. Perhaps the *World* had found itself in in a jam, feared trouble and had simply cast her off.

The possibility had haunted her from the start. What if she were trapped here for life? What would her mother do? Soon, Momma would begin to worry that she hadn't heard from Nellie, but it would never occur to her to search the asylum. Nellie would simply become another young woman who had vanished without trace in the city, leaving a grieving family behind. *Don't think of it, God, don't think of the mess you're in.*

As they took their places at the table, Sofia said, 'You don't look happy. Are you all right?'

'Well, no. I'm feeling agitated,' said Nellie, who was racking her brains for other ways to get released. Suddenly, she blurted out: 'I shouldn't be here. See, I am quite sane. I'm actually a reporter doing an undercover investigation.' She clapped her hand over her mouth, aghast at having spilled the secret she'd been trying so hard to keep. It wasn't as if Sofia could get her out.

Sofia was staring at her. 'Of course you're a reporter,' she said, 'and I'm the Virgin Mary.'

'I am serious. I don't belong in an asylum.'

Sofia gave her a puzzled look. 'Are you sure you're all right?'

'Why do you keep asking?' Nellie shook her head to try and clear it.

'I fear you're having some kind of delusion,' Sofia said gently. 'I mean, everyone knows women don't do that kind of work.' Under the table, her knee started jogging up

216

and down. 'I care about you. Please don't get sick, like the others.' She frowned, then began to pick at her meal.

Nellie looked down at her filthy dress, her chapped hands with their raw knuckles, the nails bitten to the quick. Was she like the others? At that moment, there was nothing to distinguish her from them. Even their struggle against inhumane treatment had become hers. She felt the last fragments of her identity as a reporter disintegrate. Despite the cold, she had begun to perspire, and her collar felt tight around her neck. She had to fight to keep from crying out, from beating her head against the wall. She forced herself to take deep breaths and drink some water. By the time the meal was over, she felt a little better.

Afterward, they were lined up again and led outside. A full moon hung in the sky, soothing the grim buildings with a quiet, milky light. It was the first time Nellie had seen the moon since arriving at the asylum. In her ordinary life, she didn't have time to pay much attention to the night sky. She took it for granted – noting if the stars shone particularly brightly, but never stopping to gaze and dream – until she'd got herself locked up like a criminal. The night had been taken away from her then. The nurses put the patients to bed at sunset and didn't let them stir from their cots. But unintentionally, while giving them an entertainment, they had also given them the moon-drenched night. As Nellie walked, her heart and soul flew up into it, and everything else fell away. She was drunk with wonder and moonlight. They were making their way to one of the empty pavilions that had been fitted up as a theater with rows of chairs. Nurses were positioned at intervals to direct them. Nellie took a seat between Tillie and Sofia, near the front. When the women were seated, the men filed in.

There were fewer male patients in the Blackwell's Island lunatic asylum. To ease overcrowding, another asylum for men had been built on Wards Island, further north in the East River, and most of the men had been moved there; although some were kept back to do the heavy jobs the women couldn't manage. Nellie wondered what made men sick. They didn't look half as bad as the women. Perhaps because it took less effort to make a man look presentable, these ones seemed perfectly ordinary; not smart or assured, but one wouldn't have given them a second glance in a crowd. Not one of the women, with their soiled dresses and matted hair, could have blended into any crowd apart from the one she was in now.

Dr Kinier came in and sat down next to Nurse Grupe, pressing his thigh against hers. Nellie looked around for Dr Ingram, felt a stab of disappointment when she did not see him. The oil lamps were dimmed. There was electricity in the air as the inmates awaited whatever was coming next.

'Good evening, ladies and gentlemen! My name is Micky McGee,' announced the showman, a portly individual with a bristling red mustache and chin whiskers. 'Welcome to my lantern slide show, bringing the world to life in pictures. Sit back, relax and enjoy the spectacular entertainment!'

Using a hand-held magic lantern – a boxy apparatus with a protruding snout – he began to project images printed on glass slides onto the wall. His assistant, who looked like his son – a slimmer version of him without the whiskers – accompanied the show on a glass harmonica.

After such a long time without a single diversion, it was positively astounding to see phantasmagorical images of goblins and ghosts fading in and out on the pavilion walls, iridescent yet insubstantial, sometimes appearing to dance. The disorientating effect was heightened by the eerie, ethereal chimes of the glass harmonica.

The inmates were transfixed. From time to time someone got up and pointed or yelled, but otherwise the audience was no more disorderly than in a normal theater.

They watched a cane-wielding instructor demanding silence, an impish boy in striped stockings tossing a cat into a lake, and three mustachioed generals who, when rotated ninety degrees, appeared to be three horses with bit and bridle. The patients giggled and cried out, and every now and then they broke into applause.

The highlight of the show was 'The Ratcatcher'. A man in a red woolly nightcap with an enormous beard and a protruding belly slept on a bed. His snoring bulk of flesh moved the bedclothes in great rippling gusts and his mouth opened and closed. Micky McGee invited the audience to make their own snoring noises in time to his movements and they joined in with relish. Then a rat appeared on the bedclothes. The lunatics gasped – the man snored on monstrously. Suddenly, at the very moment the man's mouth opened wide, the rat made a dash across the bed and dived down the man's throat, into his stomach. The inmates erupted with laughter.

Glancing up, Nellie saw Dr Ingram standing by the door. He must have come in late, without her noticing. He wasn't watching the images on the wall. His eyes were on her, enjoying her enjoyment. It was a moment of grace, a realization that perhaps her life mattered after all, and she felt warmth rippling through her body. Perhaps it was all right if she never got out of the asylum. Perhaps these moments of richness with Dr Ingram were enough.

She brought herself up short, horrified. What a mad thought! Dismissing it at once, she turned her attention back to the show. The next time she glanced in the doctor's direction, he had opened the door and was quietly slipping out.

As she watched him leave, all the happiness drained out of Nellie, cutting her adrift. She must really be insane to let herself entertain romantic notions about him. He saw her as another poor lunatic, without prospects or hope. Besides, she knew nothing about his life. He likely had a wife and a houseful of apple-cheeked children, and was on his way to have supper with them now.

The show ended and the lamps were lit. Micky McGee and his son began to pack up their apparatus. The male patients stayed in their seats; the women were ordered to stand and get in line. A humming sound rose from their ranks, soft at first, but rising in pitch and volume till it sounded like a swarm of angry bees. *MmmmMMMM...*

Nurse O'Grady blew on her whistle for silence. 'I hear one more peep from any of you and you'll all go to the Lodge!' she shouted. 'Now, get back in line! Move it! It's bath time.'

When Nellie reached the front of the line in the bath hall, her clothes were stripped off and Nurse O'Grady shoved her hard against one of the bathing troughs. It was made of cast iron, heavy and sharp-edged, and Nellie cried out in pain.

Nurse O'Grady shot her that dagger stare. 'You better keep your mouth shut 'cause your precious doctor has left for the night. There's nobody to hear you but us and we ain't listening.'

She manhandled Nellie into the dirty, ice-cold water and Nellie began to shake from the shock of it. She bit hard on her lip, praying that the pain would take her mind off the freezing water. Then the nurse grabbed her by the throat and pushed her under the surface. Nellie held her breath, waiting to be let up. But the fingers maintained their steely hold and pressure began to build in Nellie's chest. She thrashed in panic, clawing at the nurse's hand, unable to stop a spasmodic breath that dragged water into her mouth and windpipe, flooding her with terror. Was she breathing in or out? She couldn't tell. No thought but *get out of the water, get out of the water, get out of the water.*

All at once, she knew with piercing clarity that she was going to die. She felt connected with every other woman whose life had ended in a violent struggle. A sort of delirium came over her, there was a ringing in her ears, and everything went dark. At that moment she heard Nurse Grupe say, 'Oh, my Lord! Let her up – quick! She's gone black in the face.'

Nellie felt the unbelievable relief of being pulled out. She was gasping for breath, coughing up water, her chest burning. Without bothering to dry her, the nurses thrust her into a short flannel slip, their faces swimming in and out of focus. Moments later, she felt a warm trickle on her thighs and realized that she had wet herself. Urine dripped onto the floor, gathering into a puddle.

'Filthy creature needs the bathroom,' Nurse Grupe remarked with quiet contempt, and Nellie had never felt so humiliated.

Nurses Grupe and O'Grady took her by the arms and dragged her, feet slipping in her own piss, to the stalls. Pushing on Nellie's shoulders, Nurse O'Grady shoved her onto a toilet seat and leaned on her until her buttocks dipped in the filthy water. Nellie struggled in the nurse's grip, cold sweat running down her back. The stink was so thick and foul in her nostrils, it made her gag.

Nurse O'Grady had several sheets of hard toilet paper scrunched up in her hand. 'Spread your legs,' she ordered. 'Babies who can't get to the bathroom by themselves need wiping.'

She ground the paper into Nellie until she was writhing and begging for mercy. Then the nurse clamped one hand around Nellie's chin, pinching her jaws so that her mouth was forced open. Nellie saw her lifting the wad of paper toward her mouth and tried to scream, but only groans and whimpers came out. She looked at Nurse Grupe, pleading with her eyes for help, but the other woman glanced away, busying herself at the sinks.

Nurse O'Grady smiled, she smiled! 'Open wide, my lady,' she said. 'You think you're better than the rest, but sooner or later, everyone eats their own shit in here.'

She started to pack the paper into Nellie's mouth. Nellie retched. A spout of vomit came up and was blocked by toilet paper. She tried to swallow it, but choked, her lungs exploding. No air, *no air*... Black spots danced before her eyes, the walls of her skull seemed to cave in, and she was sucked into nothingness.

When Nellie came to, she found herself on a hard mattress in a tiny space. From the high, barred window and the eye-watering smell of sewage, she recognized it as the punishment cell where she had spent her night of solitary confinement. Her hair and nightdress were clammy with vomit, and her throat felt raw. She was shaking so badly that she couldn't stand up. She called as loudly as she could for help and waited, but nobody came. Time moved differently when one was locked up in the dark alone. It ground right down to a standstill.

She could hear the rapid breath of a woman shivering. Was there someone in the cell with her? She realized that it was herself, her own breathing. From the floor above came a loud thud and the rattling of bars. 'Murder!' a voice shrieked. 'Police!... *Help me!*' Then a ghastly sobbing.

There was a tightness inside Nellie's temples, a needling pressure, and it made her fear that her mind was about to go awry. She cried out again, hoarse and frantic, but still nobody came. She kept calling until tears boiled over and dissolved her voice, and she began to shake and choke. Dark feelings came up like a tide: shame, fear, despair; the sense that some terrible calamity was coming, but she didn't know its nature. The door to her past was flung open and her mind began to dredge up all the distressing scenes she had ever lived through. Jack's drunken rages – smashing plates and bottles, overturning chairs, the children stumbling, cut and terrified, on spilled beer and broken glass. The sound of his shovel splintering bone; her horror and fear, and his twisted pleasure.

As the graveyard scene replayed in Nellie's mind, she was once again the heavy-hearted adolescent witnessing incomprehensible brutality. And then she was not herself: she was the skeleton. She could feel the agonizing bite of the shovel in her neck, the spasm getting deeper as vertebrae and spinal column shattered. Pain was a hot, blinding whiteness that surrounded and filled her, and she was in it.

With all her strength, she pushed the image from her head. Her thoughts went reeling about and came to land with the recognition that she only had herself to blame for the mess she was in. *You had health, strength and work – and you threw it all away! Madden was paying decent money for your articles, but you had to go and overreach yourself. You've lost everything now, and you did it to yourself...*

Finally, worn out by fear and turmoil, she fell into a restless sleep.

When Nellie woke, she felt thirsty and dizzy, and she had a headache. Light was coming through the tiny window – it was morning. She heaved herself into a sitting position, but it made her head swim, so she gave up and lay back down. Nurse McCarten stumped in with a piece of the blackened asylum bread on a plate and a crock of water. She set them down without a word.

'Why am I in here?' Nellie asked.

The nurse looked at her steadily but didn't answer.

Nellie tried again. 'What's going on? When are you going to let me out?'

Nurse McCarten moved slowly and heavily toward the door, and Nellie saw that she had given up on the patients and most likely on herself, become part of the collective despair of the institution.

'What about my session with Dr Ingram?' Nellie called. 'I always see him in the mornings. Please take me there, he's expecting me.'

Nurse McCarten stopped and turned to face her. 'I'm not supposed to talk to you,' she said gruffly, 'but I'll just say this. Nurse O'Grady cancelled your session.'

Nellie felt hit, just below her ribcage. 'W-why?' she stammered.

The nurse sighed. 'She told him you got violent. Said you're dangerous and beyond the reach of any talking cure.'

'But that's not true!' cried Nellie. 'Nurse, please listen to me. I am not mad at all. I'm a reporter, sent here by the *World* newspaper to write a story about the asylum.' She was past caring about blowing her cover and ruining the scoop.

Nurse McCarten's eyebrows shot up in disbelief. For a moment, she stood staring at Nellie. Then she nodded once, as though something had been confirmed for her, and went out, closing the door with a bang. Nellie heard the bolt sliding shut.

224

She sprang to her feet. It was cold in the cell, but sweat was pouring off her. She hammered on the door until her hands were swollen and bruised, but nobody came. She began pacing up and down, beside herself. The cell was only a few steps long and the constant turning made her feel like a caged animal.

What is Dr Ingram thinking? Is he disappointed in me, is he worried? Surely he'll come and get me – he knows I am not mad.

Now and again, screams or crying came from other parts of the building and, each time Nellie heard the noises, her mind cried, *Help me help me help me.* When she had worn herself out, she sat on the pallet and tried to swallow the bread, but her throat hurt too much, so she took a few sips of water. It restored her a little. She called out to be released, but still nobody came.

By her second night in solitary, Nellie was weeping at the bars on the window and howling to be rescued. She could feel her mind slipping away from her. She tried to keep hold of herself by thinking of addresses, nursery rhymes, fairy stories. She counted forward and backward. She recited the alphabet, but the letters and numbers mashed into each other. She was tottering on the edge, the cracks in her psyche opening onto vistas of glittering madness. She tried to get back to herself by calling up Dr Ingram: the touch of his fingertips along her jawline, his voice. *Her face is the brightest I have ever seen for a lunatic.* But the words disintegrated, leaving a thousand echoes. *Brightest... lunatic... lunatic...*

I am going mad.

Her hands reached out, clawed at empty air. Her blood was racketing. The darkness was thick and solid, a weight bearing down.

I'm scared, help me. Help, I can't breathe in the dark—
But I am breathing. Steady. I must keep steady.

Her stomach twinged and nausea spread through her, like a stain. *I will go mad if they don't let me out soon. If I don't choke on my vomit.*

She began to slide in and out of awareness, falling through weird, foggy dimensions in her head. She heard a weak cry coming from the basement. It came again and again. Her brain struggled to make the connection... a baby. Yes, there was a baby down there. The thought of an innocent babe being born into such a chamber of horrors made her shudder. Then a gray mist began to drift across her mind, spreading and thickening. At first it frightened her, but she soon welcomed it, for she could not go mad while she slept. Letting go, she allowed the merciful darkness to fold over her.

Nellie struggled to open her eyes. The top of her head felt as if a great weight were pressing on it. Perhaps Nurse O'Grady had killed her, after all.

Looking around, she realized that she was back in her bed in the dormitory off Hall Six.

'Let me go home! I want to go home,' said a voice. 'I'll call the police if they don't let me out.'

'Shut yer mouth,' said another patient wearily. 'Shut it and let me sleep.'

'Don't you speak to me like that,' said the first voice. 'Just because I'm down, it don't mean you can get at me. I'll call the police.'

And then someone else started up a small, thin sobbing. Nellie lay like a carcass, letting the sounds wash over her. Her mind was strangely blank and dark, and she felt detached, as if she were on the other side of a gauze screen. She vaguely remembered hearing a baby's cry, but she couldn't hold the thought. When the nurses came in to get the women up, Nellie let them dress her. She was covered in scratches and bruises, yet she hardly felt them. She did not cry out or protest. She sat on her narrow cot in the cold dormitory and, like the other patients, stared into space.

Later, during the sitting, Nellie found herself on the bench facing the windows. She looked out and found that the outside world had lost all its color and depth; it was flat, like a picture. She gazed at the drop to the ground, thinking of the relief of falling.

'Goodness, Nellie,' said Dr Ingram when he came to do his rounds. 'You look terrible. What's been happening?'

'She is still disturbed,' Nurse O'Grady cut in, before Nellie could form a reply. 'She had a seizure last night and attacked me. She was out of control – screaming, puking and soiling herself. I cleaned her up as best I could, but you can still smell it on her.' Nellie realized that she stank of sewage and vomit.

'I know you were pleased with her progress,' Nurse O'Grady continued, 'but that's all changed now. She's a very sick woman. See, she even thinks she's a reporter writing a story about us.' She smiled sardonically. 'I've heard some wild tales during my time here, but that sure beats everything. Look, I'm not a doctor, but if I were you, I would put her in the Lodge.'

'Absolutely not,' said Dr Ingram. 'She is one of my most promising patients. I'm not giving up on her so quick.' He was silent for a few moments, considering. Then he said, 'I would like to talk to Nellie on her own, if you will excuse us.'

Nurse O'Grady stalked away, glowering.

Dr Ingram led Nellie to a quiet corner of the hall and sat her down on a bench. 'What's the matter?' he asked gently. 'I can see you're not well. Can you tell me how you feel?'

'I feel... I feel like I...' She waved a hand helplessly; her mind was swathed in wet, gray cloud. The doctor waited for a reply, his eyebrows lifted in encouragement.

'Try again, Nellie,' he finally said. 'I shall do my best to understand, so I can help you. You see, I... I care about what happens to you.' A flush rose on his cheeks.

And although a part of Nellie wanted to stay right here and be looked after by Dr Ingram, she realized that the best help he could give her would be to discharge her from the asylum. She better explain she was a journalist, clearly and convincingly, before she lost her mind for good. She opened her mouth, but nothing came out. She closed it and opened it a couple of times, like the mouth of a fish.

'Oh... oh, my head's not right,' she blurted at last, regretting the words as soon as they'd left her lips. And then she started to wail. It was an ugly sound – a keening, almost. She hung her head in her hands, trying to stop, but she couldn't. Despair rolled through her. Her gift for language had always been her saving grace, getting her through bad times, giving form to the world. And now it was gone. Without it she was nothing and no one.

Dr Ingram offered her his handkerchief, she waved it away. He let out a deep sigh and she saw that he had revised his opinion of her. Any regard he had held her in was destroyed. And even if she managed to tell him she was a reporter, there was no way he would believe her now.

'Nellie,' he said sadly. 'Oh, Nellie. You were doing so well.'

Nineteen

A FTER NELLIE'S ORDEAL AT the hands of
Nurse O'Grady in the washroom, she developed a cough, and each time she coughed, it
felt like her chest was on fire. The outside world was
becoming less and less real; her moorings were cut.
Conditions were so far removed from normal living,
they only increased her sense of rupture rather than
clearing it up. The story she was supposed to write
slipped clean out of her head; she could hardly remember why she was here. Her ability to reason or struggle
vanished; she grew dulled and confused, vague and
aching shapes of mist and memory flitting around
her mind.

Her monthlies began and Nurse Kelly brought her two
small sacks. One of them contained rags torn into strips
for her to use. When a rag was soiled, she was supposed
to put it into the other sack, and when her period was
finished, she was responsible for washing the whole lot out
for reuse. No pins or belts were allowed in the asylum;
patients had to hold the rags in place by clamping their
thighs together. In her dazed state, it was a struggle to
manage. She would forget to change her rags or hold her
legs together and, before long, a patchwork of bloodstains
appeared on her underskirt.

Something strange was happening to time. It either moved with excruciating slowness, dripping lethargically through her blunted perceptions, or it lurched forward so fast, she lost great chunks altogether. She couldn't control it. She would be sitting in the hall and it was morning, and then suddenly, it was time for bed. What had happened in the interval? She could not recall having eaten, but she knew that she must have gone to the dining room; she couldn't remember the daily walk, although she had certainly been outside. In the world of the mad, a day might consist of weeks or – and this was terrifying – time would pleat and a day scarcely lasted for a minute.

Sofia tried to keep Nellie going, talking to her, feeding her fruit whenever she could get it. On the tenth morning, she asked her to play the piano.

'I used to play,' Nellie stammered, 'but I don't think I can any more.'

Sofia gave her an appraising look. 'May I give you some advice?' she asked, chafing Nellie's cold hands between her own, and Nellie nodded. 'If you want to get better, occupy yourself. Music is the best activity, but it doesn't matter if you only wind and unwind a ball of wool. Do it a hundred times if you can't find anything else, but do something and do it all the time.'

'Sure. I'll try,' said Nellie, but she knew she had lost the will to get well.

Later that day, she took her place in the line for their walk. The routine felt normal, like she belonged here. She had grown accustomed to it all; the deathly claustrophobia, the sudden blows from the nurses, the tang of disinfectant and urine. As she put on her hat and shawl and started the dismal walk with the others, she was sure that her face was as dulled and resigned as theirs.

Outside, the sky was a smudge of gray and the lawns were flattened by wind. Everywhere one looked, long lines of inmates were shuffling along, a stream of faces. The rope gang passed by – screeching, pulling, staggering, crying – driven like animals by a cold-eyed nurse. One of the women shook and clutched at her throat, as though about to vomit. 'Help me! Please help me,' she implored Nellie, but the nurse hit her on the legs with her truncheon and ordered her to keep moving. Near them, a patient crumpled to the ground in a faint while another nurse was trying to force her to walk.

A trim man, dressed in a gray suit and carrying a briefcase, was coming up the path toward Nellie, accompanied by Dr Ingram and Nurse O'Grady. They stopped beside her.

'Step out of line,' Nurse O'Grady commanded, and it felt as if all the air was sucked out of Nellie's lungs.

The stranger came up close. What did it mean? Had Nurse O'Grady finally succeeded in getting her sent to the Lodge? Was this the day Nellie Brown disappeared for good, without trace?

But the man was smiling. His eyes were full of respect.

'My name is Peter A. Hendricks. I am your lawyer,' he said to Nellie, adding in a whisper: 'The *World* sent me to get you out of here.' Then, in a normal voice, 'I have arranged for you to be released into the care of your friends in the city.'

The river roared in Nellie's ears like an ocean. The ground tilted beneath her feet. 'Is... is this for real?' she stammered.

'Yes, it is. The papers have been signed off – you're really free.'

'It's a mistake, I'm telling you,' Nurse O'Grady said coldly.

'Why?' Mr Hendricks asked.

'She is crazy and a danger to the outside world. She belongs on the Island.'

Gulls screamed overhead. Nellie looked from one to the other, petrified that Mr Hendricks would change his mind.

At last Dr Ingram said, 'I don't agree she's dangerous,' and Nellie breathed out in relief. 'I am prepared to vouch for her, on condition that you will accept full responsibility,' he told Mr Hendricks.

'Yes, I'll gladly do that,' said the lawyer.

The nurse let out an incensed puff of breath. 'You'll be sorry. Mark my words,' she warned.

Dr Ingram put his hands in his pockets and rocked slightly from heel to toe, ignoring her. 'Can I give you a few words of advice?' he asked Mr Hendricks.

'Sure. Go ahead.'

'We recommend that a recovered lunatic stays in the house she's discharged to for at least three weeks. She may have gentle outdoor exercise, but no unsupervised wandering. Oh, and be careful about who she comes into contact with. She shouldn't have any unhealthy or overly exciting influences.'

'Got it,' said Mr Hendricks. 'Makes perfect sense.'

Then, while Nurse O'Grady scowled and the lawyer looked on benignly, Dr Ingram turned to Nellie. 'So, I expect you feel a bit apprehensive about returning to the outside world. It's normal,' he said, smiling at her. 'But remember, your little setback will soon pass. You'll be relieved of your symptoms and restored to yourself. Goodbye, Nellie Brown, and good luck.'

'Goodbye, Dr Ingram,' Nellie replied, trying to stop her voice shaking. 'Thank you for everything. I'll never forget you.'

Reluctantly, Nurse O'Grady handed her a package containing the clothes she had arrived in and her handbag.

'All right then, let's go,' urged Mr Hendricks. 'There's no time to change. The boat is leaving soon.'

Dr Ingram stood back to let Nellie past, but she hesitated, unable to tear herself away. Mr Hendricks took her arm and guided her toward the gate; he seemed to realize how destabilized she felt. Almost in a trance, Nellie said goodbye to everyone she knew as she passed them. She hugged Tillie and Sofia.

'Where are you going?' Sofia asked.

'I'm leaving. I've been released.' Suddenly, Nellie's eyes glazed over with tears; she blinked them away.

'Say what?'

'I'm getting off the Island.'

Something shifted in Sofia's face. 'Oh, my Lord,' she said incredulously. 'You really are a journalist, aren't you? I thought you were raving when you told me, but it's the truth.'

'Yes. There's no time to explain, but I'll come back for you.'

Sofia's face hardened. 'Oh, sure you will. And I'm the Pope.'

'But I *will*. I promise.'

Sofia only shrugged. Nellie kissed her fingers to Tillie, who was gazing blankly and unflinchingly at a spot to the left of Nellie's head, seeing Lord knew what.

The boat swayed away from Blackwell's Island. Nellie sat at the bow, breathing in salt from the river, watching Manhattan draw nearer. She had looked forward so eagerly to getting out of the asylum, and yet she felt bereft about leaving the others, especially Tillie and Sofia. For ten days she had been one of them. It was dreadful to abandon them.

The clouds began to part and the air was piercingly clear. The sun was mellow gold, throwing sequins of light on the brown river, turning thousands of windows ablaze. New York was waiting for her. She felt bewildered by the magnificence of it and oddly unprepared. Would she remember how to talk to people, or how to react while they were talking? When to sit down and when to rise; how to use a knife and fork? She was no longer sure she knew how to navigate the real, tricky world of manners. She had faked madness to get into the asylum. Now she was out of it, she must fake sanity.

Twenty

T HE BOAT DOCKED AND Mr Hendricks helped Nellie into the covered carriage that waited for them on the wharf. The inside of the carriage was snug and clean, and Nellie worried that the way she smelled must be noticeable, but Mr Hendricks gave no sign of being bothered by it. They set off at a brisk pace, overtaking traffic, and she began to relax, savoring the wide streets, the many-storied buildings, the sense of being in but shielded from the city. Mr Hendricks explained that they were on the way to the Fifth Avenue Hotel on 23rd Street, where the *World* was putting her up at their expense to recover from her ordeal. She would find clothes, toiletries, everything she needed in her suite. He didn't like the sound of her cough, he added, and would send a doctor to have a look at her in the morning.

They alighted from the carriage and walked up the broad steps of the hotel, which seemed to Nellie like a palace in a storybook. She could hardly take her eyes off the scene in the lobby – the well-dressed men and women, the flowers, the lights, the perfume. It was all so colorful, so lush; it was almost unbearable.

She thanked Mr Hendricks and said goodbye to him, and the lawyer shook her by the hand and wished her luck. Nellie wondered if he said that to all his clients, or only to those in particular need of luck. A bellboy in a gold-braided uniform showed her up to her room. It was generously proportioned, with rich brocade drapes, deep armchairs and a four-poster bed. The fire in the grate was lit and the air was warm as toast. It eased her chest.

'Is there anything else I can do for you, Miss?' the bell-boy enquired.

'Why yes, there is. I need to send a note urgently. Can you please wait while I dash it off and get it delivered for me?'

He showed her where to find paper and pen in the drawer of a large, green-topped desk, and she sat down to write.

It's not a pretty story, Colonel Cockerill. But I got it.

As soon as the bellboy had taken the note, Nellie went to the bathroom. The walls were hung with full-length mirrors. The tub was huge and there were plenty of soft, fluffy towels. Clean, hot water gushed from the taps. She tore off her Blackwell's Island clothes and stuffed them into the trash basket, wishing she could burn them. She braced herself to look at her reflection.

It was worse than she thought. Her body was wasted and bruised, her ribs and hip bones protruded sharply. Her head seemed too large in proportion to her scraggy neck. In her own eyes, she saw the vacant depths she had sometimes noticed in other madhouse patients. It was a look that reminded her of Poppa in his coma, as if all the spirit had drained out, leaving an empty shell behind.

Repelled, she averted her gaze and climbed into the tub. The warmth and the delicately scented soap were intoxicating. She lay up to her neck in hot water, musing about losses and scars. She was safe, yet everything felt precarious, herself a stranger. Grateful though she was to have her freedom, it was lonely. She missed Sofia's intelligence and Tillie's sweetness prior to falling ill – she remained terribly worried about Tillie. It struck Nellie that this was the first time she had ever made friends. She'd never allowed herself to get close to anyone outside her immediate family; she had been too angry and driven, too barricaded up inside. And there was someone else she missed. An image of Dr Ingram crept into her mind, sitting at his desk, smiling up at her as she stood in the doorway, one hand on the frame.

'Well,' he had said. 'Well, Nellie. How are you feeling today?'

What she had felt was an overpowering longing to touch him, to erase everything else and just do that. But now she wondered if those feelings had been madness, delusion, or if they were genuine. She could not trust her emotions.

Nellie closed her eyes, held her breath and slipped under the water. It closed over her head like silk. Coming up for air, she soaped her body and her matted hair, producing a lacy film of bubbles on the surface of the water when she rinsed herself. Afterward, she towelled herself dry and put on the navy-blue dressing gown that hung on a hook on the bathroom door, relishing the feel of the silky fabric against her skin. She sat for a long time gazing out of the window at the tops of buildings suffused with the coppery glow of the setting sun, and Madison Square stretched out like a green carpet beneath her.

She ordered dinner in her room, as she didn't feel strong enough to face the dining room. A waiter in tails brought lamb chops, roast potatoes, buttered carrots and a slice of apple pie swimming in a lake of cream. He set up a table for her with linen of dazzling whiteness, glittering glass, silver dishes and a white rose in a vase. Nellie ate all the food, scarcely chewing, gulping it down, ravenous. She ate until her stomach hurt and she had to lie down. From her bed, she saw the streetlights come on. It was a magical moment, turning the city into a glittering kaleidoscope of light. New York was ravishing, but indifferent. It always had been, but she was more aware of it now. It gave her a hollow feeling.

It still seemed strange to be free. She thought it should feel different, but it didn't. She was weirdly stuck in the asylum. It would not let her go.

A knock at the door interrupted her thoughts. It was the bellboy. He handed her an envelope and left. She recognized Cockerill's handwriting and sat down to open it.

Well done, Miss Bly, well done indeed! Now go tell the world.

Nellie stared at the words until they stopped making sense, turning into squiggles that looked like stick insects marching across white ground. She hoped she was capable of telling the world, but she wasn't sure. Her mind had been blasted into a place from which it might never return. She took a breath.

Think. Think out the story you want to tell.

She closed her eyes, waited for ideas to arrive. At first there was nothing, just opaqueness, like a cloudy pond. But after a while something started to surface: her story was about the women who had been locked up and silenced. Yes, that was it. The women were at the heart of it, and she wanted to give them back their voices. But she also wanted to smash the myth of Blackwell's Island and get the asylum closed down, or at least bring about proper reform. Then the moment of clarity passed and Nellie's thoughts started breaking up. She tried to keep hold of them, but they slipped back into the murk and vanished, leaving her suffused with grief.

I cannot write the story because I am too crippled by the damage done to my mental health. This is the coda to my time in the asylum: a ruined mind and knowing it was all for nothing. I cannot help the women.

Despair arrived, a poisoned feeling in her body. She thought she couldn't sink any lower. She wiped her forearm across her face, which was wet because she was crying. This was the behavior she must avoid when she was with other people: weeping for no reason, making an exhibition of herself. It was the route back into the quicksand of madness.

She climbed into the huge bed, desperate for sleep to come and blot out the feelings. The fine cotton sheets were soft against her skin; her head sank into the feather pillows. After the cold, harsh nights of Blackwell's Island, the comfort was astounding. Sleep took her suddenly, like an invisible assailant stealing up from behind.

She dreamt that she was eating supper in the asylum, and her teeth began to crumble and fall out inside her mouth. Fragments of enamel overflowed from her lips. Horrified, she spat out the soft, rotten pieces.

Nurse O'Grady was glaring at her. 'Stop that!' she commanded in her loud, flat voice, and Nellie smelled her tobacco breath. 'Stop it at once! Finish your food.'

Nellie tried to stop. She bit down on a hard crust, but her remaining teeth disintegrated against it, filling her mouth with debris faster than she could spit it out. She began to choke; she couldn't swallow, couldn't breathe...

She woke with a start, bathed in sweat and shaking all over. The fire had gone out. She felt for the lamp and lit it. She felt disorientated, panicky. What was she doing here? Where was she?

At last she got a hold of herself. She sat up, reaching for her robe, and walked to the window to look out at the city. From here it seemed distant and enchanted: light and shadows and a dusting of stars. The darkness of the sky had begun to lose its intensity, dawn was not far off. She watched a carriage creeping down the deserted street, and returned to bed, tossing and turning till daylight began to filter through the curtains.

She thought she might as well get up. She went to the closet and opened the doors. The clothes the *World* had given her were neat and functional, in sober colors: grays and browns and navy blues. She shut the doors; she didn't feel like getting dressed. She put toothpaste on her toothbrush and thought, why bother? She forced herself to write a note to her mother explaining where she'd been, but downplaying the horrors she had endured. Once it was dispatched, she went back to bed, pulling the covers up to her chin. She'd known despair before, but never this deadly tiredness and lethargy. She wanted to cry, but tears would not come. She felt worthless. Everything she did was useless and no help to anyone, least of all herself.

A rap at the door. She opened it to find a serious-looking man with a bald head and thick, wire-rimmed glasses on the threshold. 'I am Dr Henry Gordon,' he said. 'Peter Hendricks asked that I stop by and take a look at you.'

'Oh, hello,' she answered dully. 'Well, here I am.'

Dr Gordon felt Nellie's pulse, shone a light in her eyes and throat, and listened to her breathing. He pronounced her exhausted and undernourished, with a nasty chest infection. He prescribed pills and syrup for her cough, and plenty of good food and rest. 'You have been through a test that would drive most women mad – and many men,' he said gravely.

But what about the invisible wounds? What can you do for those? she wanted to ask. She felt deadened, brutalized, as though part of her had been cut away. She thought that she could never again believe in the fundamental goodness of life. All she could see in front of her was misery and bleakness. She no longer had the energy to fight; she didn't how to work through the feelings and move on, as she had always managed to do in the past.

Over the next few days, Nellie went through the motions of living – getting dressed, taking her medicine, chewing her way through one meal after another. Her body was healing, but her mind had not – everything seemed shifting and insubstantial, and she felt deeply estranged from her life. Only Blackwell's Island was real: real and vivid, a subworld running right next to Manhattan that most people were unaware of. In the asylum, no one said, 'Don't make a display of yourself,' or, 'Why do you always answer back?' or, 'What will people think?' The mad simply voiced what everyone thought but were too afraid to say out loud, the things that lay beneath regular conversation like a city under water. All the trappings of society – the laws and customs, the mask of civility and propriety that papered over everything – they seemed to Nellie like lies, and the madness was underneath. That was the truth.

She was having strange, vivid dreams. She dreamt she had been shot in the leg, but couldn't feel anything. She knew that if she looked at the wound, she would die. She fought the urge with all her strength, but her eyes were helplessly drawn to the red-black hole, and she felt her heart stop beating.

She dreamt she was watching Tillie climb a flight of stairs that disintegrated as she reached the top, sending her plunging downward, her arms flung out, her skirt opening like a parachute. She did not hit the ground, but kept falling and falling, and Nellie could not catch her. She woke breathless, with the dropping sensation in her own stomach and the room reeling around her.

She dreamt her father was on the porch, calling her to come and look at the stars. She was deathly afraid that by the time she got there he would have slipped back into his coma, but he was himself again. Weak with relief, she took her place beside him; it was as if he had never been away.

'Look, there's the Hunter,' he said. 'There's the Pleiades, the North Star... see how brightly it's shining tonight?'

She nodded, dazed with starlight and awe. The breeze was warm and scented, and an owl hooted from the trees. Poppa turned kindly, serious eyes on her and said, 'What you saw in the asylum changes everything. You know that, don't you, Pinkey? It's time to use your evidence.'

He vanished and she woke up with his voice echoing in her head. *It's time to use your evidence, Pinkey. It's time...*

The clock by her bed said seven minutes to six. Though Poppa's absence struck her all over again, she felt more rested than she had for weeks; the cottony, clogged feeling in her head had gone. She ordered breakfast – eggs, bacon, biscuits, coffee – and ate greedily, licking butter from the biscuits off her fingers. She sipped at her coffee, thinking of everything her father had taught her about collecting evidence and arriving at truth. She thought about Momma's talent for storytelling. And she understood that if she drew on the gifts of both parents, if she presented her evidence clearly and compellingly, she would save the women of the asylum. In the process she would heal herself, as writing had always been her salvation.

She was galvanized. She washed her hands, brushed her teeth and sat down at the desk. She dipped her pen into the inkwell. How to begin?

She wrote 'lunatic' three times and scratched it out. She hated the word. During her research, she had learned that it came from the Latin *luna*, from the belief that cycles of the moon caused intermittent madness, which implicated women in a way she could not tolerate. She thought for a few moments, then started over.

Could I pass a week in the insane ward at Blackwell's Island? I said I could and I would. And I did.

She got up and went to the window. Below her the streets were coming to life. Delivery men unloaded crates of vegetables, traffic honked, a newsboy in a short jacket hawked the early-morning editions. She drew energy from the sight – no matter what happened, the city went on. She returned to her desk.

In giving this story, I expect to be contradicted by many who are exposed. I merely tell in common words, without exaggeration, of my life in a madhouse for ten days.

I always had a desire to know asylum life more thoroughly; a desire to be convinced that the most helpless of God's creatures, the insane, were cared for kindly and properly. I took it upon myself to enact the part of a poor unfortunate crazy girl and was committed to the insane ward at Blackwell's Island, where I had an experience I shall never forget.

The Insane Asylum on Blackwell's Island is a human rat trap. It is easy to get in, but once there, it is impossible to get out.

As Nellie wrote, the facts began to come alive, and so did her own anger. The anger invigorated her. Her pen moved faster and faster, the thoughts bubbling up so quickly that her hand could scarcely keep pace. It was an accurate account of her experiences, save for a few evasions. She wrote in the persona of plucky girl reporter whom nothing could stop. She recorded what she had seen, but she glossed over her suffering, keeping back her trauma at Nurse O'Grady's hands. She was aware that what was unsaid had a presence, like a looming shadow. It made her account seem rather misleading and she hoped that nobody else would notice, but it couldn't be helped. To expose how debased and wretched she had been, to turn it into news for public consumption, would have compounded the violation of her soul. It would have plunged her back into the raging humiliation of the Jack Ford days, and she had sworn long ago never to return there.

Nellie turned back to her pages. There was so much to say – she hoped it would make a series. While she wrote, her memories were bearable and she felt released, thankful for the free-pouring current of expression. Her gift was not lost after all. But the moment her pen slowed, pain started leaking out of her again, like a juice.

When the first instalment was finished late that morning and she had sent it off to the *World*, a leaden melancholy settled on Nellie. She was familiar with the pang of loss when a story was wrapped up, but this was worse than anything she had experienced before. She felt hollowed out, scooped away at the center.

She thought about all the newspaper reporters she had known, unable to take the pressures of a business they couldn't quit, drinking themselves into a stupor or working themselves to death within a few years. Even Joseph Pulitzer had sacrificed his health and his eyesight to pursue tomorrow's headlines. It was a gambler's life of feverish excitement and fleeting achievement. So far, thousands of ideas had come from Nellie's teeming brain, millions of words from her pen, yet the hungry presses always wanted more. How could a person have new ideas all the time? And when she hit the inevitable phase of aridity and burnout, what then?

Twenty-One

R AIN FELL. DAY AFTER day, cold gray down-
pours, and Nellie sat in her hotel room writing
the second instalment of her series while she
waited for the first to be printed.

Once words started flowing, everything else fell away,
and she only wanted to keep going. She was filled with an
energy she hadn't felt since before her asylum stay. The
work was alive, electric in her hands. It gave her another
world to step into, a world that she could order and control
as she wanted, unlike life. But she wasn't healed yet; the
asylum would not let her go.

It waited for sleep, then rose up with such force that it
severed gravity and sent everything spinning. She dreamt
about her suffering at Nurse O'Grady's hands. She
dreamt she was searching for Tillie, continually walking
into halls Tillie had just been taken out of, not knowing
if she was all right, if she was surviving without her. She
would wake in a cold sweat, half expecting to find herself
locked in, eight to a room, shivering under a mildewed
blanket that was too short for her, with the nurses gossiping outside.

Her story was printed as a series. A copy of the first
article was delivered to her room the following Sunday
morning. Titled 'Behind Asylum Bars', it described

how she had formed her plan to enter the asylum as an undercover patient, and her dramatic performance as a madwoman leading up to her incarceration on the Island. It had been laid out by the *World* as almost an entire page, with nothing else to detract from its importance. Nellie held the paper in her hands and gazed at it for a long time, wondering what sort of reaction it would spark.

It was dynamite, rocking the city. By the end of the day, there was hardly anyone in New York who had not read or heard about it. The public couldn't get enough of Nellie's tales of cruelty and madness, and the *World* could scarcely keep up with the demand for copies, printing more and more. The newspaper ran its own editorial on her story, calling it, 'an act of humanity' and 'the talk of the town and the nation'.

The second instalment appeared the following Sunday, sparking an even bigger sensation. To her surprise and delight, her name was actually part of the headline. 'Inside the Madhouse with Nellie Bly' covered her ten days in the asylum; the women she had met there, and the dangers they had faced from the inhumane conditions and the sadistic nurses.

Newspapers across the country picked up the story and printed their own articles about Nellie's stunt; mail addressed to her poured into the offices of the *World*, and Cockerill forwarded everything on to her at the Fifth Avenue Hotel. Some of the writers were outraged that women could be sent to asylums on the certificates of doctors who were in collusion with relatives wanting to have them put out of the way. Others dwelt on the appalling conditions. But most of the comments expressed alarm that so many experts could be fooled by a young girl posing as a lunatic; a girl who didn't even have training as an actress. The *New York Journal* wrote:

> This young woman was perfectly sane, and yet she deceived a police judge, a company of doctors and a lot of hospital nurses. After this one will feel inclined to doubt the judgment of the experts. If they can be so easily mistaken, what protection has a sane person? Is he not liable at any time to be sent to a lunatic asylum and kept there? There is enough in this whole business to set people to thinking.

In a short time Nellie had not only caused the sensation she'd hoped for, she had become one herself. But it was bittersweet, as she was desperate to keep her promise to Sofia and Tillie to get them released.

Pulitzer and Cockerill called Nellie into the office. It was a fortnight after she had arrived at the hotel and the first time she'd ventured out of it. The weather was dull, with heavy masses of cloud working across the sky and a cold north wind. The streets were muddy and bleak. It began to rain. Lightly at first, and then it pounded down, water pouring from the edges of Nellie's umbrella, splashing her as horses and vehicles ploughed through puddles. Soon the sidewalks shone with rain and the air smelled washed and earthy, like the countryside. As the security guard waved her through the lobby of the *World*'s offices, she remembered her last visit there – the humiliation of making a spectacle of herself in order to be seen.

The downpour intensified as she reached the newsroom, big drops pelting the windowpanes. The smells of wet ink, hot lead and tobacco, the sounds of telephone bells and clacking typewriters, the hustle and commotion that nevertheless possessed its own singular order gave her a pang of recognition. It made her realize how much she had missed being a newspaperwoman. It was in her blood and marrow.

The reporter nearest the door caught sight of her and nudged his neighbor, who whispered to the man on his other side. In no time at all, every face had turned toward her and then they rose to their feet as one body and began to applaud. She didn't know where to put herself. Rain fell harder and harder, the noise mingling with the clapping, rising to a sustained climax till she couldn't tell which sound was man-made and which came from heaven. There was a resounding crack of thunder, followed by a zigzag of lightning. Through the windows the sky was gray and sullen, with a hazy violet light seeping out from behind the rain clouds. Time slowed, stretched out like gum.

Finally, Cockerill raised his arm for silence. He shook Nellie by the hand, his face alight with admiration. 'You did good, Miss Bly! You're more than good! You not only got the scoop, you *became* the scoop.'

Taking her by the arm, he led her over to an empty desk. 'The job is yours,' he said simply. 'We're giving you free rein as a crusading reporter with your own byline, so it's only right that you should have your own desk. I'll admit that before we met, I thought women were only good for writing fluff or tear-jerking stories. But you've changed my mind. You performed a feat of journalism that very few men have equalled.'

She was speechless, her eyes blurring with tears. She knew that a byline was almost unheard of for a new hire, no matter how brilliant his or her achievement. She had conquered this tobacco-infused male environment; she'd been accepted as one of them, as a serious journalist. The victory was sweet.

'Three cheers for Nellie Bly! Hurrah for her pluck!' yelled one of the reporters and thundering cheers rang out, drowning the sound of rain. The men were still on their feet as Cockerill took her into his office, where Pulitzer waited for them.

There seemed to be more newspapers than ever piled on the floor and the half-drawn curtains shrouded every-thing in a dusky light. Pulitzer looked painfully thin. There were dark smudges under his eyes and his skin had a grayish tinge. He greeted her warmly, clasping her hand.

'Your work is excellent. Excellent!' he said. 'It's vivid and horrifying, yet you write with such compassion. I felt like I had walked right into the asylum.' He paused, look-ing into her eyes, and she saw that he understood what it had been like for her. 'I appreciate the personal sacrifices you made.'

'You are one gutsy girl,' Cockerill said admiringly. 'But rest assured, we will pay you handsomely for it.'

'We won't let your sacrifices have been in vain,' Pulitzer added. 'We're going to lobby for radical reform,' and Nellie felt a weight roll off her.

'Our job isn't simply to report the crime, but to get the mayor and city officials to do their duty,' said Cockerill. 'I'm going to make it my own personal mission.'

'Oh, please do,' Nellie said, with rising joy, 'and if you can pull it off, I'll feel that it has all been worthwhile.'

'If anyone can do it, Cockerill can,' said Pulitzer, smil-ing at his managing editor. 'He is a fighter, if there's fighting to be done, and he can write pungent paragraphs like nobody else.'

Cockerill grinned. 'Leave it with us, Miss Bly.'

'Thank you, she said. 'Thanks for everything. I'm honored to be working with you.' She took a deep breath. 'There are a couple of things I'd like to discuss.'

'Go ahead,' said Cockerill.

'Firstly, please can I have a few weeks' break before I start? To regain my strength and take care of some personal business.'

'Of course, Miss Bly. Take as long as you need. What else?'

She straightened her back. 'I would like to get two friends released – Tillie Maynard and Sofia Fierro. They were wrongly committed and I'm desperately worried for them.' Her eyes searched their faces. 'Please help me.'

Cockerill's fingers drummed on the desk. 'I suggest we wait,' he said. 'Try not to get caught up in the emotion – I know it's hard. There's going to be an investigation. Your friends will get the help they need then.'

'Yes, we haven't even started campaigning yet,' agreed Pulitzer.

'But there's no time to waste!' she burst out. 'The asylum is too dangerous to leave them there for a single day longer than necessary.'

'The point is that the request would be far more effective as part of an investigation than coming from us on our own,' said Cockerill calmly.

Nellie seethed with frustration. *Let's try anyway – we have nothing to lose*, she wanted to say, but she bit back the words because she could see that their minds were made up and trying to change them was useless.

The *World* demanded an investigation of conditions at the asylum and, two weeks later, Nellie was summoned before a grand jury, headed by District Attorney Vernon M. Davis, a sturdily built man with dark, serious eyes beneath

252

heavy brows. She found them to be gentlemen and the summons was not an ordeal. She swore to the truth of her statements, and the jurors asked her to accompany them on a surprise visit to Blackwell's Island.

'I'll be glad to go with you because I want to help the women,' she said. 'Really, the asylum should be shut down.'

'We'll take a good look at what's going on. But the aim is reform rather than closure because the patients still need the shelter of an institution,' Mr Davis said, massaging the short hair at his temples.

'Well, in that case it needs desperately needs money, so that the patients can have nutritious food and decent accommodation. Competent doctors and properly trained nurses, too.' She paused, for she was tired and out of the habit of speaking so much.

'I quite agree,' said Mr Davis. 'The thing is, nobody cared what happened to the insane as long as they were hidden away out of sight. But now there's an open scandal; the public and newspapers are screaming for reform. Hopefully, the publicity you've generated will force the hand of city officials.'

It was a very different voyage across the river. This time the delegation sailed on a clean, new boat. The jurors were kind and tried to engage Nellie in conversation, but she was so preoccupied, it felt like they were speaking behind glass, a sheer screen separating her from everyone else on board. The water was silt-brown and choppy, lapping against the hull. They were getting close to the Island and she could see the grim buildings clearly. Memories of her time there came flooding back. Her stomach clenched and a wave of blood rushed up to her head.

She tried to focus on her reunion with Sofia and Tillie, but she was frightened of them; or, rather, frightened of letting them know who she really was. The line that divided her from them had reappeared. They would realize she had made friends with them under false pretences and they would feel betrayed, no matter that she had grown to love them. She was anxious too about what state she might find Tillie in – assuming Tillie was still alive. If there was another reason for her trepidation, she refused to admit it to herself. As the boat docked, she tamped down all thoughts of Dr Ingram and tried to get herself together.

The gangplank went down, and they filed off the boat and headed south on foot, taking the river road. The sky was an opaque white, and the air was cool and breezy, twining Nellie's skirts around her legs. A gust stirred the sparse leaves clinging to the trees, sending a few drifting to the ground. They passed the ragged man Nellie had seen on her first journey to the asylum. He was wearing breeches too large for him, belted with a piece of string, and his tail was unravelling.

'I's Johnny the Horse. I runs races. People bets on me,' he announced, pawing the ground.

'Hello, Johnny,' Nellie greeted him.

'Would you like a ride in my wagon, Miss?'

'It's kind of you to offer, but no thank you. It will do me good to stretch my legs.'

Sofia had told her that Johnny had been an inmate of the asylum since boyhood. Nellie could hear her saying, 'His derangement is that he thinks he is a horse, but he's harmless, so they let him roam freely. He sleeps in the stables and only eats vegetables. I slip him an apple when I can.' She experienced a fresh surge of gratitude to Sofia for explaining how the asylum worked and for keeping her going during her time there. It cemented her resolve to get her out. Johnny trotted with the group to the asylum gates, before taking his leave with a whinny and a wave.

Dr Alexander E. MacDonald, the general superintendent of the New York City Asylums for the Insane, was waiting to greet them at the entrance of the Octagon. He had an open face and a cordial manner. Superintendent Dent was by his side, his face like thunder. Dr MacDonald ushered them into Dent's office: a well-appointed room with large French windows that opened out onto the grounds, bookshelves stuffed with fat medical volumes in leather covers and paintings of sleek horses on the walls. Extra chairs had been brought in so they could all sit down. They took their places, dignified and expectant.

Vernon Davis cleared his throat. 'I've suggested to Dr MacDonald that we begin proceedings with a question-and-answer session with him and the superintendent. This will give us a chance to gain a better understanding of the institution's workings and how to improve its shortcomings. They will then show us around the facilities and introduce us to the rest of the staff.'

There was a moment of silence while the doctors and the jurors eyed each other warily, like chess players.

'Actually, I'm glad Miss Bly wrote her exposé,' Dent began, with a smile that wasn't reflected in his eyes. 'Yes, I am. In fact, had I known her purpose, I would have helped her. We have no means of discovering such facts, except by doing as she did.'

Nellie gave him a long, flat look and the superintendent's face got red and tight. 'Look here, I don't think we should be faulted for pronouncing Miss Bly insane when she did everything she could to make us believe she was,' he blustered. 'What reason did we have for not accepting that her behavior was genuine?'

255

'It's a good point, sir,' said Nellie, and a light of relief sparked in the superintendent's eyes. '*Except*,' she continued crisply, 'on several occasions, I asked to have my reason tested. Apart from your assistant superintendent, not one member of staff listened to me.'

The tension in the room shifted and then Dent became busily occupied in brushing a speck of dust from his sleeve.

'Let's address some of the points in Miss Bly's articles, shall we?' Vernon Davis suggested. 'The cold baths, the food, the treatment given by the nurses.'

Dent looked up and held his eyes. 'I have no way of knowing if the baths Miss Bly was forced to take were freezing cold, or how many women were put in the same water,' he admitted. 'But listen, I'll be frank with you about the problems of running this institution.'

'I realize that the food isn't what it should be and the system of locking patients into cells is unsafe, but it's quite simply due to pressure of numbers and lack of funds. What's more, I can't tell if the nurses mistreat patients when the doctors aren't around. But I do know this much – that it's hard to attract and keep good nurses on the Island because the hours are long, the work is harrowing, and salaries are only about seventeen dollars a month, which is less than what servant girls get. The doctors' wages are also low and I struggle to find the best medical men. Although those on the Island are more than capable,' he added quickly.

The grand jury listened and made notes, and then they all went on a tour of the facilities. They saw the kitchen first. It was immaculate, with two barrels of salt open and strategically placed near the door. The bread was beautifully white and wholly not the bread patients had been given to eat while Nellie was in residence. The wards, too, were spotless. Beds had been upgraded. Worn buckets had been replaced with shiny new basins. Nellie noticed rat traps in the corners. Even the patients looked cleaner, and they had been supplied with books and warm clothing.

As she took it in, the ground seemed to shift beneath her feet. Were her memories of what she'd endured skewed? She gave her head a shake. No, she wasn't going crazy again. Although their visit was supposed to be a surprise, the administration must have known it was inevitable, thanks to her articles, and they'd had time to prepare.

The delegation was welcomed by the other doctors and the nurses. Nellie and Dr Ingram greeted each other carefully. Her heart raced and she blushed to the roots of her hair, unmoored by the fact that he knew more about her than anyone else and she could talk to him in a way she couldn't to other people. They turned away from each other at once, but she could feel his awareness of her, even as he answered the jury's questions.

In real life, Nurse O'Grady was smaller than the space she occupied in Nellie's nightmares. While the jurors were questioning the other staff, she sidled up to Nellie and said in a low voice, 'I hope there are no hard feelings, eh? I didn't mean anything by it. I was just doing my job.'

Nellie held herself steady through a paroxysm of white-hot rage. 'Take a look in the mirror, Nurse O'Grady,' she said. 'Take a good, hard look. You are caring for the most vulnerable of God's creatures, and yet you never show them one shred of decency or kindness. How can you live with yourself?'

Nurse O'Grady's nostrils tended to flare out when she was angry and they were flaring out now, but she said nothing. A slow flush crept up her neck. Under examination, she and some of the other nurses made statements that contradicted each other, and also Nellie's story. Everyone avoided responsibility for the conditions, saying they didn't know how the treatment, the food, the clothing came to be as Nellie had written it. Finally, they admitted that the jury's visit had been known to them and to the doctors.

At last Nellie had the chance to ask the doctors where her friends were, for she hadn't seen Sofia or Tillie anywhere.

'My dear, you must be confused,' said Dent. 'We don't have anyone called Sofia Fierro here. We do have a Tillie Maynard, but she is too ill for visits.'

Nellie's eyes widened. She could not believe that Dent had said Sofia didn't exist. Had she been discharged, transferred or moved to another part of the asylum? Or had something more sinister happened? Evidently, Dent didn't want the jury to find a sane woman shut away against her will.

'We would like to see Tillie,' Mr Davis said firmly.

'She is a very sick young woman,' warned Dent. 'The sight of so many strangers could shatter her mind altogether.' Dr MacDonald shot him a stern look. Dent opened his hands, turned them palms-up and sighed, 'Oh, all right then, I'll take you to see her. May I suggest you don't go into the room, but look at her through a grille in the door?'

He led them to a solitary cell in the basement and they took it in turns to gaze through the small, wire-mesh rectangle. In the dim light, Nellie could see a creature trussed up in a straitjacket and tied to a bench, pounding its head slowly and methodically against the wall, trying to end its life. Nellie felt sick with horror and pity. She wondered where Tillie was, but then she looked again and realized that it *was* Tillie. She clenched her lips together to stop herself screaming. The hair was missing from one side of Tillie's scalp and she was mumbling to herself. Nellie shut her eyes, but she could still hear Tillie banging her bruised skull.

She thought back to the sweet-faced girl who had sung with her at the piano on their first night at the asylum. It was horrifying to see where Tillie had ended up and to know, beyond a doubt, that her treatment at the asylum had led her there. Nellie banged on the wire-mesh grille, trying to get her attention and, for a moment, Tillie looked back at her. But there was not a flicker of recognition in her staring, empty eyes; she had vanished completely into the lightless regions inside her head. She was as robbed of her soul as Poppa had been, and chills ran through Nellie, making the muscles of her stomach heave.

She turned to Dent, crying, 'You have got to do something for her!'

'I agree,' said Mr Davis. 'This is totally unacceptable. You must find a more humane means of caring for her. I suggest a padded room and round-the-clock nursing.'

'I know. I know. I didn't realize she was hurting herself. I'll change the arrangement at once,' Dent promised sheepishly, and Nellie wasn't sure if he was truly ignorant of Tillie's suffering, or if he was simply covering himself. But at least Tillie would get better treatment than this.

As they were leaving, Nellie saw Dr Ingram coming toward her. Her heart surged. She smiled tremulously at him, but he didn't smile back. He took her loosely by the arm, out of earshot.

'I must tell you how ashamed I am about the appalling failures of care,' he said. 'If only I'd known, I would have stamped them out at once. The fact is, I wasn't vigilant enough. I'll never forgive myself.' His face was pale and strained.

Nellie was unsure how to respond. She recalled his kindness to the patients, how he had asked for warmer clothes for them. But she also remembered that he had thought her truly mad. He belonged to the establishment of the institution; thus, he must at least be partly complicit. Thinking about it made her head and heart hurt.

'You did what you could,' she said finally, letting him read into that whatever he wished.

There was a silence. Then he said, 'One more thing...' Their eyes met and she saw the hurt in his. 'I wish you had told me who you really were. I thought you trusted me. You know I would have helped you.'

'There were times I wanted to, but I couldn't risk how you might react.'

'It makes me wonder if what you said in our sessions was true. Or was that all fabrication too?'

She looked him in the eye, relieved to be able to speak a simple truth. 'Every word of it was honest. I have never spoken as frankly to anyone as I spoke to you.'

He flushed. 'Oh. I... I'm glad.'

'You helped me understand myself and I'll always be grateful for it,' she smiled. The smile faded; she took a breath. 'Actually, there's one last thing I would appreciate your help with.'

'Yes, gladly.'

'Please tell me what happened to Sofia? She isn't mad, you know, so perhaps you could look at releasing her? Tillie too – I would find her proper care until she got well.'

Dr Ingram looked taken aback, but before he could answer, Mr Davis joined them, saying, 'It's time to leave for the boat, Miss Bly.'

A fist squeezed tight around Nellie's heart. Her throat was closing up. 'I'm not sure you know where Sofia is,' she said hurriedly to the doctor. 'But if you have any news of her, please let me know. I'm staying at the Fifth Avenue Hotel on Twenty-Third Street.'

He opened his mouth to speak but changed his mind. 'Goodbye, Miss Bly,' he said.

'Goodbye, Dr Ingram. I wish you happiness, success, and the other good things of this earth.' She allowed Mr Davis to lead her away.

On the boat ride back to Manhattan, she made a great effort not to cry, but tears overtook her all the same, splashing onto the deck. The jurors tried to comfort her, but she turned away from them, mortified at the display of weakness she couldn't control.

On the face of it, the asylum was running fine, and she didn't think the grand jury would accept her account after what they had seen. All her hard work, all her suffering had been in vain. She could not save the women. That was it, she realized; she would probably never see any of them, or Dr Ingram, again. It crushed her. The sound of Tillie beating her brains out against the wall wove through all her thoughts, a relentless metronome.

Twenty-Two

THE REVERBERATIONS FROM NELLIE'S asylum exposé took a long time to fade away. Families who'd had relatives committed to asylums wrote to her, asking if she would investigate those institutions, find out if their cousin or grandmother was being cared for or being abused. Heartbreaking letters came from people who had once looked out at the world from behind bars and the snug embrace of a straitjacket, both those who had recovered from their illnesses, and those who swore that they'd been wrongly diagnosed and should never have been committed at all. There were letters denouncing Nellie and calling her a disgrace to the female sex, and letters containing marriage proposals. But there were also carefully reasoned letters from civic leaders who had been lobbying for reform in public institutions; they praised her work as trailblazing and believed that it would pave the way for future reforms.

Nellie answered each one conscientiously. But on the inside, she was frantic with worry for her friends, with yearning for Dr Ingram, and because she was impatient to learn the grand jury's verdict. It was a queer, seething limbo, as incapacitating as a real illness. Ten days after her visit to the asylum came a letter that changed everything.

Dear Miss Bly,

I hope you are well and have fully recovered from your time in the asylum. Life is busy as ever here. We are working on reforms, but are hampered by lack of funds.

I have news about the inmates you were asking for, and would very much like to call on you to tell you, if I may?

Yours sincerely,
Frank Ingram

Nellie smoothed the paper, feeling happiness unfurl through her, as if she'd been kept in an icebox for a long time. It was followed by a pang of alarm. What if he had bad news about Tillie or Sofia? And even if there was no bad news, was she well enough to see him? There was still a strange undercurrent of sadness, a tug from the asylum that brought it back at odd moments and knocked her off her feet. Her mind would begin to formulate terrible questions; questions she had no answers to. *Why are we here?... How do we know reality?... Why do we have to suffer so much?...* She wondered if the doctor was really what he seemed. He could be nothing but an ideal of her own devising, formed from her longings, and she'd better be prepared.

Then she told herself not to overthink. It was enough to know that Frank Ingram was in the world and that he thought kindly of her and wanted to give her the news she had asked for. Fetching pen and paper, she wrote back to him, asking if he was free to call on her the following Wednesday at six o'clock.

Nellie waited for the doorbell with electric anticipation. Four days earlier, she had moved into a simply furnished apartment on the Upper West Side; an easy transition because she had so few belongings. To make it her own, she had bought an assortment of cushions and rugs in apricot, deep red and tan. Setting the apartment to rights had given her such satisfaction; it was like giving her mind a good spring cleaning too. As she glanced around, she thought how cosy and inviting the living room looked, its wooden floorboards, generous fireplace and cream-colored walls bathed in soft lamplight.

The bell rang at six on the dot. After checking her hair one last time in the mirror, she hurried to open the door and her stomach fell away at the sight of him.

'How are you, Nellie Bly?' he asked, putting out two hands.

'Swell, Dr Ingram. I'm glad to see you again.' She took his hands, wondering if she'd said too much. She had observed that a girl saying what she felt was not approved of. She should play covert, untouchable, indifferent: perfectly convincing as a lady. But that was hardly how she lived her life.

'I'm glad to see you too,' he said. 'But can we please address each other by our first names?'

'Certainly. I'd like that... Frank.'

She stepped aside to let him in and he looked around approvingly.

'Can I make you coffee, or something stronger?' Nellie asked.

'Something stronger, if you have it.'

'Oh, sure. I keep a bottle of brandy for emergencies.'

'Ah, emergencies. Such as?'

'Cold weather. Tight deadlines. Your average, everyday kind of emergency.' She smiled at him and he smiled back.

In the kitchen Nellie took the brandy out of the cupboard, opened it and brought it through to the living room with two glasses on a tray. They sat down and she poured.

'We should drink to you,' said Frank, raising his glass. 'To your courage, compassion and social conscience.'

Nellie liked being praised as well as anyone. 'You're too kind,' she said as they clinked glasses. He swallowed a mouthful of brandy. She watched his head tilt back and his throat move.

'You look well,' he said, wiping his lips. 'You've recovered from your, er... ordeal?'

She hesitated. 'I think I will always bear the imprint of the asylum, but I am almost better,' she said quietly. 'I took time off work and am getting ready to go back. Actually, I'm looking for the next scoop. The asylum is proving a hard act to follow.'

'Oh, I can imagine. You set the bar pretty high for yourself.'

He moved closer to her on the settee. His jacket sleeve brushed against her arm, sending shivers racing through her.

'I feel such a fool for not realizing you were sane,' he admitted, flushing. 'It was clear from the start that your case was unusual. I was puzzled and intrigued by you; I even hoped to cure you. But I didn't for one moment guess you were a sham.'

Nellie felt guilt cut into her. 'I am sorry I lied to you,' she said. 'But don't blame yourself for not spotting I was an imposter. I mean, why would any sane woman put herself through that ordeal?'

'That's true enough,' he said, with a rueful smile.

They seemed to have steered themselves into some sort of conversational dead end. There was silence but for the sounds of traffic, the streetcars clanging past. Nellie took a sip of brandy. 'I have a recommendation for you,' she said.

'Of course. What is it?'

'Well, while I was an inmate, I found Nurse O'Grady to be cruel and tyrannical. She is not fit to care for animals, let alone defenceless women. I recommend that you fire her.'

His eyebrows shot up. 'Oh? I always thought her a competent nurse.' He gave Nellie a slow, thoughtful look. 'On the other hand, I have total faith in your judgment. Why don't I look into it and come back to you?'

'Thank you. That gives me immense relief.' Her fingers crossed and clenched in her lap. 'Um, what was the news you wanted to tell me? Is it about Tillie or Sofia?'

'Yes, I have news of both,' he said, frowning. 'I applied for Tillie's release, but Dent refused it on the grounds that she is incurable and unfit to re-enter society. I'm so sorry.' He shook his head. 'I've seen to it that she is comfortable and has everything she needs, but ultimately, Dent has the power over what happens to the patients.'

Nellie's heart felt as if a weight were pressing on it. 'So you're telling me there is nothing you can do?'

'I'm afraid not.'

Nellie contemplated the horror of Tillie's fate and all the others like her – deserts of suffering. She felt a deep and terrible sadness. Anger too – had Frank really fought hard enough? Tears came to her eyes.

'What about Sofia?' she asked, blinking them back. 'Surely there can't be any argument about releasing her. She is perfectly sane.'

'I have sad news about Sofia,' he said, his eyes fixed on hers. 'Are you all right for me to tell you? It's going to be a shock.'

She sat up straighter. 'Yes, yes, I'll be fine.'

Frank took a drink of brandy. 'Well, listen,' he said. 'A few days after you visited with the grand jury, Sofia's brother, Francesco, returned from work at sea and went to see her. She had been moved to another ward and was no longer under my care. I am sorry to say that he found her emaciated, badly bruised and frightened of her attendants.'

Nellie felt a choking pressure around her heart. 'Oh, God,' she breathed.

His fingers beat against the arm of the settee. 'Yes, well, the nurses said that Sofia's injuries were due to falls and fights with the other patients, but she swore this wasn't true. Francesco enlisted the help of a lawyer to get her released, and he brought her home to his rooms at East Fifth Street. I believe Sofia is estranged from her husband – did you know that?'

'Yes, she spoke a little bit about it.' *I'm going to think of you as dead, and you are*, Sofia's husband had told her. *My real wife is dead.*

'Her brother seems to be the only person who cares for her,' said Frank. 'I went to speak to him to find out if there was anything I could do. He told me that she arrived at his apartment a week ago and was scared to name the people who had harmed her. Apparently, things had been all right to begin with, but then a new nurse came, who took an irrational dislike to her. She beat her, bound her wrists and ankles, and left her like that for several hours.' Frank gave a sigh. 'I'm so sorry to break this to you, but... well, Sofia died two days after moving in with him.'

Nellie held her head in both hands. All she could say was, 'Oh no, oh no,' because a chasm was opening up and swallowing her down. She was falling through darkness; she couldn't breathe. Then came rage that this could still happen. It burned across her brain, blinding her. She wanted to tear the room apart with her bare hands, to be as violent and destructive as the sickest woman in the asylum. If she opened her mouth to speak, she was scared she might start screaming. *Just concentrate on breathing*, she told herself. *Draw air in and push it out again.*

A cold, dank realization was settling in her, making her shiver. She had not righted anything. For the poor and helpless, New York was still a place of anguish and degradation. She hadn't been able to save her friends. She had failed all the women.

Frank reached for the bottle of brandy and filled her glass. She downed it in one gulp, coughing a little. 'Thank you,' she said. 'I needed that.'

He patted her hand. 'Sometimes drink is the only remedy.'

Nellie was thinking about what Sofia must have suffered in the days leading up to her death. It would have taken a harsh punishment to break her strong spirit.

'I guess this means that in spite of my work, nothing's changed,' she said in a low voice.

Frank regarded her compassionately. 'Look, Nellie, on the strength of your story, reforms *are* happening at the asylum. It's a huge achievement – and we haven't even heard the grand jury's report yet. But your job is to expose corruption and bring injustices to people's attention, not to cure those ills. That is my job. Clearly, we need to establish better safeguards for the hiring and monitoring of staff, so that only sympathetic and conscientious people are appointed. I am determined to make it happen.'

Nellie opened her mouth to answer but found that tears were rising instead of speech. She tried to quell them, but they built into a torrent, spilling out of her.

'Nellie,' said Frank. 'Nellie, I'm so sorry.'

After a moment's hesitation, he put his arms around her and she caught the scent of peppermint and shaving soap. It was strange for one moment, but almost at once it was as if she recognized his body and had known it always. He held her while she wept, not saying anything, just letting her be sad.

Her mind went back and forth between Tillie's wrecked life and beautiful, spirited Sofia, whose only crime had been to fall in love. How could this have happened? Too often, things went wrong in life that didn't get fixed or put back together the way they were before. Too often, things stayed broken, or got worse. Nellie thought about her own life and wondered what sort of person she would have been if her father had lived. Would she have been content to follow an easier path; would she be married by now with a family of her own, happy and secure? Nothing was right and everything hurt, and she only wanted Frank to go on holding her.

Presently, her nose began running, so she went to her bedroom to fetch a handkerchief. She blew her nose, splashed cold water on her eyes and returned to the living room, feeling slightly more composed.

'Are you all right, my dear?' Frank asked gently.

She gave him a shaky smile. 'I'm not sure. Let's talk about something else.'

Frank topped up their drinks and said, 'How about we talk about *you*?' His look was admiring, but uncertain. He wasn't completely sure of himself and she liked him all the more for it. 'I'd love to hear about your newspaper career.'

Then, in bits and pieces, she found herself telling him everything: the editorial in the Pittsburgh *Dispatch* that had made her blood boil, working for Madden, the stir her articles had caused, and the gamble of moving to New York.

He listened, tilting his head thoughtfully and, as the tales of her past came out, he had nothing but admiration for her.

What a relief it was to unburden herself; to reveal all of herself and feel really seen. It was even better than talking to him in the asylum because the doctor-patient boundary was gone. It gave her a sense of comfort and replenishment. This was what had been missing her whole life, she realized, and she hadn't even known she was looking for it. They were sitting very close, thigh to thigh, and strange new feelings were coursing through her, a shimmering warmth. She kept her eyes demurely lowered, so he wouldn't read what was happening in them.

When she got to the end, she said, 'So, now you know my whole life history.'

He gave her a slow, sweet smile and said, 'You've had more than your fair share of struggles, but look how well you've come out of it.' He put his hand on her hand, then removed it. 'I've never met a woman like you. You dare to live outside a woman's proper role, yet you're straight and true, and you have a strength that's been forged by walking through fire. I don't think about much else, to tell the truth.'

The longing to touch him absorbed some of her grief for Sofia. She leaned in closer, feeling his warm breath on her cheek. He ran a finger along her cheek and then his lips grazed her neck, his body pressed against hers, warm and dense. She could feel his heart beating fast. He kissed her and their noses bumped awkwardly along the way. She felt the scrape of bristles around his lips and the softness of his mouth, and her body began to fill with pleasure, dissolving into his. After a few minutes, she pulled away.

'Oh, Nellie,' he said, and she heard his throat catch. 'Will you marry me?'

She was so shocked, she couldn't speak. A welter of emotions rose up through her: joy, exaltation, incredulity. Resentment too, for this had come too quickly and at the wrong time. She wasn't at all sure what love was, but she thought this might be it: this sweetness trembling through her, being *recognized* by him and loved for all her quirks. But she also knew that he needed things from a wife she could not provide. She couldn't manage his life seamlessly and create a haven of peace for him to come home to; she had no interest in doing so. She had no interest in proper feminine pursuits, like bridge parties and sewing bees and church socials. On the contrary, she had a propensity for diving down avenues most women would cringe from. And how could she even contemplate marriage with Sofia scarcely cold in her grave? If Sofia's experience of being a wife had taught her anything, it was that marriage was a death trap.

Frank's brown eyes were searching her face. 'What's wrong?' he asked.

She pressed her hands to her burning cheeks. 'I am honored and moved by your proposal. It's just... well, I'm so sad and confused about Sofia right now. May I have time to think about it?'

'I was hoping you'd say yes, but I understand,' he said, stifling a hurt look. 'I shouldn't have asked so soon – I couldn't help myself. I know you are in shock, and grieving for your friend.' He stood up to leave. 'Take your time and I shall give you the space you need. Please just promise that you'll write if you feel sad and want to talk. I am here for you.'

'Bless you,' she said. 'You are the kindest and most considerate of men.'

He waved her words away, smiling. 'Take good care of yourself, Nellie. Till soon, I hope.' He touched her cheek, lightly, a butterfly's soft brush.

Twenty-Three

AFTER FRANK HAD GONE, Nellie drew the
curtains and went to bed. For three days she lay
in the dark, curled up like a baby, moving only to
fetch a glass of water or use the toilet. She sent a note to
the *World* telling them she was ill, and indeed, the waves
of pain moving through her felt as real as any illness.
Sleep eluded her – when it finally came, it was short and
fitful. In her dreams, she wandered endlessly through the
halls of the asylum, searching for Tillie and Sofia. She
was shot with arrows she could not feel, but she knew
that they were killing her. Once, she dreamt that she was
kissing Frank, lost in sweetness, and she woke breathless
and tingling all over. She knew that she had to answer his
proposal, but trying to figure it out left her confused and
miserable.

She wondered if her reason was slipping, if she would
lose it again. But then she remembered the period in the
asylum when day and night had mashed into each other,
and the loss of time had terrified her, and she felt thankful
for the unvarying ticking of the clock on her mantelpiece,
measuring away the seconds at their usual reliable pace.
There was nothing wrong with her brain. She was suffering from grief, and that was the long and the short of it.
There had been so many losses, each one taking away part

of her with it, each one leaving the world a little worse off, a little more denuded of meaning.

She searched her mind for something that would restore her to herself. Writing had always been her *raison d'être*, stilling her demons, anchoring her to a sense of self that was definite and constant. Even more than that: being a reporter had *become* her. It was who she was. The best of her, the truest, purest version of Nellie that existed, was to be found in her articles. She knew it was work that would give her courage to get up in the mornings.

Before her collapse she had been thinking about taking up the cause of the working girl again. Because of the flood of immigrants arriving in New York, these young women were in an even tighter jam than in Pittsburgh. They were hired for a pitifully low wage, then sacked and fed into the underworld. But as yet, there wasn't a story crying out to be written as the asylum story had done, and she didn't feel up to looking for one. She would need to find something that was better than the asylum, and the pressure was just about paralyzing her.

A knock on the door disrupted her thoughts. Who could it be? There was no one she wanted to see, so she decided to ignore it, hoping that whoever it was would go away. But the rapping came again, more insistently. She dragged herself out of bed and went to open the door. On the threshold stood a skinny, freckled messenger boy, who handed her a fat cream-colored envelope and left, tipping his cap to her. She tore the flap open with her thumb, wondering what was inside.

It was the grand jury's report, forwarded by Pulitzer. She began to read it, blood thumping in her temples.

The October grand jury's investigation is the immediate result of Miss Nellie Bly's articles in the *World*

newspaper about life in the Female Lunatic Asylum on Blackwell's Island.

After visiting the Asylum with Miss Bly, the grand jury concludes that certain aspects of its management are woefully inadequate and unsafe, and that changes are urgently needed. The grand jury requests that the Board of Estimate and Apportionment grants more money for the Female Insane Asylum for the coming year, so that improvements can be immediately carried out.

Relief was flooding through Nellie, making her feel so wobbly in the legs that she went back to bed to finish reading. The grand jury recommended warmer clothing and better-quality food for the inmates; better heating and ventilation; and the construction of larger premises. They called for a bigger medical staff and sufficient salaries to employ trained nurses, competent junior physicians, and at least three female doctors. The grand jury especially recommended that patients be examined more carefully before entering the asylum, so that only the genuinely ill were admitted. Finally they urged that the law be changed, placing the poor and insane under a different commission from the one controlling criminals.

At the bottom, Pulitzer had written:

As you can see, your work has been game-changing! It is the very essence of the journalism I have in mind. Bravo, Miss Bly! Bravo indeed!!

Nellie put the pages down and stretched her arms above her head. Before the report had come, she'd been oppressed by a sense of failure and the futility of human life, but its contents had restored her faith that change was possible. She had failed to save Sofia and Tillie and she would always be racked by that, but she had managed to alleviate the suffering of some of the most wretched women on earth. Something deep inside her stabilized and clarified, and she felt the resurgence of her life's purpose – to show what a woman could do.

A few days later, the *World* ran an editorial headlined 'THE WORLD THEIR SAVIOR: How Nellie Bly's Work Will Help the City Insane'.

> An appropriation of $850,000 for Blackwell's Island recommended by the grand jury headed by District Attorney Vernon M. Davis has been given by the city. An additional sum has been granted for other city asylums for the insane. A consensus had been forming for some time to increase funding for the care of the mentally ill, and Nellie Bly's articles added valuable heft to the decision to do so. Improvements in the inmates' care are expected to be implemented with immediate effect.

Although most newspapers had commented favorably on Nellie's story, the *Mail* and the *Sun* had called it blatant sensationalism, most likely in retaliation for being duped by her so publicly. They had lambasted Pulitzer for allowing a young girl to take such risks. Here, then, was vindication – for her and for the *World*.

Mary Jane came to New York to see Nellie. When she knocked on the door of the apartment, Nellie it threw open and they flung themselves into each other's arms.

'Oh, Nellie!'

'Momma! I'm so glad to see you.'

'I am proud of you, darling. I always knew you would succeed.'

Momma released Nellie, holding her at arms' length to examine her. 'Lord, but you're so altered I hardly know you.'

Nellie had been expecting this, aware that her face was marked by stress and sadness. 'I'm fine, Momma,' she said. 'It's nothing that time won't heal.'

She showed Momma all around the apartment and Momma pronounced it perfect. Then Nellie made coffee and brought it to the living room with a plate of small sugar-dusted cakes. They sat in the armchairs in front of the fireplace and Nellie poured the coffee. Momma took a mouthful. 'Mmm, this is delicious,' she said.

They ate the cakes and talked about the family, about how Charles and Albert were doing in their jobs and about the two younger children at school. Nellie gave her mother an envelope stuffed with dollar bills to help with the housekeeping.

'Thank you,' said Momma. 'But are you sure?'

'Yes, of course I am!'

'I feel bad. I mean, it ought to be me who's providing for you.'

'Oh, I'm on a good salary now,' Nellie replied, waving it away.

For an instant, she thought of confiding in Momma about Frank. But she held back because she was still undecided about his proposal; equally stuck between wanting to be with him and wanting her independence.

Momma set her cup in its saucer. 'Your stories were wonderful,' she said. 'So riveting and suspenseful, it was like reading a novel.'

Nellie flushed with pleasure. 'Thank you! But I learned storytelling from a master – you.'

Momma smiled at her, then frowned. 'To tell the truth, I can't stop thinking about what you must have seen and suffered in that place.' She bit her lip. 'I can see the toll it took and I'm worried about you. There must be easier ways to earn a living.'

'But this is what I want! Serious journalism is my life-blood!' Nellie's voice rose.

Something inside her was simmering, and she was aware that it was an old anger, with a thread of grief and pity caught up in it. In the past, she had always managed to keep a lid on her feelings, but now she was so worn down, they were all over the place.

She wondered if the loving care she had shown her mother over the years had simply been a mask for the anger. After all, it was the only acceptable way of dealing with feelings so unseemly: they had to be buried deep. But now the mask had been stripped away and Nellie was face to face with a lot of things she hadn't let herself see before. Take the money she'd just given Momma – it was as if she had to show her, by inverse example, how a responsible person cared for their family. Nellie had never forgiven her mother for putting them through the horror of living with Jack. If only Momma had been stronger, Nellie wouldn't have had to be so strong herself.

In her mind's eye, she saw Momma cowering on the floor, her arms over her head to try and protect herself while Jack raged and hit her. Yet not until the very end had she let go of the belief that she was better off with a man. And the whole time, this thing in Nellie had simmered and seethed.

The thoughts brought tears to Nellie's eyes and she feigned a coughing fit to disguise their cause. Mary Jane was still her mother and the woman who had given her life. It was impossible to confront her for the weaknesses

278

that had failed her children so drastically, however much Nellie might want to. Nellie was convulsed with sympathy and fury.

Jack's mean face, flushed with drink, came sharply back to her; and the fear of him, and their disgrace. She thought about how he had brought her mother to the brink of madness, and how easily Momma's fate could have been the same as Tillie's or Sofia's. The whole system was stacked against women. And yet Momma had found the courage and strength to defy it by divorcing Jack and starting over. In a flash, Nellie saw how remarkable her mother's actions had been. The realization settled in her, creating an extraordinary feeling, like coming into a safe harbor after being lost at sea.

Suddenly Momma said, 'I think I'm starting to understand the passion you feel for your work. The fact is that you are doing a great deal of good and I am proud of you.'

Nellie felt surprise, then joy. With tears in her eyes, she said, 'Thank you. That means everything to me.'

'I am glad,' said Momma, taking her hand. 'Look, I have an idea. Why don't I move to New York for good with Henry and Kate? That way I could at least look after you while you're on your assignments; cook, help keep the place clean. It would be company for both of us.'

'Yes,' said Nellie, without hesitation. 'Yes, please. I would like that very much.'

The café was Italian, with roughly whitewashed walls, checked cloths and a coal stove at either end of the room. Appetizing smells filled the air. Frank was sitting at the back, wearing a charcoal-gray suit. He stood up when Nellie walked over and kissed her on the cheek. He looked drawn and it made her heart ache.

'Hello, Nellie. I am glad you suggested meeting. How are you?' he asked. Fragments of traffic noise drifted in every time the door opened and got drowned out by his voice.

They sat down and a waiter took their order for coffee and cake. Nellie's heart was rocketing around against her ribcage – it was impossible to make small talk. She was still unable to decide about his proposal, and she hoped that seeing him again would give her clarity.

Frank leaned toward her and rested his forearms on the table. 'I have good news, for a change. I am pleased to tell you that Miss O'Grady has been discharged. She will never again get work caring for vulnerable people.'

'Oh, thank goodness!' said Nellie. 'I'm awful glad.' Her eyes were welling up and, noticing it, Frank's hand crept to cover hers. Her hand tingled and floated in his warm grasp. They fell silent, listening to the hum of voices around them.

'I have something for you,' Frank said at last. He took a notebook from his jacket pocket – black with silver edging; bent, dog-eared and dirty. Nellie drew in her breath – it was the book that had been confiscated when she'd arrived at the asylum.

'H-how on earth did you get it?' she stammered.

'Someone left it on my desk, I don't know who. One of the nurses, probably.'

'Thank you,' she whispered, and the hairs on her arms rose as she took it from him. She turned it over and over, remembering how she'd felt when Nurse Grupe had mocked her crazy writing and confiscated it. The note-book had been restored to her and so had her liberty, but what of the women who had lost everything? Nellie had kept her promise to go back for Tillie and Sofia, but she had arrived too late, and all she could feel was guilt and unspeakable loss.

Gradually, lucidity began to break through the turmoil. Her resolve to bring similar atrocities to light strengthened. She felt more focused than ever on her quest – it would be an act of remembrance to her friends. She drew herself upright, thinking about how flat and dreary the world seemed when Frank wasn't there. But she had reached her decision.

'Frank,' she began, and the hope in his eyes made her heart constrict. 'I am so very flattered by your proposal. Being your wife would be a privilege, but I... I'm afraid I can't accept.'

'Why not?'

She clenched and unclenched her hands. 'This is the hardest decision I ever made. I feel terribly torn. See, I love you.'

'I love you too, Nellie. So what's the problem?'

'Well, listen. I'll tell you. You need a traditional wife and, for as long there are injustices like the ones at the asylum, I cannot be that person.'

'Who said anything about a traditional wife? I couldn't be prouder of your achievements.'

She shook her head. 'It wouldn't work. See, I am inspired by the change I helped make at the asylum, and devastated that it didn't happen in time to save Sofia and Tillie. I want to lobby for other essential reforms. It will mean being single-minded about my career and doing even more daring things as a woman. I would be a liability to you. We'd both be miserable.'

She got to her feet and the hurt on his face made her wince. She kissed him gently on the forehead and walked out of the restaurant without looking back. She thought her heart would break.

It was a crisp, cold night, and she made her way along Broadway, which was filled with light and crowds. Shop windows gleamed with Christmas scarlet and holly, wood and brass glittered as the endless procession of carriages flashed past. There were shoppers and workers returning home, revellers coming out for the night, a newsboy crying, 'Young girl strangled in her bed – read about it here!' An old man stood on a corner, dressed in a threadbare velvet jacket, plucking at his long gray hair with trembling fingers and shouting, 'You are all playing with hellfire! You're walking around and around your destruction, but you will fall in the end!'

She took in every sight, sound and smell, absorbing the energy, the unquenchable life. *All this will carry on beyond my lifetime*, she thought. *And on, and on.* It brought a lighter feeling to her, a lessening of pain. She felt that she could carry on walking for ever – the street was a place of unending interest. Anything could happen here, anything at all. It was where worlds collided. Where her next story would come from.

Tomorrow she would return to the streets to look for it. She had a hunch that it would be about working girls, about misery and injustice. There were no stories about happiness and easy lives, because happiness had no momentum. It was struggle, loss and longing that propelled the narrative forward. She felt a pang of yearning for Frank, but tamped it down at once. She had closed that door behind her; it was time to look forward. She did not know what the future held, but one thing was certain. There was always another story to be found.

Biographical Afterword

Nellie's Bly's articles about her ten days on Blackwell's Island in 1887 highlighted the predicament of the mentally ill in American state asylums. They reached out to a huge audience, taking up a subject that had previously been off limits. Those who suffered mental illness were often cast out by their communities and shut up in remote asylums, along with women who were not ill, but were simply deviant by the narrow standards of society. There they were largely forgotten, both by their families and the state. In short, the asylum was a socially acceptable way of disposing with inconvenient women.

In the wake of Nellie's blistering report, administrative changes were implemented at the lunatic asylum on Blackwell's Island. But although there were some improvements in the patients' care and conditions, the abuses and the appalling conditions were not wiped out, and the image of the asylum as a human rat trap lingered. It was an epitome of the unrealized goals and failures of care so extensively covered by the press. The asylum closed in 1894 – seven years after Nellie's exposé. All that remains of it today is a domed octagonal structure that was once the centerpiece of the institution.

Nellie's articles captured public imagination, and turned her into a celebrity, a fiery national presence. Her feat also catalyzed a new journalistic movement known as stunt or detective reporting, the acknowledged forerunner of full-scale investigative journalism. Nellie pioneered a path for future women reporters. According to her biographer, Brooke Kroeger:

> It was the advent of both the stunt girls and the large separate women's sections that created the first real place for women as regular members of the newspaper staff and an important part of the editorial mix... Stunt girls, with Bly as the genre's leader, formed the human chute down which the next generation of women reporters plunged into journalism's mainstream.[1]

Nellie continued to write about poverty and politics with a special focus on women whom no one else would speak about. In 1889, she proposed a new story. She would travel around the globe, attempting to smash the record of Phileas Fogg, the protagonist of Jules Verne's novel *Around the World in Eighty Days*. She made the trip in seventy-two days, six hours and eleven minutes – beating Fogg by a week. The feat turned her into an international sensation.

Dr Ingram left the lunatic asylum on Blackwell's Island the same year as Nellie's exposé and went into private practice. On occasion he would testify as an expert witness on insanity. (He attended the electrocution of two calves at Thomas Edison's laboratory, which was intended to demonstrate that the electric chair was more merciful than hanging.) Nellie and Ingram maintained their friendship after she was released from the asylum, and there were constant rumors that their relationship had developed into romance. After completing

---

[1]Brooke Kroeger, *Nellie Bly*, New York, Times Books, 1994, p. 127.

her round-the-world trip, Nellie visited Ingram in his hometown in Indiana. A local reporter asked if there was any truth to the rumor that they were engaged. Nellie declined to answer but explained that she knew Ingram 'intimately'. Ingram denied the rumor, adding that he was nonetheless an ardent admirer of Nellie Bly. The paper accepted the denial, but the pair's responses seemed to indicate that they were, or had been, lovers. Three years later Ingram would die unexpectedly of a heart attack, tragically echoing Nellie's father's sudden death.[2] Ingram was thirty-three years old.

In 1895, aged thirty-one, Nellie quit her career to marry 73-year-old industrialist Robert Seaman. When her husband died in 1904, she took over his business, the Iron Clad Manufacturing Company, and became one of the leading female industrialists of the day. She went on to patent several inventions related to oil manufacturing, many of which are still used today, such as the first practical 55-gallon steel oil drum. However, employee fraud, her lack of experience and a sequence of legal issues forced the company into bankruptcy and Nellie went back to journalism.

In 1914 she started working for the New York *Evening Journal* as America's first female war correspondent. For nearly five years, she reported from the front lines of World War I. She returned Stateside in 1919 and died of pneumonia in 1922.

[2]Stacy Horn, *Damnation Island*, North Carolina, Algonquin Book p. 87.

A Note on Sources

Readers in search of factual material about Nellie Bly are directed to the following excellent works, which were also my research sources: *Nellie Bly: Daredevil, Reporter, Feminist* by Brooke Kroeger, *Ten Days a Madwoman* by Deborah Noyes and *Damnation Island* by Stacy Horn. For Nellie's own account of her time in the Blackwell's Island Lunatic Asylum, see *Ten Days in a Mad-House* by Nellie Bly.

I found many other books helpful, but most especially *Mad, Bad and Sad: A History of Women and the Mind Doctors from 1800 to the Present* by Lisa Appignanesi, *Alias Grace* by Margaret Atwood, *Nellie Bly, Reporter* by Nina Brown Baker, *Women of the Asylum: Voices from Behind the Walls, 1840–1945* by Jeffrey L. Geller and Maxine Harris, *I Never Promised You a Rose Garden* by Joanne Greenberg, *Legally Dead: Experiences During Seventeen Weeks' Detention in a Private Asylum* by Marcia Hamilcar, the Irene Adler series by Carole Nelson Douglas, *Nellie Bly: First Woman Reporter* by Iris Noble, *The Amazing Nellie Bly* by Mignon Rittenhouse, *A Mind That Found Itself: An Autobiography* by Clifford Whittingham Beers, *Voluntary Madness* by Norah Vincent, *The Snake Pit* by Mary Jane Ward. My novel bears traces of them all; however, any factual errors are mine alone.

Acknowledgements

Every published book is a group effort, and my thanks go to Toni Kirkpatrick for being my first reader and the first person to believe in my writing. Miranda Vaughan Jones for outstanding editorial input and always being a joy to work with. Stephanie Duncan for being a wonderful mentor and friend. Suzanne Goodman for introducing me to Nellie Bly – without you this novel would not have been written. The wonderful book bloggers, who have supported and continue to support my work – I appreciate each and every one of you. The Library of Congress, and especially Amber Paranick, for invaluable help with research. My friends and family for always being there for me, for giving me space to write, and for seeing me through the ups and downs of the writing life. My greatest thanks go to the wonderful team at Bloomsbury Publishing: firstly, Nigel Newton, for his enthusiasm and support. I owe an enormous debt of gratitude to my publisher, Alexandra Pringle, for her wise and inspiring input; to my editor, Sophie Wilson, for brilliant guidance that lifted the book onto another level; and to my copy-editor, Kate Quarry, for her skilled and sensitive work. It was a joy and an honor to work with you. I would like to thank Sarah Ruddick, Allegra Le Fanu, Francisco Vilhena, Ros Ellis, Maud Davies, Beth Maher, Emma Ewbank and everyone at Bloomsbury who helped bring the book to life. Also Kathleen Carter, publicist with a magic touch. Huge thanks go my children, Adam, Imogen and Alexandra for supporting my writing, despite the many times my head was so full of the story that I dropped the ball at home. I love you more than words can express and I am so proud of the incredible people you have grown up to be. Finally, I want to thank George MacMillan for reading numerous drafts, for helping me understand American and Native American history and culture, for your heart of grace and for boundless love and inspiration that I hope to spend a lifetime reciprocating.

Note on the Author

LOUISA TREGER, a classical violinist, studied at the Royal College of Music and the Guildhall School of Music and worked as a freelance orchestral player and teacher. She subsequently turned to literature, earning a PhD in English at University College London, where she focused on early-twentieth-century women's writing and was awarded the West Scholarship and the Rosa Morison Scholarship 'for distinguished work in the study of English Language and Literature'. She is the author of the novels *The Lodger* and *The Dragon Lady*. She lives in London.

Note on the Type

The text of this book is set in Baskerville, a typeface named after John Baskerville of Birmingham (1706–1775). The original punches cut by him still survive. His widow sold them to Beaumarchais, from where they passed through several French foundries to Deberney & Peignot in Paris, before finding their way to Cambridge University Press.

Baskerville was the first of the 'transitional romans' between the softer and rounder calligraphic Old Face and the 'Modern' sharp-tooled Bodoni. It does not look very different to the Old Faces, but the thick and thin strokes are more crisply defined and the serifs on lower-case letters are closer to the horizontal with the stress nearer the vertical. The R in some sizes has the eighteenth-century curled tail, the lower case w has no middle serif and the lower case g has an open tail and a curled ear.